A DEADLY WALK
IN DEVON

A DEADLY
WALK
IN DEVON

NICHOLAS
GEORGE

Kensington Publishing Corp.
www.kensingtonbooks.com

KENSINGTON BOOKS are published by

Kensington Publishing Corp.
119 West 40th Street
New York, NY 10018

All Kensington titles, imprints, and distributed lines are available at special quantity discounts for bulk purchases for sales promotion, premiums, fund-raising, educational, or institutional use. Special book excerpts or customized printings can also be created to fit specific needs. For details, write or phone the office of the Kensington Special Sales Manager: Attn. Special Sales Department. Kensington Publishing Corp., 119 West 40th Street, New York, NY 10018. Phone: 1-800-221-2647.

Library of Congress Card Catalogue Number: 2023949858

ISBN: 978-1-4967-4526-2
First Kensington Hardcover Edition: April 2024

ISBN: 978-1-4967-4528-6 (ebook)

10 9 8 7 6 5 4 3 2 1

Printed in the United States of America

To all the walkers of the world

Acknowledgments

The writing process is a paradox. There's a lot of time spent alone, hunched over a laptop, trying to piece together a good story with interesting characters. But there's also a lot of time spent with others, responding to their feedback, gaining strength from their encouragement and support, and learning from their perspectives and experience. Here I'd like to acknowledge many of those who've helped make this book a reality.

The seed for this book began (not surprisingly) on a Wayfarers group walk in Devon, when Betsy West (wife of company co-founder Michael West) learned I was a writer and suggested I write a murder mystery that takes place on a walk. She may have been joking, but when I returned home I hammered out a first draft, basing two characters on walk leader Sarah Hudston and fellow walker Ginny Thomas. I then workshopped chapters through a stellar array of writing group compatriots (in person and online): Stephen Brown, Cristina Stuart, Cody Sisco, Suki Yamashita, Susan Emshwiller, Bill Loving, Larry Keeton, Jack Maconaghy, Amy Bosworth, Phillip Larson, and Jen Watkins, among many others.

When I felt I had a decent final draft, I enlisted the help of editors Dominick Wakefield and Nathan Bransford to provide additional fine-tuning. My dear friend David Link gave the book a valuable beta read.

All that expert help took me a long way, but I still had to tackle the formidable hurdle of securing representation. I was extremely fortunate to link up with my incredible agent, Michelle Hauck at Storm Literary, who led me to Kensington and my equally amazing editor, John Scognamiglio.

Of course, I get my ultimate support from my wonderful husband Bert Engelhardt, who patiently endures my creative tantrums and often serves as a valuable sounding board.

Thanks to one and all!

Chapter 1

"Chase! *Watch out!*"

I leaped back onto the pavement as a red Vauxhall sedan raced past, missing me by inches.

A short woman with tightly curled, ginger-and-gray hair rushed over and gave me a quick, warm hug. "Haven't changed, have you? Honestly, Chase. Why can't you learn how they drive here in England? They even have 'look right' and 'look left' written on the street in front of you."

"Billie!" I said, with a rush of relief as I returned the hug. "It's good to see you, old friend." My longtime companion from many walking trips was clad in one of her colorful self-knit sweaters. "How the hell are you?"

Flashing me a smile, she said, "Much better now that I know you won't need to be scraped up off the street." She led me across the road to the train station, both of us looking left and right as we pulled our cases behind us. When we reached the other side, I said, "I can't believe I made it here. I was afraid I'd gotten totally lost."

She shook her head. "I can never understand how the venerable Rick Chasen, a man with an uncanny talent for

sniffing out deadly criminals, somehow has no sense of direction."

I took another glance at her sweater, a purple-and-
yellow creation with a pattern that looked like moose per-
forming a ballet. It reminded me of when I first met her on
a walk in Northumberland—what was it, six years before?
Our shared love of England and literature made us fast
friends. My late partner, Doug, had been fond of Billie too.
He'd accompanied us on a walk in Sussex and, even though
he wasn't the jealous type, was pleased I'd found a friend
who wasn't a younger, good-looking man.

"When did you get in?" Billie asked.

I told her about my long journey the day before: the
five-hour flight from San Diego to Atlanta, and the six-
hour flight from Atlanta to London. "I spent the night
right here in Barnstaple, at a refurbished vicarage. It was
quite respectable. I did, however, sense hints of a scan-
dalous past within its walls."

She gave a small laugh. "Well, what else would you expect from a vicarage?"

We entered the station, its imposing stone façade and
ornate brickwork a stark contrast to the bland commer-
ciality of the massive Tesco superstore across the road.

"You arrived here in England a week ago, didn't you?"
I asked as we wheeled our suitcases through the ticket hall
on our way to the lunchroom, a utilitarian space with five
plastic tables. We parked our cases beside one.

"I sure did. I'm sorry you couldn't have joined me in
London, Chase. Museums, concerts, theater. A veritable
cultural orgy! I'm so worn out that I don't know if I can
take another step."

Despite her supposed fatigue, she briskly walked up to
the counter and ordered a cucumber and cheese sandwich,
while I requested an American coffee, black. I was beginning to feel calmer, though still shaken from my earlier

misstep. I simply hadn't been watching where I was going. Panic attacks had been common in the first weeks following Doug's death, more than a year ago, but I thought I'd been doing better lately. What had triggered this one? I always had looked forward to a long walk in the English countryside. Maybe the prospect of putting on a brave face for strangers had pushed me over the edge.

We took our seats, and Billie gave me a once-over. "You look good, Chase. Your beard is fuller, and maybe a little grayer. It becomes you. You've lost weight, though."

I've always been a big guy, owing to my hefty build as well as my love for a good meal, but she was correct. Since Doug's death I'd dropped several pounds. "This trip should revive my appetite."

Billie took a bite of her sandwich and made a face. "If all the food here is like this, that might not happen. But other than not eating, what else is new with you?"

"Same old, same old. I sit around and watch ball games on TV."

"You know what I'm asking. The last time we spoke, you sounded so defeated. Even now, you still don't have your old spark back."

Was it that obvious? I took a sip of coffee. I could pretend to be fine but decided to come clean. "I admit it's taking me longer than I'd thought to get over Doug. Yes, I know there's no set timetable for grieving, but some days my mood seems to be getting worse rather than better."

I could have launched into a real pity party, complaining about my reluctance to keep up with mutual friends or even my cousin, Emily, in Seattle, my only relation other than my sister, Allison, who refuses to speak to me. But I didn't want to go down that road.

Billie formed a knowing smile. "You know what I think? I think you've lost your purpose. You retired right around the time Doug got sick, didn't you? Looking after him and managing his medical treatment became your new job. With Doug gone, you have no goal. Am I right?"

"Um . . . is this supposed to make me feel better?"

"All I'm saying is that you need to find a *new* purpose, Chase. You can't expect to go from a life of being an ace police detective to one of watching ball games on your sofa. Depression is bound to sneak in, especially after the death of someone you dearly loved."

I ran my finger around the rim of my cup. "Everything you're saying is true. But what can I do? The force won't let me have my job back at my age, no matter how sharp I still may be. And I have no interest in taking any old job just to stay busy."

She patted my hand. "You know what you do? Exactly what you're doing now. Go places. Get outdoors. You're only, what? Sixty-seven? That's still young! Find something that delights you, something that will open up your mind to other possibilities. Doug would be telling you to do the same. He'd have been so proud that you made your way back here."

I finished my coffee. "You're right as ever, Billie. Just be patient with me, okay? It only takes a stray thought of Doug to turn me into a blubbering mess."

She raised a finger. "I have a remedy for that too. I call it Flip it, Vanna."

"Flip it what?"

"Flip it, Vanna. You know, that lady on *Wheel of Fortune*. Every time a negative thought comes to mind, just say, 'Flip it, Vanna!' The thought turns around and becomes a brighter one on the flip side."

Where had she come up with this one? "It's worth a try, I guess. But I'm also worried about you."

Billie's eyes widened. "What makes you say that?"

"Small things. Your steps were more hesitant than usual just now when we were crossing the road. You're wearing different-colored socks on each foot. And most telling of all, your sweater pattern is completely wrong. Moose? In England, you always wear patterns of local animals—deer or foxes."

She chuckled. "Still the detective, aren't you? Well, you're right. The moose sweater was for London, where I saw *Come from Away*. It's a musical that takes place in Canada. I didn't mean to wear it today, but it's true, I'm preoccupied. Yesterday I got word that my younger sister, Janice, has breast cancer. They've conducted scans and found a tumor, so she needs surgery to see how far it may have spread. I wanted to rush home to be with her, but she wouldn't have it. 'You need to live, Billie,' she said. But . . . oh, Chase." Billie's lip trembled. "She needs to live too."

I reached over and held her hand.

She straightened her shoulders. "Still, whenever I get down, I just do a Flip it, Vanna! So what if Janice is having a health scare? The doctors can treat anything these days if they catch it soon enough."

Her comment struck home. Doug might still be alive if he'd undergone a routine colonoscopy, as I'd repeatedly suggested and he'd repeatedly ignored. I fell into another spell of maudlin navel-gazing, broken by the stationmaster announcing the arrival of the 3:45 train from Exeter.

"Oh dear," Billie said. "I thought we would be able to chat a bit more before the others arrived."

"Don't worry," I said, getting to my feet. "We're here for an entire week. There'll be plenty of time for us to catch up." As I turned toward the station's main hall, though, my resolve began to falter. It had been a while since I'd felt comfortable in the company of groups. When I lost Doug, I also lost my facility for conversation and small talk, something my old pals in the department would have thought impossible.

Billie and I wheeled our bags to the ticket hall, where

passengers were coming in from the platform. It wasn't difficult to spot those signed up with the Wanderers. There were five of them, each eyeing their surroundings as an alien might regard its first encounter with Earth.

A bright voice rang out. "Wanderers!" A smiling, young, brown-haired woman carrying a clipboard strode briskly to the center of the room. "If you're with the Wanderers, please gather round."

Billie and I stepped forward and were joined by two couples: a paunchy man wearing a loose shirt and trousers standing beside a woman with graying, sandy hair sprouting from beneath a floppy hat. Next to them was a tall, slender young woman with long, russet-colored hair and a wide mouth with firehouse-red lips and a young, square-faced and broad-shouldered man, his jet-black hair combed straight back. A similarity in the shape of their brows and chins suggested they might be related. The young woman gazed around in wonder, while her companion maintained a bemused, tolerant expression. The final member of our group was a small, nearly bald, rotund man wearing a blank expression. He seemed so inconsequential as to be nearly opaque.

From the list mailed to me, I already knew they were, like myself, Americans—the Wanderers' target market. From past walks, I also knew Wanderers clients were largely a genial bunch, diverse but like-minded in their appreciation of a slowly taken view of other lands and cultures. Beyond their names and hometowns, though, I knew nothing about them.

When we were all assembled, the brown-haired woman said, "Welcome, everyone! I am Sally Anders, your walk leader. I trust all your bags have identification tags? Be sure to place them over there, near the station entrance. Our walk manager, Howie, will collect them and take them to the van. From this point, you need not worry about anything. The Wanderers will take care of it all! Now bear with me as I check your names against my roster." She began to circulate through the group and eventually came to Billie and me.

We told her our names, and she glanced at her board. "Oh, yes. Mr. Chasen. Miss Mondreau. I've heard quite a bit about you."

"Mostly good things, I hope," I said.

"Very much so." In an undertone, she added, "Actually, I'm new to the Wanderers organization—this is my first assignment—so the staff has filled me in as much as possible. I understand you two have walked with us many times before, which will make things a bit easier."

"I'm sure you'll do fine," Billie said.

Sally maintained her smile. "This walk is a new one as well, you know. We've never offered it before."

"That's what appealed to me," I said, and assumed a stentorian tone. "Exmoor, that fabled corner of England with its rugged seacoast and sweeping, mist-swept moors! Majestic and mysterious home to numerous tales and legends! And please . . . call me Chase."

Sally laughed. "I'll do that."

I scanned the room. "I thought there would be more of us."

"You're correct," Sally said, her eyes darting to her clipboard. "Mr. and Mrs. Gretz have yet to arrive. Apparently, they weren't able to make the train and have hired a private car. If they don't show up in the next few minutes, we'll catch up with them later at the hotel." She turned to the group. "Everyone! Please make your way out to our van. It's the yellow one; you can't miss it. We will be leaving in a few minutes."

Everyone headed outside, a few steps behind Howie, the short, stocky walk manager, tweed cap atop his head, pushing a large cart laden with our bags.

At that moment, a black Bentley roared up and came to a stop that I would have termed "screeching" if Bentleys could screech. The doors swung open, and a stern-faced man in a blue polo shirt and brightly patterned slacks stepped out, followed by a platinum-haired woman whose bosom was prominently displayed in a low-cut, tight-fitting dress. She carried a small leopard-print handbag. The man was in his late sixties or so, the woman considerably younger.

"Those must be the Gretzes," I said to Billie. "I don't normally check people online, but when I saw his name on the list, it rang a bell. I'd seen it in the business pages. He's some kind of a tycoon in health care, and that's his latest wife—the third, if I remember correctly."

Their driver loaded their cases onto a cart. From the quantity, it looked like they were embarking on a months-long ocean voyage. He began wheeling them toward the Wanderers van.

"You see, you moron?" the man barked to his wife as they followed their driver. "You and your worrying! We made it, just like I said we would. Now, shut your trap."

Billie leaned close and murmured, "We're going to have to put up with *him* all week? Now I understand the two ex-wives."

Another train had pulled up, and more passengers soon spilled onto the platform. Billie and I were weaving our way through the throng when we were jostled by two young toughs, yelling and pushing. One of them—long-haired and wearing a blue hoodie—bumped roughly into Gretz. It appeared to be intentional.

"Hey!" the man said. The youth scurried off.

My interior "something's not right" alarm signaled. I darted after the boy, but he was moving fast, so I broke into a run. When I neared him and reached out to seize his arm, he took off at an even faster pace. Well, that tears it, I thought. As fit as I may be, I was no match against a kid. Fortunately, he ran straight toward a small gaggle of nuns and one—a surprisingly agile lady with quick reflexes—picked up on what was happening and thrust out her leg. The boy tripped over it and fell to the ground.

I ran over, thanked the nun, yanked the boy to his feet, and pulled him over to Gretz, who was looking shell-shocked. I thrust the lad toward him. "Give this man back his wallet."

The boy tried to wrest himself free, but I held fast. "Wot you talkin' about?" he said. "I ain't got no wallet."

With my other hand, I reached into his hoodie and extracted Gretz's billfold. "What do you call this, then?"

"Wot do you know!" the youth said. "How'd *that* get there?"

I took the lad over to a nearby security officer. "This boy just stole that gentleman's wallet," I said, nodding toward Gretz.

"I never did!" the boy protested.

The officer took hold of him and inspected his other pockets, producing two more billfolds. He thanked me and led the boy away. I handed Gretz his wallet.

"Th–thanks," he said, taking it. His eyes were hollow, and his hand was trembling. This seemed an overreaction to what happened, and yet having your wallet taken was unnerving, certainly.

Gretz's wife smiled at me. "We owe you a big thank-you, Mr. . . . ?"

"Rick Chasen. I'm on the same Wanderers walk as you."

"I'm Summer, and this is my husband, Ronnie. We're in your debt, Mr. Chasen."

"Please call me Chase. And it was nothing. Just doing my civic duty."

Sally stepped up. "We really must get going. Please board the van so we can keep to our schedule."

As the group followed her, Gretz remained frozen.

"Come on, sweetie," his wife said as she took his arm. "We've got to go."

His eyes were vacant. "Don't you see? It's happening."

"What's happening?" his wife asked.

He gave her a frightened glare. "Someone's out to get me."

Chapter 2

"Out to *get* you?" Summer said. "Don't act crazy, baby! It was a pickpocket, that's all. And thanks to Mr. Chase here, you got your wallet back. Come on."

Gretz hesitated before following his wife to the yellow Wanderers van. He eyed Howie hefting his bags and said, "Careful with that one, boy. If I find anything broken, I'll know who to blame."

Howie, hardly a boy, flashed him a glare. What sort of fragile items was Gretz carrying? I joined the others inside the van and found my capture of the pickpocket had become the main topic of conversation.

"It was like something out of a crime show," the raven-haired young woman said. "You're a real hero!"

"Chase used to be a police detective," Billie said. "He's got lots of stories. Ask him about the time he—"

"Billie's exaggerating," I interrupted, flashing her a warning. "I was just an everyday investigator. Nothing exciting."

"Nevertheless, that took guts," the woman in the floppy hat said. "My husband would never do anything so brave."

The man beside her said, "Now, listen here, dear—"

"I'm Phaedra Meyers, by the way," the woman said. "This is my husband, Justin."

"You're from upstate New York, isn't that right?" I asked.

Phaedra recoiled slightly in surprise. "Why, yes."

I'd read that in the list I was sent, but Doug had been an actor who specialized in vocal work, and over the years, I'd absorbed his knack for identifying accents. "I detect subtle glottal stops and raised vowels."

"What about me?" asked the raven-haired woman. "Can you tell where I'm from?"

"Hey, don't put him on the spot," said the young man beside her.

The monophthongal Southern slide in her pronunciation of "I'm" was unmistakable. "I would say the Southeast, perhaps South Carolina."

Her mouth dropped. "That's *amazing*! I'm Corky Nielsen, and my baby brother, Brett, here and I are from Charleston!" She spoke exclusively in exclamation points.

"*Baby?*" Brett snorted. "We're practically the same age. Only ten months apart."

"You're still my younger brother, however many months it is."

"Is this your first time on a Wanderers walk?" Billie asked.

"This is my first time in *England*! It's like a dream come true. I mean, everywhere you look"—her eyes turned to the vista outside, at that point still the parking lot—"it's so *British*!"

"Please forgive her," said her brother. "She's been like this ever since the plane landed. She's a chronic Anglophile."

Corky gave him a withering stare. "Honestly, Brett. You make it sound like a *disease*."

Billie and I introduced ourselves, and turned inquiringly

to the diminutive man with the dour face. "Lucien Barker," he said in a barely audible squeak. "Denver, Colorado."

"Pleased to meet you," Billie said.

"And we're the Gretzes from North Carolina," said Summer. Her husband remained silent, still shaken.

Howie secured the van's doors, hauled himself into the driver's seat, and fired up the engine. "We'll be at our hotel in a few minutes," Sally announced as we exited the car park. "Just make yourself comfortable."

I gazed out the window as the buildings of the town gave way to the green fields of the countryside. Once again, I was struck by the singular beauty of rural England, its springtime colors pulsating with the vibrancy of a high-resolution video. Soon we were passing country fields and lanes, dotted with Devon's classic limewashed, thatch-roofed houses. This verdant landscape was a completely different world from the desiccated hills of northern San Diego, where I lived, and it was a welcome change.

I turned to see if my fellow walkers were similarly entranced. Only Corky and Billie seemed drawn to the view outside. The rest appeared unimpressed, as if they were on their way to a business meeting. Sally studied her papers. Phaedra looked straight ahead with an air of impatience. Justin and Brett were glued to their cell phones. Lucien dug for something in his knapsack. Summer checked her appearance in a pocket mirror.

It was Gretz I was concerned about; he still looked spooked, staring straight ahead. With a shaking hand, he extracted a fat cigar from his pocket, lit it up, took a drag, and let loose a toxic cloud of smoke.

"Mr. Gretz," Sally said with strained patience. "There is no smoking in this van."

He turned toward her. "What are you talking about? Winston Churchill loved his cigars. It's a British thing, isn't it?"

"It's also an unhealthful thing," Phaedra said.

"Mrs. Meyers is right," Sally said. "I must insist that you put it out."

"For what I'm paying? I'll damn well smoke if I want to."

"Not here, mister," Phaedra said. "Keep that up and we'll all have stage-three cancer within minutes."

Gretz growled, lowered the window, and tossed his cigar outside. "You happy now, lady?"

"Don't talk to my wife like that!" Justin said.

Gretz turned to him. "Then tell her to mind her own—"

"Look at that church steeple!" Corky said. "It's like something out of Jane Austen!" Everyone peered out the window.

"It's the poets we're best known for," Sally said, grateful, I suspected, for the diversion. "Wordsworth. Shelley. Coleridge. We'll be walking on some of the trails that inspired them."

As the van passed through a small cluster of trees, Billie said, " 'One impulse from a vernal wood may teach you more of man, of moral evil and of good, than all the sages can.' " Turning to the group, she said, "That's from one of my favorite Wordsworth poems."

" 'Moral evil,' " Brett said. "That doesn't sound very comforting."

"Evil is everywhere if you look for it," Phaedra said. She asked Sally, "Speaking of which, isn't there a Beast of Exmoor? I heard someone talking about it."

Sally gave a small laugh. "You've caught up with some of our local folklore."

Corky's face tensed. "Don't tell me there's some kind of monster on the loose around here!"

"It's what you would call an old wives' tale," Sally said. "The most popular theory is that a few pumas and leopards were released into the wild around here, back in the sixties, after a law was passed that made it illegal for them to be kept as pets in captivity outside of a zoo."

"Oh, dear," Corky said.

"Rest assured, no one has ever documented their existence, let alone been attacked by one," our guide said.

The van abruptly swung to the left and back. "Sorry 'bout that," Howie said. "I needed to avoid a stray lamb in the road."

"I think you wrenched my back," Ronald Gretz growled.

"I'll give you one of my rubdowns," his wife purred. "You like those."

"Can't you keep your trap shut?" he snapped. "Everyone doesn't have to know about your damn rubdowns!"

Summer fell quiet. Billie leaned close to me and whispered, "I think the Beast of Exmoor is real after all."

No further outbreaks marred the rest of the journey. I continued to be captivated by the roadside vistas: neatly trimmed hedges bordering pastures on which sheep and cattle grazed, green meadows unfurling beyond toward forested hills. Overhead, small cotton-ball clouds floated in the deep blue sky.

After a few minutes, we pulled onto a side road and headed up a narrow drive toward an imposing, gray-stoned building looming in the distance. On the side of the drive, an elegantly lettered sign read, DOWNSMEADE GRANGE.

There were appreciative "oohs" and "aahs" as the Victorian gothic manor house came into view. I'd seen images of the building, built in the 1700s, on the Wanderers website, but it was far more impressive in reality: a classically proportioned structure perfectly situated in the fold of a green valley. The van pulled to a stop on the gravel drive before the entrance.

"This is more like it," Phaedra said as she stepped out, took a deep breath, and surveyed the leafy alders bordering the broad lawns and gardens.

"It's perfect!" Corky gushed, her mouth open in awe. "Look over there—they even have a garden maze!"

As the others climbed out, Sally clapped her hands. "Listen up! Howie and I will bring your bags into the hotel. Once you're checked in, it would be helpful if you could carry them to your room. If you would rather not, or you are not able, please let me or Howie know and we will make sure your bags are delivered."

"I sure as hell am not going to haul my own luggage," Gretz said. "Where are the bellmen?"

"There are no bellmen, Mr. Gretz, I'm sorry to say," Sally replied. "This is a boutique hotel without that kind of staff. However, as I said, Howie can assist you if you're unable."

"I'm not 'unable,'" he barked. "But for what I'm shelling out for this boondoggle, I'll be damned if I have to be my own servant."

The rest of us hurried inside the studded wood entrance door and queued at the front desk to receive our room keys. My haste—and I surmised that of the others also—was motivated more by avoiding Gretz than by any desire for efficiency. I found myself standing with Billie behind the Meyerses.

"Are we to put up with that horrid man all week?" Phaedra said.

"Give him a day or two," Billie said. "People tend to mellow once they're out on the path."

"Or after a pint or two of British ale," Justin said.

I looked to my left. "Speaking of which, there's the hotel bar." I pointed left toward a warmly lit room fashioned like a country alehouse. It had a low, wood-paneled ceiling, colorful taps lined up along the bar, and a small fire sizzling in the brick fireplace. All that was missing was a sleeping hound on the slate floor.

Sally told us to all gather in an hour at the hotel's famed restaurant, Gables, which, she reminded us, had recently earned its first Michelin star. I turned to give my name to the desk clerk, who checked me off her ledger and handed me my room key. To Billie I said, "I don't know if I can wait an hour for a drink. Meet you in the bar in fifteen minutes?"

She nodded, received her key, and followed me past the row of suitcases lined up in the entrance hall. I cast my eyes over the bags. One in particular caught my eye. There was something about it that didn't make sense, although I couldn't quite put my finger on it.

"No elevator? What kind of dump is this?"

I looked up. Ronald Gretz had found something new to complain about.

The others had rooms on the upper floors, but mine was in a small annex at the rear of the main building. The room was a bit glam—an imposing, multicolored Ellsworth Kelly print hung over the bed—but not overly glitzy. One window overlooked a small green courtyard between the room and the main house, and a larger window beside the bed provided a view of a grassy rise behind the hotel, atop which sat another building that, I surmised, must be the Michelin-starred restaurant. The sun had begun its descent, and the tall oak trees cast long shadows across the manicured lawn. I noticed a flat-screen television mounted on the wall opposite the bed and was tempted to find the Red Sox–Tampa Bay game. Nope, I reminded myself. That wasn't why I was there.

But something else was on my mind besides baseball. Back home, I'd become accustomed (mostly) to being alone again over the past year, but this was the first time in quite a while that I'd traveled by myself. A mutual passion for visiting other lands had helped first draw Doug and me together, and over the years, we grew to appreciate each other's additional interests—particularly my love of walking and England, and his for regional theater and mimicking local accents. These had become so entwined that, when Doug passed, it felt as though half of my own identity had been taken with him.

It had taken me many long, dark months to begin to believe that I could truly function on my own. And now, just when I thought I'd become adept at not thinking of Doug every minute, his absence again made itself known and was creating a familiar void that was darkening my anticipation of the days ahead.

Maybe Billie's weird strategy would work. I shut my eyes, said, "Flip it, Vanna!" and waited for my mood to shift. When nothing happened, I opened my eyes, unpacked, changed into my dinner clothes, took a quick look in the mirror to make sure my beard hadn't strayed too far into Crazed Woodman territory, and headed to the hotel bar. It was deserted except for a young couple, perhaps newlyweds, holding drinks and gazing into each other's eyes. How nice it would be, I thought, to look at someone that way again.

Again, Doug came to mind—the smile on his handsome face the first time I saw him, at a birthday party for a mutual friend in La Jolla. I knew at that moment that my life would never be the same.

I realized that I was standing beside a long table on which sat thirty or so bottles of local gin. I picked one up and was examining the label when a man beside me said, "Daunting, isn't it?"

I hadn't heard him approach. He was about my age (late fifties or early sixties), a bit shorter, slender, with a healthy swath of salt-and-pepper hair and the kind of smile—

lopsided, playfully sneaky—that makes me weak. He wore a sports coat and an open-necked shirt.

I smiled back. "I know there's been an upturn in gin production here, but I hadn't expected anything like this."

" 'Upturn' is putting it mildly," he said with a laugh. " 'Explosion' is more like it. Some say the attraction is our water—it is exceptionally pure—while others claim it's the locally grown botanicals. Many of the distilleries around here use as many as ten." He picked up a crystal-blue bottle with an intricate design. "This is a good one. Want to try it?" He twisted the top off, poured a finger of gin into a glass, and handed it to me.

I took a sip and raised my eyebrows. "That's nice."

"Do you taste the anise and caraway?"

I took another sip. "I wouldn't recognize caraway if I was swimming in it, so I'll take your word for it. You're certainly well-informed. How long have you worked here?"

He chuckled. "Oh, I'm not an employee. I just dropped by to see an old friend who's up for the weekend. We dated years ago, but that never worked out. He and I still keep in touch, however."

Suddenly, this conversation had become a lot more interesting.

"As you made an assumption about me," he said, "let me make one about you. American, correct?"

"Guilty as charged. From Southern California, north of San Diego. Where do you call home?"

"I'm a local lad. Born and bred outside Dartmoor. Nothing too exciting, unfortunately."

I let my eyes travel over him. "Oh, I don't agree with that."

He broke into that off-kilter smile. I felt like whimpering. He leaned close. "Did you know you have a pair of stockings hanging from your dinner jacket?"

I looked down and laughed. "It's a Boston Red Sox pin. An American baseball team."

"Do you play for them?"

I laughed again, but stopped when I realized he might not have been joking. "I'm a bit too old and out of shape for that, I'm afraid."

He looked up at me. "Old? Not from where I'm standing. And your shape looks just fine."

A sudden buzz made him fish his phone from his coat pocket. He frowned as he looked at it. "Oh, blast!"

"Not bad news, I hope."

He pocketed his phone. "A work matter, nothing unusual. But it means I must take my leave of you, which is bad news indeed."

Blast was right. "That is bad news. My name is Rick Chasen, by the way. But everybody calls me Chase."

" 'Chase.' I like that. I'm Mike. Will you be here tomorrow? Perhaps we can sample more of the gin."

"That would make my day." He gave me another heart-melting smile, topped it with a wink, and walked away.

The encounter left me feeling gut-punched, but in a good way. I hadn't flirted, or been flirted with, for ages. It was exhilarating, but unnerving. I couldn't help feeling I was betraying Doug.

Chapter 3

Sunday, late afternoon,
Downsmeade Grange Bar

It was at this low point that Gretz walked in.

"There you are," he said. "I need to talk to you."

I took a deep breath. He was the last person I wanted to deal with at that moment. "What is it you want, Mr. Gretz?"

"Call me Ron; everyone does. Listen. I saw how you handled that creep at the train station. Pretty smooth work. Then I learned you used to be a cop."

"A police investigator," I corrected.

"Even better. You're just the kind of guy I could use right now. Let's sit down, okay?"

Gretz began walking toward a table but hesitated when he spotted my lapel pin.

"Don't tell me you're a lousy Sox lover," he said.

"Let me guess. You're a Yankees fan, right?"

"Damn right. Best team in the whole damn world."

I let this pass. Sports team rivalries are not worth squabbling over. We sat, and a bowtie-wearing barman appeared to take our drink orders. I suggested the gin Mike and I had just sampled, and he promptly filled two glasses. Gretz swallowed his in one gulp and leaned close.

"Let me get right to the point. Someone is out to get me. I don't know who or when or how, but I've got a feeling it's gonna be soon."

I took a sip from my drink. This explained why he looked so shaken after the pickpocket incident; he'd been expecting something to happen. What was it? Normally, I relish a challenge, but this was in the wrong place and at the wrong time. Still, I was intrigued. "When you say someone is 'out to get you,' what do you mean?"

"What do you think I mean? Someone's looking to bump me off!"

"Why would anyone want to do that?"

Gretz waved his hand. "Never mind. Believe me when I say that someone is gunning for me. Since we got over here two days ago, I've received . . . threats. Text messages. Emails."

"Threatening what, exactly?"

"They don't come right out and say. It's stuff like 'you'd better watch out' and 'you're going to be sorry.' "

"Sorry for what? What have you done?"

"I haven't done anything, I tell ya! But I've been getting these ever since we got here. And now we'll be walking around in the wilderness. God only knows what could happen."

"Do you have any idea who's sending these notes?"

"Nope." He pulled out his cell phone and showed me one of the posts, which said simply, "You're going to pay." It was signed "An Avenger."

I thought for a moment. Was the name "Avenger" a reference to the popular superhero characters? Doubtful. It was more likely that Gretz had cheated someone in a business deal and they wanted payback. I asked, "Could the person who's sending these be someone in our group? Do you recognize any of them?"

He leaned closer. "Never saw any of 'em before in my

life. But that's just it, you see? It *must* be one of these guys! We're going to be together for a whole week. That'll give this guy time to try something. I need you to find out who it is before it's too late."

I took another sip of gin. Although I tried to maintain a calm façade, the pros and cons of Gretz's proposal were battling away inside of me. The pros: His offer was tempting; it was something I could get my teeth into. I could go back to doing what I love—sniffing out danger and finding a bad guy. The cons: I'd been out of the game too long. I was over here for relaxation, not to work. And . . . what if I failed?

The cons won out.

"I'm not a police investigator anymore, Mr. Gretz, and even if I was, I wouldn't have any authority over here. I suggest you contact local law enforcement. They could put a trace on these threats and get to the bottom of them."

Gretz slammed his fist on the table. "Don't you understand? I can't get the law involved in any of this! If I were back home, I'd know what to do, but over here, I'm fair game. All I'm asking is for you to keep your eyes open, like you did today."

I shook my head.

"You want money. Okay, then. Name your price."

I'd had enough of this. "Look. I came here to have a pleasant walking holiday, not be someone's bodyguard. I'll keep my eyes open—I always do—but if your concern is genuine, then maybe you should just go home. Either that, or notify the police."

"I tell you I can't!" He paused a moment and said, "It's a Yankees thing, right? Still sore because you traded off the Bambino, right?" He was referring to the infamous sale of Babe Ruth's contract by Red Sox owner Harry Frazee to the Yankees in 1919.

"That was over a hundred years ago." I downed the rest

of my drink and stood. "I don't hold grudges, and certainly not for that long." Looking at my watch, I said, "We're supposed to get together with the others in a few minutes. Are you going to join us?"

Gretz didn't respond. I walked off and found Billie in the foyer.

"If you don't mind, let's not go into the bar right now," I said.

"You look spooked. Is everything alright?"

"Why don't we go up to the restaurant? We need to meet up with the others there soon anyway."

We headed up the hill behind the hotel, where the restaurant's namesake gables towered above us, silhouetted against the night sky. Inside, the large dining room was lit with bright votive candles and a crystal chandelier. To our right was a more intimately lit nook. We went there, and a young male server in a green waistcoat appeared.

"I've been craving a pint of local ale all day," I said, even though I'd just had two glasses of gin. "Sound good?"

Billie nodded.

"Your best local ale for us," I told the server.

"Two Exmoor Golds coming up," he said with a smile.

"Now tell me what's going on," Billie said. We sat in a pair of armchairs, and I related my conversation with Gretz.

"Leave it to you to get caught up in cloak-and-dagger intrigue right off the bat."

"I'm not 'caught up' in anything. I told Gretz in no uncertain terms I was not for hire. He refuses to go to the police with his concerns, but he won't explain why."

Billie cocked her head. "Why did you turn him down? This sounds right up your alley. Tackling a puzzle would fire up those brain cells you've been ignoring."

I sighed. "In case you've forgotten, I came over here to walk, not work."

She reached out and clasped my hand. "Do I have to tell you again? You've been adrift without a puzzle to solve. Now one falls right in your lap and you throw it away! I wish you'd reconsider."

I'd expected Billie to support my decision, not be a cheerleader for Gretz. "I can't deny that I'm tempted. These days I welcome anything that will take my mind off Doug."

Billie smiled. "Joyce Carol Oates described her grief process beautifully: 'My discovery is each day is livable if divided into segments. More accurately, each day is livable *only* if divided into segments. It is not possible to endure an entire day.' *A Widow's Story*. I suggest you read it."

Our walk leader, Sally, appeared, looking fresh in a yellow dress. She smiled and approached us. "I thought the rest of the group would be here by now. I hope I don't have to go round them up."

I checked my watch. "We still have a few minutes. You're dealing with Americans, you know. We're not the most punctual people on the planet."

Billie said, "You mentioned this is your first assignment as a guide."

Sally gave a nod. "That's right. It's practically ready-made for me, in view of my background. I've done a fair amount of country walking, rock climbing, and whatnot. Plus, I'm a born organizer. I've led groups on a volunteer basis in the past, so I figured, why not get paid for it? I even got to plan some of the itinerary. The Wanderers came up with the general route, but I contributed specifics—my favorite path segments and places to stop for meals."

"What work did you do before?"

Sally's face darkened slightly. "I was in the hospitality

industry. You know what that's like; you've seen some of the demands here at the Grange. It can become very tedious and often . . . toxic. But how about you two? Oh, excuse me, Chase, you did some work with the police, didn't you? That sounds exciting."

"That was a few years ago. And yes, some of it was exciting, when I was able to get out in the field, but it was mostly desk work. Not the stuff of TV shows or action films at all. Billie here probably had more interesting adventures than me."

"Were you in police work as well?" Sally asked her.

Billie chuckled. "You might say I worked under cover. Book covers, that is. I was a librarian for nearly fifty years."

Sally smiled. "Brilliant. And what coerced the two of you to join this tour?"

Billie and I traded looks. I said, "We both love walking, we both love England, and neither of us have been to this part of the country. Plus, I recently . . . lost a family member. I hope a change of scene will clear my mind and put me back on the right course."

Sally's eyes assumed a faraway look. "Families can be distressing, can't they? I have found it's best not to grow too close to them."

An uncomfortable silence followed, broken when the Meyerses walked in. I barely recognized Phaedra: she had tamed her loose grayish-blond hair, which was no longer covered by a large hat. She was dressed simply in an evening dress. Justin, casually clad for dinner as well, greeted us with a smile.

Corky and Brett were next to appear. "Look at this room!" she gushed. "Isn't this all so perfect? The paintings! The chandelier! The furniture! It all looks so . . ."

"So *British*, we know," Brett said. "Give the shock and awe a rest for a while, Cork, okay?"

"I can't help it. This place is like something out of a mystery novel. I half expect Lord Peter Wimsey to walk in any minute." As if on cue, Lucien Barker entered wearing a tweed jacket, a gold waistcoat, and a bright red bowtie.

"And there he is!" Corky said. "Good evening, Lord Peter!"

Barker looked mystified.

"The only thing that's missing is a raging storm outside," Corky added.

Everyone froze, expecting to hear a peal of thunder. When none came, Phaedra said, "Well, short of a storm, what about a murder?"

Her comment was greeted with uncomfortable laughter. The Gretzes arrived next, which was surprising; not only did I think Ronald would still be angry about my refusal of his offer, he seemed like the type who lived on room service. Yet there they were—Summer in a white dress with a plunging neckline, and Gretz in a polo shirt and slacks.

"Hi, everyone!" Summer said. There was that overly sensualized voice again—part Marilyn Monroe, part Jessica Rabbit. It was theatrical but passably credible. Doug would have had a field day analyzing it.

Gretz noticed the glass in my hand. To his wife he said, "Go get me a beer. Make it cold. None of that piss-warm crap they serve over here."

"The server will be here momentarily," Sally said. "There's no need for your wife to do anything."

"I want a beer *now*," Gretz bellowed.

Summer scurried off like an obedient servant.

Phaedra leaned close to me. "Unbelievable," she whispered. "I'm surprised she hasn't killed him."

A moment later, the server appeared with the Meyerses' drinks and turned to Corky, who requested a Corpse Reviver.

"A what?" the server asked.

"Corpse Reviver. You know. Brandy, sweet vermouth, an apple slice, calvados."

Brett laughed. "Honestly, Cork. Where do you think you are, at one of your chichi Glenwood hangouts? Order a decent drink, for God's sake."

"I'll see what I can do," the server said and walked off before someone requested another exotic concoction. Summer returned with a large frosty glass that she handed to her husband. He gulped it down without a word of thanks.

Another awkward silence descended. The server returned with Corky's cocktail. She took a sip and winced. "Whatever this is, it sure isn't a Corpse Reviver." The server offered to take it back, but Corky waved him off. "When in Rome, isn't that what they say?" She tasted it. "Not too bad, as it turns out. Very Devonian!"

Phaedra eyed her wineglass critically. "We should have cheese as a balance. There's disagreement about that, of course, but one must admit that the two fermented agricultural products complement one another beautifully and provide a . . . shall we say, magical? . . . result when consumed in equal amounts. Very soothing to the psyche."

"The 'psyche' is very important to my wife," Justin noted.

I said, "I love cheese and I love wine, so I'm on your side."

Sally stood. "Before we go to dinner, let me propose a toast. To a wonderful week of illuminating walks and exciting discoveries!"

We all raised our glasses. "Hear, hear!" Billie said.

"For those of you who have not visited this corner of Britain before, prepare for a varied experience. We'll be walking across the fabled moors, through fields of heather, along the tops of granite cliffs, and beside streams in wooded valleys. In all, we'll walk approximately eight miles tomorrow and be back in plenty of time for everyone to relax before dinner. Does anyone have a question?"

"Yes," said Phaedra.

"Mrs. Meyers?"

"I must say that our room is most inadequate. There's a horrid painting of an elephant over our bed. How can we rest peacefully with that looming over us?"

"My dear," Justin said. "Now is not the time to bring up such a petty matter."

"*Petty?*" Phaedra shot back. "I wouldn't call bad art a petty matter. Not to mention lampshades of the most off-putting shade of tangerine, exceedingly inadequate lighting in the bathroom, and don't get me started on the carpeting—"

"I'll see what I can do about changing your room," Sally said. Turning to the others, she said, "Let's go to our table. There are place cards tonight, but on subsequent dinners you may sit where you wish."

We went into the dining hall, a high-ceilinged room illuminated by two crystal chandeliers, and found our places. A server in a starched shirt distributed menu cards. "Hmm," Phaedra said as she scanned the starters and main courses. "These selections don't scream 'Michelin star' to me. Guinea fowl, John Dory, and lamb. Merciful heavens."

Phaedra ordered the fish. Promptly, the rest of us placed our orders, and the server walked off, but soon reappeared with wine. This loosened us up, and soon we were inquiring about each other—backgrounds, professions, history. Billie mentioned her career as a librarian.

"And she knits like a whiz," I said. "She's wearing one of her creations."

Billie held up her arms. "In case you can't make out the pattern, they're maple leaves. It's a tribute to my home state." This was greeted with appreciative nods.

"What's your profession, Mr. Nielsen?" Sally asked, keeping her tone light.

Brett paused. "I'm . . . I'm what you might call an investment consultant."

Corky blurted out a laugh and put her hand to her mouth. Brett glared at her.

"Best way to make money is through good, old-fashioned work," Gretz said. "Not through stock market swindles."

Brett turned toward Gretz. "*Swindles?* I've never swindled anyone in my life!"

Billie asked, "And what exactly is *your* work, Mr. Gretz?"

"Ronnie owns a chain of nursing homes," Summer said.

"Talk about swindles," Brett murmured.

"I can speak for myself, you know," Gretz growled to his wife. Turning to the group, he said, "Golden Sunset is not a 'chain of nursing homes.' Summer's never understood my business. She thinks it's all bedpans and diapers. Golden Sunset is much more than that; our elder-care facilities provide a dignified haven for life's second chapter." His words sounded as if they came from a prospectus.

"*Dignified?*" Barker piped up. Pushing his thin voice, he said, "There's nothing 'dignified' about them! Death factories, that's all they are! Warehouses for the dying. My mother passed away in a so-called 'elder-care facility' this past year, long before she should have. It was the same thing as murder!"

"Cut the hearts-and-flowers crap," Gretz snapped. "You sound like all the families I have to put up with. They think we're going to make their dear old mommies and granddaddies young again. They got no idea what it takes to put up with those old fossils. I tell you, it's a thankless job, and—"

"How dare you!" Barker shouted, his eyes flaring. "My mother was no fossil!"

"Mr. Meyers," Sally spoke up, before Gretz could respond further. "What kind of business are you in?"

Justin was startled by the sudden question. "Oh. We . . . um . . . we . . ."

"We design living environments," Phaedra said. "Décor, color, lighting, general ambience. We make workplaces more productive, home spaces more relaxing, that type of thing."

Billie said, "That's fascinating. What exactly do—"

"Keep your hands off me!" Gretz shouted.

Summer, who had been tucking a napkin in Gretz's shirt collar, froze and assumed an overcompensating smile. She gave a dismissive laugh. "I forget how touchy Ronnie gets when I help him with his napkin."

"And stop calling me 'Ronnie'! You treat me like a goddamned child."

Howie cleared his throat. "You're in mixed company, Mr. Gretz. Watch your bloody language."

"You telling me how to talk, limey?" Gretz said. "When are we gonna eat? I'm hungry!"

As if on cue, a young woman entered carrying plates of the starters—lobster bisque, goat curd, veal ravioli. Judging by everyone's comments, these were received favorably. I sampled my ravioli. The restaurant's reputation was well deserved.

While the group was enjoying their food, I eyed Gretz. He was strangely mute, taking small spoonfuls of his bisque, his face expressionless.

"So tell me, Chase," Justin said, "how many walks like this have you been on?"

"Well, let me see now . . ."

Suddenly, Gretz erupted in violent, choking coughs. His eyes were bulging, and his face was red. I sprang up, but Phaedra was already behind him, yanking him from his chair and clutching her arms around his rib cage. She gave him a sharp squeeze, and something shot out of his mouth. He coughed a few additional times and seemed to be out of danger. Summer took Phaedra's place by his side.

"What was he choking on?" Brett asked.

Billie reached out and picked up the projectile. "It's a bone."

"We haven't been served anything with bones in it," Corky noted. "What was he eating?"

"The lobster bisque," I replied, and took the bone from Billie. It was small and delicate, easy to overlook. I scanned the faces of the others. All appeared to be horrified. Gretz was shaken but otherwise seemed okay.

"Lobsters don't have bones, do they?" Corky asked.

"They have shells," I said.

"Someone . . ." Gretz struggled to speak. "Someone tried to kill me!"

Phaedra took the bone from me. "It looks like a chicken bone. But chicken isn't on the menu."

"Guinea fowl is," Justin noted.

"Yes," Phaedra said, turning the bone in her hand. "They have small bones just like this."

"But how did it get into Mr. Gretz's bisque?" Sally asked.

"Isn't anyone listening to me?" Gretz raged, his voice stronger. "Someone put it there! To kill me!"

"I keep telling you, Ronnie," Summer said as she caressed her husband's neck. "Nobody's trying to kill you. Who would want to do that?" He had clearly not told her of the threatening notes he'd received.

The manager rushed over. Sally explained what had happened, and his face tightened with concern. To Gretz, he said, "I am so sorry, sir. I don't know how this could have happened. Our chef is painstaking in his preparations. He would definitely have noticed if there was anything foreign in your bisque."

"Your chef didn't do this!" Gretz shouted. He rose to his feet and threw his napkin on the table. "It was someone else!" He cast an accusing look at all of us. "*Someone at this table!*"

"You're out of your mind," Brett said. "Why would any of us want to harm you? We just met you!"

"If you think you can fool me, you can sure as hell think again," Gretz said. "I know one of you has it in for me. And I'm going to find out who it is!"

Summer put her arm around him. "Come on, Ronnie. Let's go back to our room, watch TV, and have burgers from room service. Okay?"

"Only if nobody here touches them first," he said. Summer led him away.

After they left, Brett said, "I know some of us have joked about killing the old guy. But nobody would actually try to do it, would they?"

"It's preposterous," Phaedra said. "If someone wanted to kill that creep, there are better ways to do it than tossing a tiny bone into his soup."

Justin said, "How far away are we from the Arctic Circle? Maybe we could put him on an ice floe and be done with it."

"Let's be real here," said Corky. "It must have been an accident, right?"

Shaken by what had happened to Gretz, none of us was in the mood for light conversation when our main courses arrived. We ate quickly and rose to leave, bidding each other good night. Phaedra and Justin said they were going to have an after-dinner drink in the hotel bar.

As I walked out, I passed Sally, looking morose. "What happened to Gretz wasn't your fault," I said in a reassuring tone. "I'm sure he'll be alright. And the meal was delicious."

"Glad you enjoyed it, Mr. Chasen." She managed to form a smile.

"There you go again with the formality. I would never call you Miss Sanders."

Her smile faded. "It's Miss *Anders*. And you have my word that I'll call you 'Chase,' although I'm so used to addressing people by their surname."

"You can do that with the rest of this bunch. Just don't let any of them intimidate you." Both of us knew whom I was speaking of.

In my room, I was about to climb into bed when I got the feeling I'd forgotten something. Then it came to me. When I was with the force, I kept a journal and would update it every night with everything I'd observed during the day, no matter how trivial. Gretz's situation didn't exactly qualify as a "case," but resurrecting my routine would get me back into a comfortable habit. I was grateful I'd packed a small moleskin notebook and a writing pen.

I sat at the small desk and began writing—my impressions of the group, the pickpocket incident, Gretz's job offer. I grinned when I noted my encounter with Mike. But when I began detailing what had happened at dinner—the arguments and Gretz's choking attack—I paused. Could he have been correct? Had someone really tried to kill him?

I was inclined to dismiss the possibility. How would anyone have engineered that? Certainly, Gretz was the type to fling out accusations. I had to admit I didn't like the guy. That he'd been the subject of threats didn't surprise me.

And yet . . . he was clearly troubled. He wouldn't reveal what might be behind the threats he'd received, and my knee-jerk reaction was that he must be guilty of some misdeed (fraud? extortion? blackmail?). Yet that was, I confess, unfair. Simply being an unpleasant person didn't make Gretz deserving of harassment.

I considered rethinking his offer. But that was not a decision to be made at that late hour. I switched off the light and slid into bed, noting I was on the left side, where I'd slept all my years with Doug. The vacant right side of the bed taunted me. Would I ever share a bed with someone again? I thought briefly of Mike, but who was I kidding? It seemed the height of self-delusion to pin any romantic hopes on a man I'd most likely never see again.

Chapter 4

Monday, 5:50 a.m.,
Downsmeade Grange

The morning sun, shining harshly through the curtains, jarred me awake. I got out of bed and peered outside to see the burgeoning sunrise. It promised to be a beautiful day to get outside and move around. After shaving and dressing, I entered the main house and was heading for the breakfast room when I heard a man's voice coming from behind a corner.

"Why else do you think I let my pinhead wife drag me on this death march? But the bastard tried to kill me last night, and I'm going to nail him. He ain't gonna get away with it."

The voice was Gretz's.

"I can't talk anymore. The damn walk is gonna begin in a few minutes. I gotta make it look like I'm enjoying myself. Right. Talk to you later."

I acted surprised to see Gretz when I turned the corner. "Good morning," I greeted. "I couldn't help overhearing you just now. When you informed me of the threats you've been receiving, you said you didn't know who'd sent them. Have you learned something new?"

Gretz studied me. "You said you didn't want to help. But let me show you this."

He pulled out his cell phone and turned it toward me so I could see the message on the screen.

Watch your step today. The first one may be your last. The sender was *Avenger 001.*

This was serious stuff. I debated pleading with Gretz to contact the authorities, but I knew where that would lead. I felt the responsibility for his fate thud upon my shoulders.

"Okay. I'll watch out for you. But I can only do so much. You need to watch out for yourself as well. If you see anything suspicious—and I mean *anything*—let me know, alright?"

He gave me a small nod of agreement and strode off. As he walked away, I saw my chances of enjoying the day's walk diminishing as well. In the breakfast room, I found Justin Meyers hunched over a bowl of porridge, checking his cell phone.

"Good morning," I greeted. "So nice to see another early riser."

Justin looked up. "I can't sleep beyond five a.m., even over here. Something genetic, probably. In this case, it's a good thing, so I can eat breakfast before Phaedra gets here. She'll go ballistic when she sees all the meat and sugar."

I eyed the food on display. "They do have cereal, yogurt, and fruit. But I'm in the mood for the sinful stuff." As I loaded my plate, I asked, "Looking forward to the walk?"

"I guess so. But I'm concerned about that Gretz man. What on earth is he doing on a tour like this? Do you suppose it's to please that brainless wife of his? What's her name—Summer? Good God. He's a mid-life crisis cliché."

I sat and took a sip of coffee. "I wouldn't jump to conclusions. As the saying goes, appearances can be deceiving."

Billie breezed in, lively as ever, wearing a green sweater with a pine-tree pattern. "Morning, Chase, Mr. Meyers. What wonderful weather! It promises to be a glorious day." She headed to the breakfast buffet as Phaedra and Corky entered.

"I'm so excited!" Corky said. "Imagine, today we'll be on the same trails where Walt Whitman used to walk."

"I believe Devon would have been rather far afield for Whitman," Billie said. "Can you be thinking of William Wordsworth?"

"Of course! Silly me. I always get those 'W' guys confused."

Phaedra eyed the breakfast selections with disdain. "Are they serious? This spread is a veritable heart attack waiting to happen."

Justin leaned toward me. "What did I tell you?" His wife sighed and filled a bowl with muesli and pears.

Barker came in and joined the others at the buffet. Gretz and Summer were the last to arrive. "Bacon and eggs is what I want," he growled. "And coffee."

Phaedra sat across from Justin and placed her napkin on her lap. "I can already feel the spell of the Old World seeping in, can't you? Even though upstate New York is very pastoral, this is a different world here. Even this hotel is charming, despite the room décor." She ate a spoonful of muesli. "As a matter of fact, there's a lovely tissue holder in our room with a carved otter on it, just the type of thing I collect. I'm tempted to steal it."

"You shouldn't be admitting something like that to an ex-policeman," Justin said with an uncomfortable smile.

Barker sat at a nearby table, looking as unengaged as ever. "Did you have a good night?" I asked.

He slowly lifted his gaze. "As a matter of fact, I didn't. I had to finally take some sleeping medication I'd brought. Andorphinol. It's a strong prescription—knocks me right out." He looked like he was still feeling its effects.

Billie joined me at my table. "Any word about your sister?" I asked.

She sighed and plopped two cubes of sugar in her coffee. "My cell phone reception has been so spotty here that I've asked Janice to send messages to the front desk. I've had a devil of a time getting them, but I eventually learned the surgery approval from her HMO got lost in the system somewhere. The incompetence is absolutely staggering."

"Enjoy your breakfast. They'll find the paperwork. Your sister will be fine."

Brett walked in, looking breathless. "I hope there's still food left."

"It's over there," Corky said. "Where have you been?"

Brett began loading a plate with pastries, jam and bacon. "I overslept. Lost track of the time."

He got his food and sat to my left. I couldn't help noticing a large, flashy watch on his wrist. He held out his arm. "Really something, isn't it? It's a Breguet Guilloché. Five separate, hand-engraved dials. Precise to the tenth of a second." How could he lose track of time with such a timepiece?

Conversation fell to a mild buzz. Gretz wolfed down the last of his breakfast, stood, and left the room without a word. Brett carried his plate to Summer's table and joined her. Soon they were chatting.

"That's kind of nervy, don't you think?" Billie murmured to me. "Making a move on the wife the minute the husband is gone?"

"She doesn't seem to mind," I noted. Brett probably was just being friendly, yet his behavior struck me as nervy too. Could he be the one sending the threats to Gretz?

As everyone was finishing their meals, Howie walked

in. "Please be out front in thirty minutes to board the van. Get there early if you can. I need to take your lunch orders."

After fetching my backpack from my room, I joined the others outside. Most wore walking gear that looked fresh off the outlet rack: cleanly pressed lightweight cotton shirts, waterproof walking pants, trendy multicolored walking boots, and aerodynamically designed backpacks. A high-end camera hung from Justin's neck. Most had on light-weight jackets. The exception was Gretz, attired in brightly checkered golfing trousers, another polo shirt, and tasseled loafers.

"Are those the shoes you're planning to wear on the trail, Mr. Gretz?" Sally asked.

"What's wrong with 'em?"

Sally looked down at Gretz's loafers. "Those aren't suitable for the rocky paths on which we'll be walking. You could easily stumble or fall. Not to mention your feet could get sore and blistered. We can help you find some proper boots."

"Get off my back, will ya?" Gretz groused. "I've walked in shoes like these all my life."

Sally stiffened. "It's my job to look out for your safety. You're not the one in charge here, do you understand?"

"Don't tell me who's in charge, lady!"

"Yes, I *am* telling you, and it's me," Sally said, her voice reaching a level I hadn't yet heard. "Got it?"

Gretz looked like he was about to explode. "I'm wearing the shoes I've got on. End of discussion." He turned and boarded the van, followed by his wife.

I walked over to Sally. "They're his feet, and they'll be his blisters. Perhaps that will change his mind."

She took a few breaths. "I'm sorry. I've never met anyone so . . . obstinate. I shouldn't have lost my cool."

We boarded the van. As it pulled onto the main road-way, Sally regained her composure. She turned to the group. "This morning our walk will begin on the South Coast Path near Trentishoe, a few kilometers from here. We'll walk eastward toward the coast near the mouth of the River Heddon, where we'll stop at a riverside inn for our morning break. Keep your eyes open for Exmoor's famous red deer. They are reclusive, but you might spot one."

The van traversed a series of hills, green with springtime growth, providing tempting views of inland valleys, spotted with gorse and clusters of oaks and alders. I should have been relishing the scenery, but my focus was on Gretz. He was no longer a fellow traveler.

He was a target.

Chapter 5

Soon we reached the trailhead, a pull-out on the road beside an imposing hill. No sooner had we stepped out of the van than Sally rallied us to follow her up the trail. Phaedra and Justin began walking behind her, followed by me, Billie, Barker, and the Nielsens. Summer and Gretz brought up the rear.

Even with the trail's uphill grade, it didn't take long for familiar walking motions—the rhythmic swinging of my arms, the steady forward propulsion of my legs, the measured breathing—to work their magic. Tension began to flow from my shoulders, legs, and neck. Each intake of fresh, clean air was followed by an expulsion of the stale accumulated chemical soup of the civilized world. To hell with Vanna. *This* was how to get in a positive frame of mind.

While there are plenty of inveterate walkers like me, for whom the pleasures of walking are best found on a country trail (Billie is one also), there are many other ways to enjoy that most human of activities. Some walk only at night, or naked, or in the shape of a cross or a circle, or for thousands of miles at a time, or in costume, or for causes, or for no reason whatsoever. People have an innate need for movement, and walking is one of the best ways to satisfy it that I know of.

As good as it felt to be back on an English trail, however, I couldn't help checking behind me to make sure Gretz was safe. He and Summer were a distance away, but it appeared they were proceeding without incident. So much for his first step being his last.

Billie and I reached a plateau where Sally was waiting for everyone to catch up.

"The weather couldn't be more perfect," Billie said.

Sally smiled. "We're fortunate. I did a trial walk up here last week to check my coordinates, and it was simply beastly. Rained constantly. I don't mind that so much myself—in fact, I quite enjoy walking in the rain. But it wouldn't be good for this group."

"The rain certainly made the hillsides green," Billie commented.

The others soon arrived, although Summer and Gretz were still a distance off.

"Honestly," Phaedra said, "if we have to wait all week for him, we'll never get anywhere. Something must be done."

"Let's give Mr. Gretz a chance," Sally said. "If his pace doesn't improve, I'll suggest that he ride in the van. Something tells me he'll be open to that."

Finally, they arrived. Gretz was slightly winded, but no more so than the others. Sally led us up to the top of the hill, where we got our first full view of the coastline— rugged cliffs stretching to the east and west, the sea lapping at the rocks below.

She pointed to a hill on the left. "Up there is the highest

coastal hill in England. It's known as 'Hangman's Hill.' Some say that is because criminals used to be thrown to their deaths from the top, but I prefer another story, that of the sheep thief who was walking across the hill carrying a stolen ewe on his shoulder. He stopped to rest on a rock, and the struggling sheep caused the cord around its legs to tighten and slip round the man's neck, strangling him."

Billie laughed. "Justice wins out!"

"Is that Wales over there?" Phaedra asked, pointing across the channel.

"Whales?" Corky said. "I've never seen any! Where are they?"

"Wales, the *country*," Justin corrected. "Or is it a territory?"

"Protectorate, territory, there is endless debate," said Sally. "Regardless, you can make it out in the distance." We gazed at the distant coastline, barely visible across the channel's choppy waters. Justin raised his camera to record the view.

Sally led us off again. As we walked in silence, I cast my eyes over the lushness of the hillsides, carpeted with heather, and the indigo sea beyond. I suspected that, for some of my fellow walkers, this was the first time they'd walked without the constant drone of automobiles nearby. I started whistling Hank Williams's "Move It on Over"; whistling his songs is a walking habit of mine that often drives Billie nuts. My father was a big fan of classic American country music, and my childhood was inundated by it.

We continued to the bluff's edge before climbing a ziggurat-like path up another hill, its steeper sections alternating with others that were more level, spaced almost evenly apart. At the top, Sally called for another stop so the Gretzes could catch up. When they arrived, Gretz said, between heavy breaths, "You didn't tell us we'd be scaling mountains!"

"These hills are hardly mountains, Mr. Gretz," Sally said with forced patience. "How are your feet holding up?"

"My feet are fine!"

She led us down and up another rise. After several more ups and downs, we rounded a bend and beheld a clearing in which the familiar yellow Wanderers van awaited us, its rear gate open to reveal an array of midmorning snacks— nuts, fruit, candy, and cups of water and fruit juices. Howie began handing out cups of a local drink made from blueberries and fresh spring water. Barker helped pass them around.

"Just what I need," Corky said unenthusiastically as she surveyed the spread. "More food."

"It will help maintain your energy," Sally said.

Corky tasted the blueberry drink. "Just being over here is stimulating enough. I want to pinch myself to make sure it's real."

"The midges biting my arm are real enough," Brett said. "Did you bring any bug spray?"

Corky fished in her knapsack and pulled out a tube that she handed to her brother.

"Thanks, Mom," he said.

"I wish you wouldn't call me that." To me and Billie she said, "Our mother worked full-time when we were growing up, so a lot of the mom-type chores fell to me."

"Where was your father?" Billie asked.

"He ran out on us when we were little. That's why our mom had to work. If I ever get my hands on that guy, I'll strangle him. Imagine ditching a wife and two small kids."

Brett shook his head. "Our mother passed away last year. Cork here took it hard. It's one of the reasons I suggested coming over here—to lift her spirits."

Howie passed around pieces of local cheese. I took a bite and walked over to Sally, checking the walk route on her mobile phone.

"We're not lost, I hope," I joked.

She smiled. "No chance. The GPS is good, but I always keep my hard-copy map handy. I've marked down the route on it as a backup. Anyway, I've been coming here since I was a little girl and know this area like the back of my hand. There's a spot over there"—she pointed her stick to a distant stand of pines and alders—"that is one of my favorites. Right on the bluff. I often go there when I need to have a think."

"Will we be walking there?"

"Unfortunately, not today. That would throw off our schedule. But you can always come back and enjoy it for yourself. It's called Stanley's Rest."

Back at the van, I was pleased to see the group mingling and enjoying their break. The Nielsens were trying out the different fruits and cheeses. The Meyerses were chatting with the Gretzes. Barker handed a cup of the blueberry water to Gretz, who nodded in thanks and drank it down. This was more like it. The walk and the countryside were beginning to cast their spell and make everyone comfortable. It was absurd to imagine any of this bunch plotting to harm Gretz.

As we finished our snacks and headed back onto the trail, I let myself relax. I became entranced by the lushly verdant ravine around us, while keeping my eyes on the trail, where rocks and holes could suddenly appear. My eyes traveled to Gretz, farther behind, and I tensed. He was wobbling, and I didn't think the reason was his shoes. Then he staggered and fell.

Billie and I rushed over to him. Summer was kneeling beside her husband, cradling his head in her hands. "Ronnie! Are you alright? Speak to me!"

Gretz's eyes were shut. I placed my hand on his forehead, which didn't seem feverish, and lifted his arm, where

I detected a pulse, weak but steady. His eyes began to flutter and open. Barker was at my side and handed me his water bottle. "Make him drink this," he said. I put the bottle to Gretz's lips. After he took a few sips, his color began to return, and he was able to prop himself up on his elbows.

"I don't know what came over me," he said. "I got dizzy all of a sudden."

"You're not used to all of this activity, baby," his wife said. "Maybe we should ride in the van the rest of the way."

Gretz took a couple more breaths and glared up at us. "You know what happened, don't you? Someone tried to poison me!"

"Poison you?" Barker said. "That's crazy! If someone did that, why are you still alive?"

"Why not sit the next leg out?" I suggested to Gretz. "It takes time to get used to a long walk. There's no shame in easing into it."

"Nothing doing. I agreed to walk, and that's what I'm gonna do!" He struggled to his feet. "If there's one thing I hate, it's a quitter. I'm like Joe Torre in 1999; he didn't let prostate cancer get him to give up the game. When he came back to Fenway, even the Sox fans cheered him, didn't they, Chase?"

"That they did," I said, remembering the Yankees manager getting an ovation on the televised broadcast.

When Sally was convinced Gretz was fit enough to proceed, I walked beside him in case he showed signs of collapsing again. He wasn't moving as briskly as the others, but he seemed okay. I discreetly got Summer aside and asked if her husband had taken any medication that would have made him woozy.

She looked down for a moment, thinking. "He takes pills

for his heart and blood pressure. But they've never made him fall down."

This incident was probably nothing more than an inexperienced, older man biting off more than he could chew. And yet the threats Gretz received couldn't be ignored. I walked on and passed Barker, who said, "That old fool should have stayed at the hotel. He's a disturbing presence."

"He paid his money like everyone else. He deserves to be given a chance."

Gretz's choking incident and collapse on the trail were on my mind as we approached a rustic inn nestled beside the river in a wooded glen. Howie, who'd arrived earlier to deliver the lunch orders, guided us inside into a bright dining room overlooking a garden. A long table was set for us. Once we were seated, it wasn't long before the food arrived. Corky moaned in delight after her first bite. "Even fish and chips taste different over here! Perfect!"

"They're awfully greasy," Phaedra commented, frowning slightly.

"That's what I mean," Corky said. "Perfect!"

Gretz scowled at his plate. "Hey! This isn't what I ordered. I wanted a cheeseburger!"

Howie consulted his notes. "Sorry 'bout that, Mr. Gretz. This morning you checked the mushroom linguine on your breakfast form. See? I have it right here."

"Why would I eat crap like that?" Gretz shot back. "For what we're paying, can't you get my order straight? I'd think this outfit would hire people who could do their damn job!"

Howie advanced toward Gretz. "Now, listen here, you nasty old bobby—"

Sally inserted herself between them. "We will get you a burger as requested, Mr. Gretz." Pulling Howie aside, she said a few words that settled him down. He went to amend the order.

"I'm not sure I can take a full week of that awful man," Corky murmured to me and Billie. "He's ruining everything."

"What did he mean when he called him a 'bobby'?" Brett asked.

I smiled. "It's Scottish. It means 'piece of shit.'"

Chapter 6

Back on the trail, we walked down a gently sloping path beside the River Heddon, which at that point was slightly more than a stream, lazily gurgling over rocks on its way to the sea. At the river's mouth, a pebble-strewn, crescent-shaped shore spread before the blue, choppy expanse of the Bristol Channel. Sally led us up a rocky mound to the open pit of a small stone kiln and stood back to face us.

"Hundreds of years ago, the people of this area discovered that they could burn limestone, carried by sea from Torquay or Plymouth to estuaries such as this. The calcination of the lime produced a residue that had many uses. Farmers could sweeten and enrich their soil with it. It was also used as cement in many buildings, and as a form of paint."

She pointed up to the cultivated slopes of the hillside rising to our right. "Lime kilns, such as this small one, had to be built near the farms where they'd be used. The quicklime was corrosive and could eat away at containers and wagons if they'd carried it too far."

We peered over the top of the kiln and down inside. Although it must have been at least ten feet deep, there wasn't much to be seen in the shadows. Justin took photos from several angles. Corky tentatively placed her foot on the low clay wall surrounding the pit and bent to peer farther inside. I looked out for Gretz and Summer, but they hadn't yet arrived.

"You can get a better look at the bottom entrance down here," Sally said, leading us down to the kiln opening. A large rock blocked the way, but Sally moved it aside, permitting the others to take turns posing for photos beside a closed, rusted gate.

The Meyerses and Lucien Barker decided to explore the beach. Corky and Brett went back to the top of the kiln to enjoy the sea view. Billie and I stayed where we were.

"Enjoying yourself?" I asked her. "Today's walk hasn't been too rigorous, I hope."

"Just the opposite. The activity—and this brisk British sea air—is doing me a world of good. How about you?"

I looked out to the sea. It was restfully bucolic, but I couldn't shake a distinct sense of danger. "I'm not sure. Do you have the feeling something is about to happen?"

"Are you thinking of those threats Gretz received? I'm not going to let them spoil my day, and you shouldn't either."

"I can't help but feel apprehensive. Look—here he comes now."

Gretz and Summer were approaching. He was moving at a slow pace but didn't seem to be suffering from the dizziness he'd experienced earlier. Summer, as usual, was walking ahead of him, but moderating her pace.

When they arrived, Gretz said, "I need to rest." Corky had come down from the top of the kiln. "You can sit up there and get a view of the sea," she said, pointing at the low wall surrounding the top of the kiln. Gretz and Summer headed up.

Billie saw me eyeing him. "You don't need to be his watchdog every minute, you know. He's not likely to be attacked when there are so many of us around."

"Maybe. But I'll go up and stay close to him just the same."

When I reached the top of the kiln, I saw that the Gretzes had perched on the low clay wall surrounding it. Not far away, Brett was gazing out at the channel. A slight cool breeze had kicked up, but was offset by the warmth of the afternoon sun. I closed my eyes, took a deep breath of the sea air, and began to relax when a woman's scream rang out.

I turned to see Gretz and Summer pitching backward into the mouth of the lime kiln. I raced over, but was elbowed aside by Brett, who stretched out and grabbed hold of Gretz, pulling him from the abyss of the kiln mouth. Summer had managed to secure a tenuous hold on the lip of the pit, and I reached down to help her up. By this time, Sally and the others had rushed up.

With Brett's help, Gretz was back on solid ground. He swung toward Sally. "This was no accident! *Someone just tried to kill me! Again!*"

"Nonsense," she said and turned to me. "What happened?"

"I was a few feet away when I heard Summer scream. I saw her and Gretz falling into the pit. I went to grab Gretz, but Brett beat me to it."

"It's that little wall we were sitting on, you see?" Summer said, pointing toward the kiln pit. "It just gave way beneath us. I was able to hold onto something, but Ronnie . . ."

"I'm telling you, that was no accident," Gretz growled. "Someone arranged it . . . on purpose!"

"Who would want to do that, sweetie?" said Summer, taking his arm.

I knelt to examine the limestone ledge. It wasn't remotely stable; I was easily able to chip off large sections with my finger. "This whole thing is ready to go."

Sally knelt beside me and ran her fingers over the porous, loose surface. "I should have warned people off. This has been corroded by the salt and the sea air."

"It's not your fault," I said as I stood and slapped my hands together to shake off the chalky dust. "Those stones look solid until you get close. And it certainly has stood the test of time; it must have been here for ages. But it easily gives way when sat upon."

I examined the other side of the kiln pit. To my surprise, the clay there was more solid, perhaps because it was sheltered from the direct sea air. Maybe this was simply a case of Gretz sitting on the wrong spot. Or . . . perhaps not.

There was no denying that three "accidents" within the space of a few hours seemed suspicious. But if the intent was to kill Gretz, why had none of these attempts been successful?

Chapter 7

Monday, late afternoon,
Heddon's Mouth

When it became clear that Gretz, though incensed at what he believed was another murder attempt, had not been seriously harmed, Sally rounded up everyone for the trek back to the van. Gretz was having none of it.

"I'm in no shape to do that. I need a drink, goddam it!"

Summer curled her arm around him. "Sweetie, there's no booze out here. I have one of your heart pills, though."

"I've had enough pills!"

She patted his shoulder. "We need to get you back to the hotel. The only way to get there is on foot."

He shook himself free. "They can send a boat for us, then."

Sally pulled out her mobile and explained the situation to Howie. She pocketed the device and approached us.

"Your wife is correct, Mr. Gretz. Walking is the only way to get back to the hotel. But we don't need to rush. We can wait until you feel refreshed, and I'll accompany you and Mrs. Gretz back. You can walk as slowly as you'd like."

"You don't have to treat me like a child," he said, but gave in to her offer.

Sally told the rest of us to return the way we came, along the upstream path to the lodge, where Howie was waiting. "He'll take you to the hotel and return to collect me and the Gretzes."

There was low grumbling as we began heading back up the river path.

"Something has to be done about that man," Phaedra said. "How can we enjoy this walk when he's bitching all the time?"

"He had another bad scare, dear," Justin told her. "You can't blame him for being frightened."

"Maybe he'll take the hint and go back home, where he can be a pain in the ass to others."

"Give him a break," Justin said. "He's just had bad luck."

I wasn't as certain. Three mishaps in one day was pushing the limits of coincidence. Yet how could someone have engineered that ledge so it would crumble? And even if someone was able to do that, who could have done it? This time Gretz wasn't the only victim; his wife had also fallen. Did someone have it in for her too?

My thoughts were distracted by a rumbling above. Dark clouds were moving in from the south, and rain started to fall. Those of us who weren't wearing jackets began pulling them from our backpacks. By the time we reached Howie, the rain had grown into a full-throttle storm. Everyone piled inside the van just as lightning flashed, followed by a boom of thunder that rattled the vehicle. Howie switched on the wipers as he drove up to the main road.

"This storm certainly won't improve Gretz's mood," Billie said. "I don't think he even brought a rain slicker."

"Serves him right," Phaedra said. "Perhaps the rain will trigger an avalanche and wash him out to sea."

"The old fart didn't even thank me for saving his life," Brett said.

The rain poured steadily all the way back to the hotel. Upon arriving, we raced inside. Howie headed back to pick up Sally and the Gretzes.

"I'm sorry our walk was cut short, but isn't it perfect in here?" Corky said as we entered the warmth of Downsmeade Grange. She wriggled out of her jacket just as another peal of thunder rattled the windows. "It's just like being in a British mystery. What was that one with that big drafty house—Thornfield Hall?"

"That's *Jane Eyre*," Billie said. "Not quite a murder mystery by traditional standards."

"You know what I mean," Corky replied. She walked to the window and looked out onto the grounds, barely visible through the rain-streaked glass. "This storm is the perfect setup for a murder. I'll be sleeping with my door locked tonight, I promise you." Under the circumstances, I didn't think that a bad idea.

She turned toward us. "Of course, all that scary stuff never happens in real life, does it? If there were as many murders in England as there are in mystery novels, the whole place would be deserted!"

Somewhere, I'd heard that approximately three hundred people were murdered each year in the UK. I suspected most of these were fairly straightforward crimes, unpremeditated acts of anger or passion. Hardly the stuff of mystery novels.

Mike was on my mind, and I checked at the front desk to see if anyone had stopped by to ask for me or leave me a message. Unfortunately, no one had.

Billie proposed cocktails in the bar. The Nielsens and

Meyerses agreed, but Barker begged off, claiming he had some matter to attend to. In the bar, a welcome fire was blazing. As the others settled themselves around a table, I offered to get the drinks. Corky accompanied me and asked me to name my favorite English locale. Several came to mind—the chalk cliffs on the Sussex Coast, the pastoral dales in Yorkshire, the broad valleys of the Lake District. How to choose? I was about to respond when Sally, Howie, and the Gretzes appeared in the main passageway. The rain had stopped, but the four were soaked.

"Can't stand this miserable place!" grunted Gretz as he stomped up the staircase.

Summer gave us a baleful look. "He just needs his nap. I'll go up and make sure he's tucked in. He'll be back to normal after that."

As she disappeared up the stairs, I wondered what "normal" would be for Gretz. Sally and Howie joined us and apologized for the day's interruptions.

"You're the one I'm concerned about," I said to Sally. "Bedraggled" was the word that came to mind; her hair was wet and stringy, her clothes soaked, and her face pale. "Gretz is more trouble than he's worth. Can't you ask him to call it quits?"

"Have done," Howie said. "The old bastard said he's gonna stick it out. Said he paid for a walk and a walk he's gonna have. He's determined to make everyone suffer."

"We'll not let him do that," Sally said. "I understand what he's been through, but that's no reason to start tossing accusations of murder around. If he gets ugly again, we'll just ignore him. I've had experience with his type; they feed on confrontation. If we don't give him that satisfaction, I don't think he'll be a problem. Right now, I need a warm bath."

She headed upstairs. Howie claimed he was ready for a

beer and went to the bar. Billie reached for her knitting but realized she'd left her bag in the van. When I offered to dash out and retrieve it, Howie tossed me the keys.

After I collected Billie's bag, I noticed Sally's rucksack on the floor of the foyer. I delivered Billie's pack to her and went to the front desk, asked for Sally's room number, and carried her pack upstairs. In the hallway, raised voices were coming the room next to Sally's—Summer and Ronald Gretz.

"I'm not taking any more of those damn drugs!" he shouted. "They're for your own good!" Summer screamed back. "Don't be such a fool!" This was followed by Gretz yelling, "I swear those pills are killing me. Is that what you want?"

I knocked on Sally's door. When she opened it, I held out her rucksack.

"Oh, thank you," she said, taking it. "I'm a bit forgetful today."

The argument in the next room was hard to ignore. "I hope they're not bothering you."

She shrugged it off. "He's probably still upset about what happened at the kiln. Oh, could you do me a favor? I meant to ask the others to bring their maps with them tonight. I want to mark the route we took today. Could you pass that along?"

The walk leader always marked everyone's maps with the day's route; it was a tradition with the Wanderers. I agreed to relay the message and went downstairs to join the others, chatting in the bar. Billie's knitting needles were flying.

"Sally wanted me to remind you to bring your maps to dinner," I said as I sat.

"Will she use them as kindling to burn Gretz at the stake?" Phaedra asked.

"She suggested we ignore him," I said. "I think that's a good idea."

I finished my ale and felt the need for a midafternoon nap. Excusing myself, I headed for my room, glancing into the library as I passed by. Barker was seated at a small table, thumbing through a thick book that looked like anything but light reading. I found that curious, but his reading habits were no concern of mine. I continued on.

In my room, I lay down for a nap but couldn't stop thinking of Mike. Why was I mooning over some guy I'd only briefly met? I tried to laugh it off—come on, Chase, you're not a hormone-riddled teenager anymore—but my desire to see him again only grew stronger. Was I flattering myself to think I'd made enough of an impression to lure him back? Fatigue eventually won out. I drifted off to sleep, Mike's image slowly fading into nothingness.

Chapter 8

When I awoke, the bedside clock read 5:40. That gave me just enough time to dress for dinner and meet the group in the foyer. When I arrived, everyone was gathered—even Gretz, stone-faced as ever. I asked the desk clerk if Mike had called to ask for me.

"Mike?" she said. "Sorry, no."

My heart sank. It looked like I'd never see him again. Why on earth hadn't I asked for his full name? Of course, he hadn't asked for mine either. Had he been toying with me?

Sally collected everyone's maps and placed them on a chair near the door to retrieve when we got back. Outside, I was glad to see that the storm had passed. A crescent moon peered through the trees.

"The hospital received the approval for Janice's surgery," Billie told me as we boarded the van. "It's scheduled for tomorrow. The doctors remain hopeful."

"That's good news," I said. However, I remembered the long days waiting for Doug to show signs of improvement. Each day was an ordeal of awaiting the doctor's pronouncements about his progress, or lack thereof. The days turned into weeks that turned into months. Through it all, the medical staff kept up a hopeful front. It made me resolve to never trust doctors again.

On the way to the pub, Sally praised its food. I asked when she'd last eaten there, and she replied she'd never been; she was relying on an app on her phone, which rated local pubs and gave customer reviews. She withdrew a notepad from her pack, scribbled down the app's name, and handed a piece of notepaper to me. Without looking at it, I stuffed it in my pocket.

We soon arrived at the Quarryman, a seventeenth-century pub with a wood-burning stove fireplace, flagged stone floor, beamed ceilings, and pewter tankards lining the shelves. We were led to a brick-walled private room with high leather dining chairs. The meals, which we had ordered earlier, quickly arrived, along with tankards of local ale.

As we began eating, I sat tensed, anticipating another "accident" to befall Gretz. After his near miss with disaster at the lime kiln, it was looking increasingly likely that somebody was indeed out to get him. But why? Who could it be? And why hadn't I been able to prevent any of these incidents from happening?

As the dinner progressed, however—with everyone enjoying the pub's menu selection, including Gretz—I began to relax. As much as I suspected the incidents Gretz had experienced may have been intentional, I agreed with Phaedra that they were laughable attempts at murder. Maybe they were just bad luck after all.

We finished our final course—seriously decadent Knickerbocker Glory sundaes, ice cream running down the sides of the serving goblets—and stood to leave. As we passed through the main room, I decided to dispel any thoughts of Gretz and make a conscious effort to appreciate my surroundings. There I was in a quintessential British pub, one of my favorite places. How could I let negative thoughts tarnish this moment?

I beheld the room as a beguiling hive of sensory input: the fire's glare reflecting off the pint glasses in the customers' hands; the burning logs emitting not only comforting warmth but a distinctive woodsy odor; enticing smells emanating from the kitchen, accompanied by the occasional clatter of dishes and saucepans; the bar awash in a din of laughter, conversation, and the drone of a news program on the television. The screen showed attendees at a *Star Trek* convention. I'd attended one once with Doug, who'd been a huge Trekkie. The whole affair had struck me as rather silly, but I remembered Doug's boyish delight in meeting members of the show's cast.

Uh-oh.

Thoughts of Doug yanked me back into the dark chambers of grief. Memories of our life together sprang forth as if to taunt me: the two of us laughing at silly things, just like those around me in this pub; that magical look in Doug's blue eyes that always stirred my soul; the press of his lips against mine . . . As my spirits hit rock-bottom, I robotically accompanied the others outside and climbed into the van. At Downsmeade, I numbly followed Phaedra and Justin, holding hands, through the main house, envying their relationship. As they started climbing the stairs to their room, however, Phaedra turned to Justin and snapped, "How dare you talk to me that way? One of these days, I swear I'm going to kill you!"

She stomped upward, while Justin turned to give me a grudging smile. "You single guys are the lucky ones."

In my room, I recorded the details of the day in my journal, but the nagging thought that I could have done something to protect Gretz hadn't gone away.

When I settled into bed, it became clear that sleep wasn't coming. I fished out two tablets of over-the-counter diphenhydramine from my toilet kit and despaired that I had none of Lucien's quick-acting drug instead. I was able to fall asleep, but fitfully. I awakened repeatedly during the night, each time thinking I was back home. Only the splatter of rain against the window—a rare sound in Southern California—reminded me of where I was.

Chapter 9

The first light of morning awakened me right on the dot of six. On my way to the breakfast room, I passed the library and spotted the weighty volume Barker had been studying, still on the small table. Intrigued, I went over. *British Estate Law: An Overview.*

What was such a scholarly tome doing in a holiday hotel like Downsmeade Grange? Even more curious, why had Barker been studying it? Whatever the reason, it was none of my business. I proceeded on, snatched a copy of the morning paper off the front desk, and went into the breakfast room, where I poured a cup of coffee, picked a fresh muffin from a basket, and sat by the window.

"Morning, Chase! Sleep well?"

Billie, already there and wearing a busy-patterned sweater of purple and gold cats, was stretching her arms as part of her morning limbering up.

"Eventually," I said.

She sat opposite me. "Take your eyes off that paper for a second. I've got something to tell you." She leaned forward and, in a lowered voice, said, "It's probably nothing more than gossip, but it might mean something."

"I'm all ears."

"Just when I was about to drop off to sleep last night, I heard someone tapping outside my room. I was a bit groggy and thought it was a bird on my window at first. Then I heard a woman's voice say, 'Brett.'"

"Let me guess. Summer Gretz."

Billie nodded. "She tapped again, and Brett must have let her in."

"A late-night tête-à-tête."

"Well, that's one way of describing it."

"Did you hear her when she came out?" I asked.

"No. But, of course, she must have gone back to her room at some point. The question is, how did she leave her husband alone for all that time, however long it was, without him noticing?"

I mentioned overhearing the Gretzes argue over his medications.

"So she's keeping him drugged," Billie said.

"Or he's doing it himself. We mustn't jump to conclusions. He had three bad scares yesterday, after all. It wouldn't be surprising if he took something to calm down."

"And his lovely little wife took advantage of the opportunity."

"Maybe," I said. "Anyway, it's none of our business." I went back to my paper, but Gretz still dominated my thoughts. I hadn't been able to keep him out of danger so far. What would the coming day bring?

A half hour later, everyone gathered by the van. Sally was all smiles, attempting to erase the unease of the previous day by making light chitchat. She outlined the morning agenda—a walk through a river gorge to a waterside café for midmorning refreshments, and later a ride up a funicular to a cliff path.

As we prepared to board the van, Gretz approached me.

"Whoever that bastard is, you know as well as I do he's been trying to finish me off. You may be a Sox lover, but you're still the sharpest guy in this bunch. Did you see who it might be?"

I had to be honest. "If those were actual murder attempts—and that's a big 'if'—the killer kept his or her identity well-concealed. I'll continue to keep my eyes open, but you need to help as well. Don't do anything stupid. And that includes losing your temper."

He paused before giving me a quick nod.

When the van reached the trailhead, we stepped out, and I did a quick scan of the terrain. To the north, a rough path disappeared into a deep gorge in which lush ferns and chestnut trees shrouded a cleft forged by a river. On the nearby hills, the dark springtime green was broken here and there by the browns and grays of rock outcroppings.

Everyone suited up, and we began walking in pairs behind Sally, stepping carefully over runnels of water before reaching the river, barely a stream at that point. The air was crisp and exhilarating.

"Glorious, isn't it?" I remarked to Brett, walking beside me.

"It's okay, I guess," he said. "I only came over here because Corky is so England-crazy that I thought it would take her mind off our mom's death. I like a different kind of travel. Cruising the Caribbean in my yacht. Driving my Lamborghini on an open highway."

"I have to resort to less pricey ways of getting my scenery," I said, not mentioning that my car back home is an old Ford in which I also do my cruising, out to the supermarket twice a week.

"Speaking of scenery, that Summer is pretty easy on the eyes, wouldn't you say?"

I weighed my comment. "I suppose she's attractive, although I'm not the best judge of that, I'm afraid. My taste runs in another direction."

"You're gay, huh? I would never have guessed, a rugged, manly type like you."

"We're not all limp-wristed drag queens, you know."

"Sure, I know. I've got lots of gay friends. Doesn't bother me."

That sounded a bit defensive. "It's none of my business," I said, "but I'm not the only one who has noticed your interest in Mrs. Gretz. Let me give you a word of advice. It's not a good idea to go after another man's wife, especially when that man is on the same walking tour."

Brett was silent for a few paces. "You're right."

"I'm glad you agree."

"I mean, you're right. It's none of your business."

After a brief midmorning refreshment break, we proceeded along the trail as it broadened through the woods. The Gretzes, as always, were the farthest behind, which made it difficult for me to keep him in view. At intervals, Sally would call for us to stop and wait for the rest to catch up. Spotting a meadow of coarse grass stretching beyond a gap in the forest, she said, "We're not far from where R. D. Blackmore placed the fictional Doone Valley in the novel *Lorna Doone*."

"Lorna Doone?" Summer asked. "Isn't that a cookie?"

Sally explained it was a famous English novel of passion and revenge. "This afternoon we'll see the extraordinary landscape of the Valley of the Rocks, which Blackmore, like many, believed was formed by acts of the Devil."

"That sounds scary," Corky said.

"*Lorna Doone* is a pretty frightening book," Billie said. "There's a lot of murder and nastiness. The lead character's thirst for revenge almost kills him and his sweetheart."

"Except that it doesn't," Sally said.

Billie nodded. "You're right. There's what some might call a happy ending."

We continued along the trail as it stayed close to the river, winding among the trees. Around a bend, we got our first glimpse of Lynmouth, a small seaside village clearly catering to visitors. Soon we were walking past shops displaying souvenir hand towels and T-shirts, interspersed among the usual assortment of toffee and fish-and-chips vendors. We rounded a corner, and the bright green funicular station came into view. Corky cautiously peered up at two steep, nearly vertical rail lines that led to the top of a bluff. A bright green car was descending on the left one, passing another car going up to the top on the right.

"I don't know about this," she said. "That looks awfully scary."

"It's fascinating," Justin said, perusing a sign beside the loading platform. "It says here that this train requires no fuel at all to run. It's all done with water power. There are two cars, you see? A cable between them keeps them in balance, with water from the river added to a tank mounted between the wheels to make them equal in weight. They let out the water from the tank in the lower car until the heavier tank forces the upper car down. The brakeman controls it all. It's ingenious, actually."

"Yeah, ingenious," Corky replied as the lower car arrived and disgorged passengers coming from the top. We climbed inside, and it began its slow upward climb. Corky kept her eyes closed. Suddenly, the car jerked to a stop and swayed sharply. Corky let out a yelp. Everyone stood frozen.

Gretz's eyes widened, and he gripped the railing beside him. After a few long moments, the car lurched forward.

Corky exhaled. "I hope *that* doesn't happen again."

I untensed as well. Whatever had caused that glitch, it didn't seem to be the work of any of my fellow travelers. A minute later, we arrived at the top, the weather notably windier and colder.

Sally led us down a couple of streets and into a small café where our lunch awaited us—Middle Eastern mezze dishes and standard sandwiches. During the meal, everyone seemed to be on their best behavior, with no arguments or complaints. As we left the café, Summer stumbled on the curbstone. Brett rushed to help her, reaching out and taking her arm.

Gretz stepped over. "Keep your filthy hands off my wife!"

Brett released Summer, now on her feet, and turned to Gretz. "I'm just lending her a hand. It was more than I saw *you* doing."

Gretz stepped up. "Don't think I don't see what you're up to, punk. You've had your eyes on my wife right from the start. If you so much as lay one finger on her again, I'm going to—"

"Enough!" Sally said, inserting herself between them. Facing Gretz, she said, "There will be no more of this squabbling, do you understand? If you can't control your temper, Mr. Gretz, I will exercise my authority to dismiss you from this tour. Do you understand?"

Gretz fought back a harsh reply. *Don't do anything stupid*, I'd warned. He gave a humble nod before flashing a warning stare at Brett and walking off.

Sally turned to Brett. "The same goes for you, Mr. Nielsen. Please refrain from provoking Mr. Gretz. Keep your eyes on the trail rather than his wife."

"But I . . ." Brett began. "Yes, okay."

"Very well then," Sally said. "Let's continue."

I was reminded that my newfound role of Gretz's protector had its challenges. Someone may have been intending him harm, but I needed to face facts. The man was his own worst enemy.

Chapter 10

To reach the cliff path, Sally led us through a web of narrow cobblestone streets so labyrinthian that I was grateful I didn't have to navigate them on my own. I certainly wouldn't have noticed the small yellow directional arrow denoting the trailhead, mounted on a post obscured by an overgrown hedge.

Sally paused. "The path will take us upward, but it's not very steep. Don't be surprised if you spot feral goats on the rocks. Keep your eyes open!"

Phaedra zipped up her jacket. "It's chilly."

Sally nodded. "It's a bit brisk, yes, and likely to get colder. But it should warm up once we get to the valley."

She set off, and we followed, passing several holiday cottages before beginning our upward climb. To our left was the rocky cliff wall, and to our right a precipitous drop to the sea. Fortunately, the trail was wide enough for us to keep a safe distance. We walked past a workman laying stones to form a retaining wall against the cliff. When Phaedra complimented him on his work, he stood and flexed his arms. Justin snapped his photo.

"The trail looks steeper than I thought," Corky remarked to Sally as she eyed the path ahead. It didn't appear to be particularly steep to me. I was more concerned about the wisps of mist that were forming, obscuring the view. Where was the sunny weather we'd been promised?

Sally said, "Trust me, there's nothing to worry about. You will be perfectly safe as long as you don't get close to the cliff edge."

Corky paused. "I can stay behind, can't I? I'm afraid I'll get dizzy and fall accidentally."

Sally didn't seem upset. "Of course. Can you find your way back to Howie at the van?"

"I'll find him," Corky said, although I doubted I could have remembered the way back through that maze of streets. To her brother, she said, "Is that okay with you?"

"I don't mind," Brett said. "But from what I hear, you'll be missing one of the best views your precious England has to offer. Sure you won't reconsider?"

"I'll do some shopping in town," Corky said. She said goodbye and started back, while the rest of us continued onward. Walking behind Sally, I noted the heavy mist forming and asked, "What happens if the fog gets too thick for us to see?"

Sally surveyed the path ahead. "I don't think it will be a problem." Turning to the others, she announced, "If you find yourself in a bank of fog, just stay where you are until it clears. The best advice I can give you is to use common sense."

Common sense. I wondered how much of that there was among this group. Each seemed to be dealing with his or her own issues. The question was, did any of those mesh with the events of the past two days?

Maybe I was looking for puzzles where none existed. I focused instead on the path in front of me. The mists bathed it in an ethereal glow that gave it a haunting quality. Behind me, I could only see Billie and Brett, the others behind them obscured by the thickening fog. I was uncomfortable with Gretz being out of sight. Should I head back to be nearer to him? He always walked right behind Summer, and it would have been awkward for me to insert myself between them.

I was determined not to think about potential disasters. I did a Flip it, Vanna! and focused on the trail, once again shimmering in patches of sunlight. As we pressed on, though, the mist again thickened, accompanied by a strong wind. I gave thanks for my Gore-Tex jacket when the mist began turning into rain; some of the others wore no rain gear at all.

My concern for Gretz surfaced again: The increasingly wet and rocky path, its proximity to the edge of a steep cliff, and his questionable footwear all combined to create the scenario for another accident. I tensed and halted. The fog was preventing me from seeing anyone ahead, and behind me I could barely make out Billie. I waited until she caught up.

"This isn't exactly the carefree walk I expected," she said.

The wind kicked up, and I struggled to retain my balance.

"Stay close to the cliff wall," I said. "We should be through all of this soon enough." I looked behind again. "I wish I could see the Gretzes. I don't have a good feeling about this."

"He's a grown man," Billie said. "He can take care of himself."

"He hasn't been doing such a good job of it so far."

We walked on carefully, keeping our eyes focused ahead, even though all we could see were the creeping mist and fog. Billie and I instinctively stopped walking when the trail became completely obscured, and continued when the way ahead became visible. The fact that none of the others seemed to be near us indicated that they were most likely taking the same approach.

"Are you enjoying this?" Billie asked. "It's creeping me out."

"I think we're almost at the Valley of the Rocks. It shouldn't be much farther."

With care, we took shorter steps through the fog, which partially cleared to reveal the trail more clearly. Billie gasped when she saw a bearded white goat to her right. It regarded her coolly and went back to looking out to sea.

A towering rock formation came briefly into view in the distance. I remembered its name from the guidebook—Castle Rock. The mist made the setting even more unearthly. I could well believe that demonic forces were responsible for it.

The fog again thickened, obscuring the view, and I slowed my walking.

Suddenly, a figure emerged from the fog, walking toward me. As his facial features became clearer, I gasped and froze.

He was the spitting image of Doug.

Chapter 11

Tuesday, midafternoon,
Cliff Path

The man gave me a smiling nod, rolled his eyes slightly at the fog, and kept walking until he disappeared into the mist.

"Chase?" Billie called out. "Are you here?"

I was so shaken I couldn't respond. Of course, the man couldn't have been Doug; that was absurd. Yet his appearance had been so eerie, and the resemblance so striking—he'd had Doug's thick black eyebrows and his piercing cobalt blue eyes—it was as if I had seen a phantom.

Billie was at my side. "What's happened? Something wrong?"

"Did you just see that man walk past us?"

"A man? No. But in the fog, I'd have been lucky to have seen my own two feet."

I paused for a moment, then realized we'd be better served to keep moving. "Let's keep on," I said, and we began walking again. Around the next bend, we heard Phaedra yell.

"What are you doing? You're trying to push me off the cliff!"

Through the mist, the Meyerses came into view, facing off to one another.

"I didn't push you!" Justin countered. "Why would I do something like that? I just bumped into you because I couldn't see you in all this fog!"

"You expect me to believe that? I know you've been waiting for the right moment to bump me off."

"You're being paranoid, darling. Please try and—"

"*Paranoid?*" she barked. "How dare you!"

"Calm down," I said to Phaedra. "Justin's right; it's easy to take a wrong step in this weather. The end of the trail isn't far. I suggest you take a few deep breaths and continue walking, staying as far away from the edge of the cliff as possible."

Phaedra darted another angry look at her husband. He reached out to stroke her neck. "I'd never do you any harm, honey. I don't know what I'd do if I lost you."

Phaedra's anger melted. "Oh, darling. Honestly?"

"Swear to God."

The couple embraced and fell into a long kiss. Billie and I took our cue and continued forward. When another gust of wind made us stumble toward the cliff edge, Billie grasped my arm.

"I don't know how much more of this I can stand," she said.

"We should be almost there," I assured her.

"So you keep saying. If only we could see where we are walking."

As if she'd said the magic word, the fog vanished, and before us a long, broad valley spread out between towering rock formations. The Valley of the Rocks! The change was as startling as if someone had switched a channel. A couple of buses were parked on the far side, and tourists were walking amid children playing.

"Thank God!" Billie said.

I spotted a vacant picnic bench not far off. "Let's go sit and collect ourselves while we wait for the others."

Once we sat, Billie asked, "Where's Sally?"

I looked around. "There she is." Our walk leader was striding toward us, concern tightening her face.

"Where are the others?" she asked. "Everyone should be here by now."

"The mist got so thick that everyone slowed down," Billie said. I glanced to the spot where the trail entered the valley to see if any of the others had arrived, but saw no one.

"That's what I was afraid of," Sally said. "The fog must have worsened right after I got here."

My senses were again on full alert. Something wasn't right. What was taking everyone so long? Finally, I saw Phaedra and Justin weaving through the crowd and raised my hand to catch their attention.

When they reached us, Phaedra said, "We've never seen fog that thick before in our lives. I thought we'd need to send up signal flares."

Barker was next to arrive, rounding the bend into the valley, dour-faced as ever, his knapsack clutched in his hand. When he joined us, I asked, "Are the others close behind?"

"How would I know?" he drawled. "With that damned fog, it was all I could do to see my own two feet."

A minute later, Brett came into view. "Thank heaven that's over," he said as he joined us. "It was like a scene from a horror movie. Corky will be glad to know that she made the right decision to stay in town."

I was expecting Summer and Gretz to show up next, but when they didn't after a couple of minutes, I grew worried. I was about to set off in search of them when Summer appeared, her hair hanging in wet strings. She was alone.

"Where's your husband?" Billie asked as she approached.

It took Summer a moment for the question to register. "He's right here, isn't he?" She looked behind her. "Ronnie!" she called out. When he didn't appear she said, "I don't get it. He was behind me just a little while ago."

"When did you see him last?" I asked.

"I'm not sure. When we started walking into all of those clouds, I couldn't see him. But I heard him behind me, complaining like he always does. Do you want me to go find him? He's probably just resting."

I kept my eyes on the cliff path. "No. I'll do it."

"That would be sweet," Summer said. "I need to sit down."

Billie turned to me. "I'm going with you."

We went back onto the trail. The mist was gone, but the winds were still fierce, stronger than before. As we walked, we found ourselves regularly pausing to steady ourselves. All the while, we kept our eyes peeled on the trail ahead for a glimpse of Gretz's brightly colored clothing. Finally, a figure began to appear in the distance.

"Is that him?" Billie asked.

The figure turned out to be a middle-aged woman, striding toward us, swinging two walking poles.

"Excuse me," I said. "Have you seen an older gentleman on the path, dressed in bright colors?"

"In that fog? Are you kidding? I haven't seen anyone until you, just now."

Billie and I exchanged glances. We started forward again, checking the rocky shoals at the bottom of the cliffs every few feet. At one point, I thought I saw something that could be Gretz, but it was just a goat, standing on a rock. The farther we walked, the more I began to wonder if the search was futile. Gretz had probably just said the hell with it and gone back to the van. After a couple more minutes, I was about to suggest heading back as well when

I looked down and spotted a sliver of yellow in the blue-green water at the base of the cliff.

"Down there, Billie," I said. "Look."

She peered down. "I don't see anything."

"Take hold of my arm."

As she steadied me, I managed to lean farther out. There was no mistaking what I was seeing—a body clad in checkered trousers and a pale-yellow polo shirt. It was facedown, and waves were lapping at his head.

It was definitely Gretz. And there was no way he could be alive.

Chapter 12

Tuesday, midafternoon,
Valley of the Rocks

After taking a quick look at my watch—it was 2:40—
Billie and I hurried back to the valley. When we arrived, we led Sally away from the others and told her what we'd seen.

"Oh no," she said with sadness but not surprise. "Are you certain it was Gretz?"

"As certain as we can be at that distance," I responded. "The man was spread out, facedown, but unless there was someone else of Gretz's build, wearing the same clothes, on the path today, he's our guy."

She nodded soberly.

"You should ring the authorities," I said.

"Oh yes. Of course." She pulled her mobile from her rucksack, punched in 9-9-9, and relayed the information I'd given her. "They said they'll be sending out a patrol boat," she said when she finished. After a pause, she added, "I suppose I must tell the others."

She assembled everyone—Corky and Howie had since arrived in the van—and explained that what appeared to be Ronald Gretz's body had been seen at the bottom of the cliff. What she didn't say, but what everyone understood, was that nobody could have survived such a fall. I should have warned her not to tell Summer until Gretz's body had been identified.

Summer let out a wail, and Brett hastened to her side. "We don't yet know if it's him," he told her, putting his hand on her shoulder. She wrapped her arms around him and continued sobbing.

Corky said, "Gretz did look unsteady on his feet today."

"He wore those ridiculous shoes," Phaedra said. "They aren't made for walking on cliff paths like this."

"But you said the path wasn't dangerous, dear," Justin reminded. This earned him another of Phaedra's glares.

Everyone struggled to find the right way to respond to the news so as not to further upset Summer. None had cared for Gretz, which made remorse hard to fake, but their shock seemed genuine. A police car appeared. Billie, Sally, and I walked over as an officer stepped out.

"You the lot who saw the body?" the uniformed young woman asked. Billie and I confirmed that we were and described what we'd seen. The policewoman said a patrol boat had been alerted and was searching the shoreline. She'd no sooner finished speaking than her mobile phone buzzed. After listening for a moment, she turned to us. "The patrol crew found the body; actually, another boat had spotted it and reached it first. It's being transported to Lynmouth, where it will be taken to the hospital for examination and identification."

We returned to the group and relayed the news.

Summer was wide-eyed and panicky. "It's all my fault. I shouldn't have brought Ron here! He didn't want to come. Why did I do it?"

Brett held her and said, "There was no way to know this would happen. Don't be hard on yourself."

The policewoman asked Summer to accompany her

back to town so she could identify the body. Brett moved to go with them, but Sally encouraged him to stay with us, explaining that, as our guide, she was the one who should accompany Summer.

Once inside the van, everyone began voicing opinions.

"It's abundantly clear, isn't it?" Phaedra said. "The old fool slipped and fell. He wasn't wearing proper shoes and looked half-dead to begin with."

"The path was definitely slippery and rocky," Billie admitted.

"We shouldn't even have been up there," Brett said. "Even I felt nervous. Any one of us could have fallen."

"That's ridiculous," Justin said. "Sally told us all to use common sense and not walk close to the edge of the cliff. How difficult is that? The mist got thick alright, but never to the point that I couldn't see where the edge of the cliff was."

"*I* almost fell," Phaedra pointed out. "And I have as much common sense as anyone else."

"It was windy too, wasn't it?" Corky said. "It wouldn't have taken much of a gust to blow someone off the edge, not if they're unsteady on their feet to begin with."

"Gretz seemed groggier than usual this morning," Barker said.

Phaedra nodded. "Do you think he might have been drugged?"

I remained silent. Everyone had raised valid points. My thoughts, however, were directed inward; I couldn't help feeling that I'd screwed up, big-time. I'd agreed to be Gretz's bodyguard, but had blown it. If only I'd stayed closer to him. If only I'd realized the danger and warned him not to attempt the walk. If only . . .

I continued to reprimand myself all the way to the hotel. When we arrived, my mood was about as low as it could get.

None of the others were blaming me, of course. The general consensus was that Gretz's death had been inevitable. Justin asked if it would have an impact on the rest of the walk.

"Why should it make any difference?" Phaedra said as we entered the lobby. "It's not as if we're all grief-stricken and need to plan a memorial service."

"That's not exactly true," Brett said. "At least one of us is grief-stricken."

"Oh, give me a break," Phaedra replied. "Do you honestly think that ditzy wife of his married him for love? More likely love of his bank account."

"That's pretty harsh, dear," Justin said.

Corky collapsed into one of the lobby's cushioned chairs. "I'm sorry the old guy is dead, but dammit, I've been looking forward to this trip! Why do we have to let that jerk mess it up just because he couldn't walk straight?"

I reminded everyone that it was Sally—or rather, her bosses at the Wanderers—who would decide whether the walk would go forward as planned. I told them of a woman who had died of a heart attack on one of my previous walks. It was not due to the walk itself—she had a congenital heart condition—and the walk continued as scheduled. I said that would probably happen in this case also, although I was far from certain.

"A heart attack is clearly a health problem," Justin said. "Falling off a cliff, though, could be . . . something else. It might require an investigation."

"An investigation?" Phaedra said. "Why on earth would that be necessary? It's obvious it was an accident."

"Is it?" I asked.

Phaedra looked as if I had asked why water is wet. "That old fool was in no condition to walk, let alone do so on such a dangerous path! Our walk leader should have clearly realized that and put a stop to it."

"If it was so obvious, dear," Justin asked, "why didn't you say anything at the time?"

"It's not my responsibility to protect people from themselves!"

"Aren't you being rather disingenuous?" her husband said. "After all—"

"Who's being disingenuous?" Phaedra shot back.

Here we go again. I said, "Let's back off from theories until we get more information. In the meantime, I'm going to my room. I need a shower." What I really needed was time away from this bunch so I could manage the many thoughts swirling in my mind.

Billie stopped me. "After your shower, want to join me for some attitude adjustment in the bar?" I sensed that there was more to her request than merely a desire for companionship.

"Good idea." I walked off as the others continued trading theories. When I crossed the small courtyard to my room, I had a chilling sense of déjà vu. It was something I'd experienced many times before—that strange, unsettling period after a sudden death. That was a terrible way to leave the world, I'd always thought. Both the victim and their families are caught off-guard and unprepared, and unless the death happened on the battlefield, they were thrust into a situation they'd never foreseen.

What to make of Gretz's death? Given the close calls he'd had, either he was the unluckiest bastard ever to take a country walk, or the "Avenger" in his emails had been working overtime to carry out his or her threats. If that was the case—and I was coming to suspect that it was— had they left enough clues for me to track them down? At the moment, it didn't look good.

Chapter 13

Tuesday, midafternoon,
Downsmeade Grange

When I entered my room, its orderly cheerfulness came as a jarring contrast to the dismal episode I had just experienced. The Kelly print above the bed—a composition of multicolored blocks—seemed to mock the gravity of the situation, as did the framed watercolors of the local countryside displayed on the other walls.

I changed my mind about a shower. A soak in the tub presented a more tempting option; it would soothe my nerves and calm my thoughts. I turned the tap on full-force and poured in bath salts. Within minutes, the tub was full and steaming. I eased myself in and felt my muscles relax and my mood improve. Yet I was still shaken by what had happened to Gretz, placing the blame entirely on my shoulders.

I drifted into a reverie. Snippets from the previous two days came to mind. The overheard phone conversation—the bone in the bisque—Gretz's collapse on the trail—the crumbling wall at the lime kiln—Summer's late-night liaison with Brett—the argument over medications between Summer and Gretz—Gretz's blowup with Howie.

Lumped together, they added up to a situation rife with danger. My first inclination was to examine everything more closely and determine where I could have interceded. When I realized that would only bring me down again, I took another view of the incidents and saw what was wrong.

There were *too many* of them. No one else in the group had suffered even one "accident," let alone three. I was always beside Gretz, ready to snap into action should danger rear its head. But someone else had always beat me to it. Phaedra was there to give Gretz the Heimlich maneuver that dislodged the bone from his throat; Barker had given Gretz water to help him recover when he fainted on the trail; Brett had grabbed Gretz's arm to prevent him from falling into the lime pit. It was as if several guardian angels had been looking out for Gretz. Yet how had all of them, including myself, failed when he needed them the most?

I began to view the incidents as pieces in a complex game of logic, begging to be arranged in the proper order so they would reveal a solution. Perhaps the best way to approach it was to again consider my fellow walkers.

The Gretzes were the most obvious mismatch: a badly tempered older man and his naïve younger trophy wife. They had been an almost laughable cliché. He had been possibly engaging in some shady business practices that had fired up someone's rage.

The Meyerses appeared to be a happy couple, but their frequent bickering suggested issues beneath the surface.

The Nielsens displayed a close brother-sister bond, yet there were issues there as well, perhaps stemming from the mysterious missing father.

And then there was Lucien Barker—reserved, unexpressive, and interested in British estate law. What secrets was he hiding?

After spending several minutes contemplating these people with no success, I realized something else was weighing on my mind: the stranger I'd encountered on the path who looked so much like Doug. Had he been real? My grief often had gotten the best of me, I had to admit, but it hadn't yet conjured up look-alike phantoms out of thin air. And yet what if it had? Hallucinations are known to occur, particularly in moments of stress. Of course, I began searching for what such a vision might mean. The stranger had nodded at me in greeting, it seemed, but had it been something else? Perhaps a sign for me to go and check on Gretz? Or to continue walking and trust that everything would work out? Or had it been an indication that Doug, wherever he was, was giving me his approval to look for love again?

Enough, I thought. *Better back off, Chase.* Going down that woo-woo rabbit hole would get me nowhere. A glass of ale might be more helpful. I stepped out of the tub, toweled off, got dressed, and went down to the bar, where Billie and the others were on their second (or perhaps third) round of beers.

That's what I wanted. I headed for the bar, and Billie came after me.

"For heaven's sake, Chase, don't you know what time it is? Four in the afternoon! It's no time for beer. It's tea time!"

I had my palate prepped for beer, but a cup of Earl Grey could do the trick as well (not to mention all the sinful treats that accompanied it). The bar staff was only too willing to oblige and promptly prepared a platter of scones, strawberry jam, and clotted cream for our group. Billie showed everyone the proper way to slather the cream and jam on their scones and said to me, "Phaedra has a theory."

"Well, I wouldn't call it a theory exactly," Phaedra said after she took her first bite of scone. "It's just that . . . as you know, I had been thinking that Gretz stumbled off the cliff because of his wonky shoes. But given that he was such a nasty son-of-a-bitch, I'm thinking maybe somebody . . . seized the opportunity and did him in."

Brett shook his head. "He was a prize asshole alright, but none of us even knew the guy. Who would kill a total stranger just because he was a pain in the butt?"

"Don't forget about the bone in his soup," Corky pointed out. "That sure looks fishy now, given what's happened. Maybe there's more going on than we think."

Barker took a petite bite of his scone. "He appeared to have been overly medicated today, in my opinion. That can play all sorts of tricks on one's coordination."

"You say 'your opinion,' but what qualifies you to make such an assessment?" Phaedra asked.

Barker mumbled a reply, his mouth full of half-eaten scone.

"You're a *farmer*?" Corky asked. "Pardon me for saying so, but you don't look like any farmer *I've* ever seen!"

Barker swallowed and cleared his throat. "I'm a *pharmacist*. And assessing the effects of drugs on my customers is something I do all the time."

"Chase, you have experience in these kinds of things," Billie pointed out. "What do you think?"

I poured cream into my tea. "I think it's far too early to start speculating. I agree with Mr. Nielsen. None of us had ever met the man before. It's not likely that anyone here would murder a stranger."

"But there is one of us to whom Gretz *isn't* a stranger," Phaedra said.

We all knew who she was talking about, but nobody wanted to come right out and say the name. Finally, Barker said, " 'And though she be but little, she is fierce.' "

"*A Midsummer Night's Dream*," said Billie. "Helena said that about Hermia because she knows Hermia will fight to be with the one she truly loves."

I couldn't see Summer fighting for Gretz's love. Besides, *she* was the one who was cheating. And yet, at one point, I'd detected a toughness beneath her cartoonish exterior. When, exactly, had I noted that?

"I can't believe I came this close to chucking this whole walking thing and cruising the Mediterranean," Brett said. "Next time, I'll listen to my gut instinct."

"You have a yacht, you said?" I asked.

"A sixty-foot Corsica, sleek and fast as a racehorse."

It isn't surprising to meet rich people on these walks; the expense is a bit steep for most folks. Money itself, however, and the possessions it can buy, is seldom discussed. Gretz was no doubt loaded. Could that have played a part in his murder? Unless there was a binding prenuptial agreement, had his wife relied on the most clichéd reason in the book to commit murder—so she could inherit his estate?

I was trying to figure out the riddle when the woman herself appeared in the doorway, accompanied by Sally. Summer looked as if she'd been through hell. Her eyes were red, a loose man's jacket was wrapped around her shoulders, and her hair was a limp, straggly mop. Sally held her arm.

"The body was Gretz, I'm afraid," Sally told us. "I'm going to help Summer up to her room. Then I'll come back down."

Once they left, Justin said, "I'm no judge, but Summer doesn't look like someone who just murdered her husband."

Phaedra said, "How on earth would you know how such a woman would look?"

He shot her a glare. "Maybe like the way you're looking at me right now."

Billie finished off her scone. "There's one thing about murder I've learned from reading mysteries: it must be *proven*. And how is anyone going to do that? For all we know, Gretz was completely alone on the path when he . . . fell."

"He wasn't alone," Phaedra said. "His wife was with him."

Brett turned on her. "Are you accusing Summer of murder?"

"Let's not get ahead of ourselves," I cautioned. "No crime has been suggested yet."

"It would have been easy for her to do, though, wouldn't it?" Justin suggested. "All it would have taken would be one quick shove. And with the mist swirling around, she could be assured nobody would see her. What could be more natural than an older guy, wearing the wrong shoes and addled by his medications, taking a step in the wrong direction? I mean, the circumstances were almost too perfect! In a way, Summer would have been crazy *not* to have taken advantage of it."

"Unless . . . she actually loved her husband and couldn't bring herself to do it," Billie said.

Phaedra gave a bitter laugh. "Get real. Do you seriously believe that?"

Corky took a sip of tea and stared in the distance. "Not everyone is cut out to be a murderer, circumstances or no circumstances."

Sally returned and sank into a chair.

"Anything else you can tell us?" I asked her.

She leaned forward and sighed. "Here's what I know. Any death such as this requires official review to determine if it was accidental or . . . something else. That means bringing in someone higher up the chain of command than the constabulary in this town. Therefore, a chief inspector from the CID will be coming in from Exeter. He will need to speak with all of us."

Corky's face lit up. "A real English police inspector? Wow!"

"Not counting on that, were you?" Brett said, his voice dripping with sarcasm. "What a bonus!"

"This is just what I was afraid of," Phaedra groaned. "The police will drag this out, and it will hold up everything. We may as well kiss the rest of our walk goodbye. Will we be compensated for the missed days? And the inconvenience? Not to mention the indignity. I didn't come on this trip to be treated like a criminal."

"Honey, be realistic," Justin said. "Someone has died."

Phaedra closed her eyes and fell silent.

"I'll need to check with my superiors to see what this means in terms of continuing the walk or issuing refunds," Sally said.

"I'm so sorry," I said. "This is a hell of a thing to happen on your first assignment."

"Baptism by fire, isn't that the saying?" she replied with a forced smile. "I just hope I'm not found liable in any way. I should have been more insistent Mr. Gretz wear the proper footwear."

"Fiddlesticks!" Billie said. "You did a great job of cautioning him. If that path was unsafe, the local authorities were the ones with the responsibility to block it off."

Sally smiled gratefully at the encouraging words.

"When will this inspector arrive?" I asked.

She shrugged. "It depends on the train schedules. Or he may drive. It's not terribly far from Exeter."

Brett stood up and stretched. "Now I suppose we'll have to act all torn up because a jerk like Gretz is dead."

"That shouldn't be something we need to fake," Justin said. "It's called common respect."

Brett said, "That's where you and I differ, then. Respect must be earned."

"Unlike money," Corky commented. Brett gave her a glare.

A tall, thin man bearing a definite authoritative air appeared at the doorway. He wore a rumpled topcoat, had a disordered mop of hair, and a ruddy face with a long, aquiline nose. Cresting his upper lip was a thin moustache. He might have been considered handsome in a lofty, Oxford don-ish way were it not for his equine face, elongated to the point where he wasn't necessarily unattractive, but definitely odd-looking. Accompanying him was a baby-faced young man with wide eyes.

"Are you the group on the walking tour?" the man asked.

Sally stood. "Most of it, yes. I'm the walk leader, Sally Anders."

The man pulled a billfold from his pocket and flipped it open to show his credentials. "Chief Inspector Teddy Kilbride of Exeter CID. This is Detective Constable Darren Bright."

His thick accent reminded me of someone, but whom? Stepping forward, I introduced myself. "My friend Billie here and I discovered Mr. Gretz's body. Have you had a chance to speak with local police yet?"

"It was an accident, of course," Phaedra said. "Wasn't it?"

Instead of responding, the inspector went to the bar and gave a hand signal to the barman, who promptly filled a pint glass with ale. He took a healthy swallow and turned toward us. "For the time being, allow me to be the one asking the questions. Of which I have a few, given the situation."

"Yes, but what *is* the situation?" Justin said. "I mean, we're sorry that old coot is dead and all that, but other than having walked a couple of days with him, what do any of us have to do with this?"

The inspector took another swallow of beer. "That's what I need to find out. Murder always complicates things, doesn't it?"

Chapter 14

Tuesday, late afternoon,
Downsmeade Grange Bar

"*M*urder?" Billie cried out.

"What makes you think Gretz was murdered?" Corky asked.

"There was a witness," the inspector replied with, I thought, exaggerated coolness.

"A witness?" Sally asked. "Who?"

"A local fisherman notified the authorities right before you did. He'd been in his boat, following the coast, when he heard someone yell. He looked up just as the fog was parting. He saw the body on its way down, with someone standing above, at the edge of the cliff, watching it fall."

The group accepted this startling piece of information in silence before Barker asked, "Well? Who was it? Who pushed him?"

The inspector sighed and ran his hand through his hair. "I'm afraid we don't yet know that. As I said, Ben—that's the fisherman's name—didn't actually see the act itself. He saw Gretz fall, and saw someone above him, and that's all. He couldn't remember much else about the person, not even whether it was a man or a woman."

"That's not much to go on," Billie said.

The inspector hesitated before saying, "He did notice, however, one important detail. The person on the cliff was wearing a green jacket."

"Green jacket?" Phaedra asked. "None of us was wearing a green jacket. I don't think any of us has worn one so far."

The rest of us mumbled in agreement.

"Then none of you will mind if the sergeant here searches your rooms," the inspector said.

"Well . . . no," Phaedra said.

"I can get you the keys," Sally offered, leaving for the front desk. A moment later, she returned and handed them to the inspector.

"Thank you," he said, and turned to us. "In the meantime, I would appreciate it if you lot would wait in the front parlor. Our search shouldn't take long. It's purely procedural, as I hope you realize. None of you, of course, are under suspicion specifically."

Grappling with the news, we moved into the parlor, warmly inviting in the afternoon light flowing through the large windows. Brightly colored carpets were placed strategically upon the wood floor, and large sofas and chairs beckoned before the decorative fireplace. It was all very luxe, even though there did seem to be an overkill of crushed velvet.

Brett seated himself and laughed. "Well, Cork, you should be on cloud nine. A genuine British murder, right in your lap!"

"Don't be crude, Brett."

"I think it's silly, all of this searching our rooms," he said. "It has to have been some local nutcase who did this. Why would any of us want to kill Gretz? We'd just met him!"

"But remember what I said," Phaedra pointed out.

"There was one person among us who *does* know Gretz—intimately."

Brett laughed. "Be serious. Can you picture Summer knocking the old boy off?"

"It does seem unlikely," Billie acknowledged. "Also, she wasn't wearing a green jacket. In fact, she wasn't wearing a jacket at all, was she?"

"She may have had one in her backpack," Phaedra said. "And she was the closest to him on the trail. We all know that."

Brett shook his head. "I've gotten to know her a little bit. Maybe not enough to swear in a court of law that she couldn't be a murderer, but it just doesn't seem possible."

Billie said, "The Gretzes are from North Carolina, and you're from South Carolina. Had you ever come across them before?"

Brett chuckled. "The Carolinas together are about the size of Colorado. It's not as if we all bump into each other at the supermarket. The Meyerses are more likely to know Gretz rather than us. You two work in the medical field, don't you?"

Justin and Phaedra exchanged looks. "To say that nursing homes like Gretz's are in the 'medical field' is being generous," Phaedra said. "Justin and I design living environments, mostly for schools and homes. But yes, we also consult with health-care facilities such as hospitals and clinics."

"No offense, but *yuck*," Corky said with a shiver. "Hospital walls always have that ugly green color. Gives me the creeps. They're as institutional-looking as prison cells."

"That is precisely the perception we're trying to change," Justin said. "At Enviro-Plus—that's the name of our firm—we've discovered that certain interiors can make a world of difference. Introducing more cheerful colors and décor, for example, or certain types of music can dramatically affect one's mood. In terms of hospitals, they can even improve one's chances for recovery from surgery."

"Sort of like feng shui," Billie said.

Justin paused. "Well, in a way, yes, but far more targeted toward health outcomes. Another example would be—"

"I can't help but admire your sweaters, Miss Mondreau," Phaedra said. "You knit them yourself?"

Billie began talking about her knitting, which can keep her going for hours. Why had Phaedra changed the subject? The others fell into general conversation about the weather and plans when they got home. For a group of people who were prime suspects in a murder, they seemed exceptionally cool and unconcerned.

After finishing her explanation to Phaedra of how she came up with the ideas for her sweaters, Billie came over to sit with me. "I notice you didn't come up with any theories for Gretz's murder," she said quietly, so the others couldn't hear. "I can understand not wanting to show off in front of the others, but what is your take on all of this? Who do you think did it?"

I motioned to the corner window. We stood and walked over. Out of earshot from the rest of the group, I said, "It could have been any of us."

Billie cocked her head. "You don't think that's farfetched, as Brett says? A group of total strangers?"

I leaned toward her. "A group of people who *claim* they're strangers. All we have is everyone's word for it. We don't know that for certain."

"Well, you're right, of course. But I find it hard to picture any of us as a murderer."

"You haven't known any murderers, have you?"

"No."

"Well, I have. They look like anyone else. And remember, everyone was at a distance from one another on that path this morning, walking more or less alone in a thick fog. It was nearly impossible for any of us to walk side by side, even as wide as the path may have been. You had to walk behind me, remember? I would venture that any of the group could have been out of sight of the others long enough to have pushed Gretz."

Billie gave a slow nod. "Yes, that's true, but . . ."

Kilbride appeared at the doorway. From his gloved right hand hung a bright green walking jacket.

"You found the jacket!" Corky exclaimed. "Where was it?"

Kilbride walked over to Brett. "It was at the bottom of a suitcase in your room—Mr. Nielsen, is it?"

"*My* room?" Brett yelled, jumping to his feet. "Now wait a minute. I've never seen that thing before in my life!" He looked at the rest of us imploringly. "Well, I haven't. Just ask . . . Cork, you'd know if I'd packed a jacket like that. You've never seen it before, right?"

His sister fidgeted, looking uncomfortable. "Honestly, Brett, how would I know which clothes you packed?"

"What? You think I'm a . . . killer?"

"Of course, I don't. But I can't automatically provide you with an alibi, either."

"Gee," he said bitterly, "thanks a lot."

I felt the need to speak up. "Hold on a second. Your witness claims they saw the killer wearing a green jacket, is that correct?"

Kilbride nodded.

"Well, there was someone else on the trail today who was wearing a green jacket. I only caught a quick glimpse of him, but the jacket was dark green. Not as light as this one. Doesn't anyone remember him?"

Everyone looked around, waiting for someone to speak up.

Brett's eyes widened. "You know, Chase is right! I remember the guy now. He *was* wearing a green jacket." He beamed, as if all suspicions directed at him had vanished.

It was reassuring to learn that what I thought may have been a hallucination of Doug had been, in fact, a real flesh-and-blood human being. But the others weren't convinced.

"I didn't notice anyone else on the trail," Phaedra said. "Did you, darling?"

"No," Justin said. "The only others I saw after we got going were Sally, Chase, and Billie."

"I didn't see anybody else either," Barker said. "I'm pretty sure I would have noticed."

Brett's smile faded. "Well, it's not me imagining things. Chase saw him too."

"Don't forget that the trail was clouded over much of the time," Billie pointed out. "It's surprising that any of us saw this mystery man."

"She's right," Brett said. "I only saw him for a second or two."

"Do you know what this person looked like, other than what he wore?" Kilbride asked.

Brett thought a moment. "Not really, other than it was a guy, not a woman. Although . . . I'm not even sure of that."

"Well, *I'm* sure of it," I said. "He had a lean, somewhat weathered face, with dark, thick eyebrows, black hair hanging down slightly in front beneath the rim of his jacket's hood, and deep blue eyes."

"I thought you only caught a 'quick glimpse' of him," Phaedra said. "It sounds instead like you sat him down and painted his portrait!"

"Chase has an eye for detail," Billie said. "He was a police detective, don't forget."

"Indeed, Mr. Chasen?" the inspector asked.

"Yes, that was my career when I was working." What I didn't mention was that the stranger's striking physical similarity to Doug made me study him more intensely than I would have otherwise.

"Quite interesting," Kilbride said. He reflected for a moment, his head down, before looking up and turning to the others. "The next matter at hand is to take this jacket to our laboratory and check it for fingerprints."

Everyone began talking at once. Kilbride's voice rose above the din. "Now listen up! No one's been accused of anything just yet. One step at a time, that's the way we work."

DC Bright produced a plastic bag into which he slipped the jacket, which was made of the synthetic material called Gore-Tex, as is much protective outdoor clothing.

"Can you identify fingerprints on that kind of jacket?" I asked the inspector.

"It's difficult, but it can be done. The Scots developed a process a few years ago called VMD—vacuum metal deposition. It uses fine layers of metals to detect fingerprint marks on plastics, glass, and even fabrics such as this."

"Well, you certainly won't find *my* fingerprints on that thing," Brett fumed. "Unless . . . fingerprints can't be faked, can they?"

"Not likely," Kilbride replied. "But, of course, in order for us to check fingerprints, we need to have something to check them against. So we must take samples of everyone's prints. The constable here has a small kit to do that. It won't take long. The process is quick and painless."

DC Bright began setting up the fingerprint kit on the bar counter. The inspector's time estimate was accurate, and within a few minutes, all our prints had been taken. The constable folded up the kit and prepared to leave with Kilbride for the local forensics lab. The inspector instructed us to remain at the hotel. After telling us he would return in the morning to begin his questioning, he gave a lighthearted "Toodle pip!" and walked off.

We were left a dazed and edgy bunch. *Murder.* None of us had reckoned that such a calamity would occur on what was supposed to be a pleasant amble through one of the most civilized countries on the planet. Worse still, we were all suspects. Brett feared that somehow he could be framed for Gretz's murder. I assured him that only happened in detective fiction, but he didn't feel comforted.

Neither, I had to admit, did I. In most of the murders I'd investigated, there was usually a group of suspects with a clear motive for wishing the victim dead. Some motives were stronger than others, but they were always *there.*

In this group, as others had pointed out, the only person with any perceivable motive for killing Gretz was his wife. For some, that alone would have made this an open-and-shut case, but it didn't feel right to me. Summer's guilt also seemed too clean, too textbook.

And yet . . . what possible motives could any of the others have? Brett was right. We'd all just met Gretz, and while he was a pain in the butt, that isn't a very strong motive for murder.

In addition, there was the mystery man on the trail. His resemblance to Doug made me think favorably of him, but he could be anyone, including the one who'd been sending death threats to Gretz.

It was a puzzle, alright. Which normally I like. But as I was one of the suspects myself, this one was striking too close to home.

Chapter 15

Howie announced that dinner would be served on the terrace, as a wedding party was holding their rehearsal dinner in the main restaurant.

"Dinnertime, already?" Phaedra said. "That can't be right. Didn't we just have tea?"

A look out the window at the evening shadows on the hotel's eastern lawn was proof the end of the day was approaching. I agreed with Phaedra; given everything that was going on, the concept of time had been difficult to grasp that day.

"I'm not very hungry," Corky said, as we walked outdoors. "This trip isn't turning out to be anything like I expected at all."

The air outside was damp and cool. Our entire group was there except Summer, who had, understandably, chosen to remain in her room. We headed to tables that had been brought together and circled with pillow-seated iron chairs normally used for afternoon tea. We all took our seats, and dishes of the starter course were promptly brought out and distributed. The wedding party, although some distance away up the hill, could be heard celebrating with lots of chatter and piano music. It provided an uncomfortable juxtaposition with the grim mood of our group.

"Can someone tell them to quiet down?" Phaedra asked.

"I'll speak with the manager," Howie offered, disappearing inside.

Soon the unseen pianist launched into a more subdued number—a slow, tinkly version of "Begin the Beguine"—and our group fell into another discussion of Gretz's murder. None believed that Brett could be the killer, despite the evidence of the green jacket. Everyone was in agreement that, while we all had issues with Gretz, none of us would have actually killed him. The only one with a motive, Phaedra said, was Summer, who would presumably be receiving a considerable inheritance.

As before, Brett came to her defense. "Look, I've said it before, and I'll say it again. I just can't see her pulling off something like this."

"We know she's not the sharpest knife in the drawer," Justin said, "but it doesn't take brains to push someone off a cliff."

"That's true," Brett acknowledged, "but it takes a lot of nerve. Summer doesn't have a ruthless bone in her body."

"And just how closely have you been inspecting her bones?" Phaedra asked.

Corky emitted a sharp laugh, but Brett scowled and stuffed an asparagus spear into his mouth.

"Well, if Summer isn't the killer, who is?" Corky asked her brother.

"I'm still not convinced there *was* a killer," said Barker.

"But we know there was!" Corky said. "That fisherman saw it happen."

Barker emitted a small, cynical laugh. "Oh, come on. How could he have seen something like that from his boat? At that distance? And with all that fog swirling around?

He probably just heard Gretz scream and his subconscious mind came up with the rest."

"If the inspector believed him, that's good enough for me," Justin said. "Why would that guy make up such a serious allegation? Yet I don't think for one minute that it was one of us who did it. I agree with Brett that it was some homicidal maniac. There must be one around here somewhere. It could have been that man he and Chase saw on the trail."

Phaedra laughed. "How convenient that this anonymous homicidal maniac should pop up and kill the most irritating member of our group."

"Not to mention be able to slip the jacket they were wearing into Brett Nielsen's suitcase," Justin said.

That was bothering me as well.

"Remember, the stranger on the trail was also wearing a green jacket," Brett said.

"Then why did someone hide one in your bag?" Justin asked. "And how did he gain access to it?"

Everyone reflected on this. Justin had raised good points. The fact that the man on the trail was wearing a green jacket could be a simple coincidence. The one placed in Brett's suitcase—if indeed it hadn't been placed there by Brett himself—indicated that someone was trying to incriminate him. And that someone would pretty much have to be one of us. How would an outside assailant know where we were staying?

"There is one bright spot I haven't mentioned," Sally said. "We weren't scheduled to remain at this hotel beyond tonight. Fortunately, they're lightly booked for the next few days, so we won't need to relocate."

"The next few days?" Barker said. "Are we going to be here that long?"

"Perhaps not," Sally said, "but as I said, we don't know, do we?"

"In the meantime, we're all prisoners," Phaedra said gravely.

"That's an awfully strong word to use, dear," Justin commented.

"Here are a few strong words for you," she said. "Shut the hell up."

"This isn't such a bad place to be a prisoner," Corky said. "Plush rooms, good food, a library. I feel like I'm in a movie!"

"Good for you, Little Miss Sunshine," Phaedra snapped. "It feels like a movie to me too. *Twenty Years in Sing Sing*. Except the prisoners in that movie didn't have pictures of elephants above their beds."

"Lighten up, dear," Justin said. "There has been a murder committed, after all."

I was expecting another of Phaedra's ripostes, but she tightened her lips and said nothing.

"Don't forget that we're all US citizens," Brett said. "That must count for something over here. They can't just lock us up indefinitely."

"Who knows what they can do?" said Barker. "They don't necessarily play by the same rules over here as we do in the States."

"What a vacation this turned out to be," Phaedra said.

The main course arrived, and conversation abated while everyone ate. No one was very hungry, and most of us just poked at our meals. When dessert was announced, all but Barker begged off.

"Except for ruining this walk, Gretz's murder hasn't bothered me at all," he said. "I'm going to have the strawberry trifle and enjoy every mouthful."

As the others stood up to leave, I saw Billie studying a message on her cell phone. Knowing she was expecting news about her sister, I went over and asked if she'd heard anything.

She turned off the phone and gave her head a shake. "It's maddening! They were all set to operate on Janice when the surgical center had to shut down because of a bomb threat."

"A bomb threat?"

"Apparently, someone spread rumors that they conduct abortions there and decided to give them a scare. So now it's a waiting game. Want to take a walk? I need to move around."

I gave her a nod, and we made our way toward a neatly tended rose garden on the other side of the lawn. There was still enough daylight remaining for us to navigate the twisty path.

"I couldn't help but notice over dinner that you weren't sharing your theories along with the rest of the bunch," Billie said. "Yet I definitely sensed the wheels spinning in your feverish mind."

"I'm not one for idle speculation," I said. "And besides, I can't help feeling partly to blame."

Billie stopped and stared at me. "Are you serious? There wasn't anything you could have done to save Gretz, Chase. As the kids say, get real."

"What about you? Do you think Summer is the killer? Or is it some local lunatic?"

"Let's just say I've been thinking about order."

"Order?"

"Yes, the order in which we were walking on the cliff path. As you know, we were all in a line, nearly every one of us in front of or behind another."

"Correct," I said.

"And, except for you and me, everyone was walking at a fair distance from one another, right?"

"Yes, that's true as well. You were always close to me, but I could only see one or perhaps two of the others with the mist swirling around us."

"And Gretz was walking at the rear of the pack, as usual. Isn't that right?"

"Now, Billie," I warned, "that would be an assumption—a reasonable one, but an assumption. Yes, he was at the rear of the pack when we started out, but that could have changed."

Billie crouched and picked up a twig. With it, she drew a line in the dirt beneath us. "Let's say this is the cliff path. And here is the order of the walkers as I remember from when we started walking. In the lead, as usual, was Sally." She drew a circle at the front of the line, followed by other circles. "Behind her was Phaedra, then Justin, then you and me, then Brett, Barker, and finally Summer and Gretz. Corky and Howie were back in the town."

I knelt and studied the circles. "Yes, that's what I remember as well."

"Very well. As I see it, the five of us at the front of the pack are in the clear. I mean, we agree that neither you nor I killed Gretz, right? And those in front of us—Sally and the Meyerses—couldn't have done it either, or we would have seen them walking past us, going toward the rear of the pack where Gretz was."

I nodded.

"The same thing applies to those behind us. Assuming that Gretz continued walking at the rear of the pack—yes, I know, that's an assumption, but it's a logical one—anyone besides his wife who wanted to kill him would have had to walk past her in order to do it. And she hasn't claimed that anyone did that."

"Not yet, that is."

"True," Billie conceded. "She might say that someone *did* walk past her, if she is, indeed, the murderer and wants to deflect suspicion. But that would be a stretch, don't you think? It would be just her word against someone else's."

"True as well. You've done a good job thinking this out."

She smiled at my praise.

"So what you're saying, if I understand you correctly, is that Summer must be the murderer."

Billie looked down at what she'd drawn. "I don't see any other explanation."

"Yes, it sure looks that way." I rose to my feet. "However, I see a couple of flaws in your reasoning. Perhaps more."

Her smile disappeared. She looked down at her diagram. "Flaws? But where?"

"Think of the path itself." Pointing to the line in the dirt, I said, "On one side there was an immediate drop several hundred feet to the sea below. That was true along the entire path, as I recall. It hugged the edge of the cliff closely. The other side of the path, however—the one facing away from the sea—wasn't as consistent. At times, we were walking right up against the side of the cliff wall, and at other times, there were recesses, some of which held an outgrowth of gorse or large bushes. There were several spots such as that, I recall. Any could have provided cover if someone wanted to hide while the other walkers passed by."

"You're right," Billie said, discouraged. "Then, once Gretz approached, the murderer could jump out and do the deed."

"Possibly."

Billie pondered this. "Hold on a moment. You almost had me going. But you didn't think it through. Yes, what you describe could have happened; someone could have hidden as the others passed. But if someone did that, wouldn't they have had to return to their original place in line so as not to arouse suspicion? And they would have to pass us in order to do that."

"Yes, I thought of that also. It appeared that everyone arrived at the Valley of the Rocks in the same order as when we started, except for—"

"Well, Gretz, of course."

"Yes, but . . . didn't Brett Nielsen appear after Barker?"

Billie thought a moment. "Yes, I think so."

"But he was walking ahead of Barker when we started, wasn't he?"

Billie struggled to remember, but gave up with a sigh. "I thought that he was, but I can't be sure. I can't believe this whole thing. It's so frustrating."

"In addition, your diagram here doesn't account for the stranger who passed us."

Billie eyed me questioningly. "Are you sure you saw someone, Chase? I know I told the inspector how foggy it was on the path, but it does seem weird that only you and Brett were able to see this person. And Brett might only have said that he did because it makes finding the green jacket in his suitcase less suspicious."

Her suspicion again raised doubts in my own mind. "What I haven't told you is that the man on the trail bore a striking resemblance to Doug."

"Doug? Are you serious?"

"Practically the spitting image. So much so that I wondered if it might have been a figment of my imagination. I'm not prone to stuff like that, but stranger things have happened."

Billie gave this some thought. "It's possible, I guess. I know Doug's passing has really brought you down. But . . . you seem much too pragmatic to let that throw you into hallucinations."

And yet, how pragmatic had I really been? "I almost walked in front of a speeding car the other day when I arrived, don't forget. Still, whoever or whatever it was I saw on the trail today seemed so real . . ." I closed my eyes to conjure up the stranger's image. "Wait a minute!" I said, my eyes opening. "I just remembered something else about that guy. He had an image or a logo on his jacket—it looked like a rooster."

"A rooster?"

"Isn't there a line of outdoor wear that has a rooster for a logo?"

"It wouldn't be hard to find out. Anyway, I'm inclined to believe that you saw a real person and not a phantom. But where does that leave us? This stranger could have been the one sending Gretz those death threats, I suppose, but how would he have known Gretz was on the trail? Chase, this has gotten so muddled."

"There's one more thing you overlooked," I said. "Your theory, sound as it is, applies only to those of us who were walking on the cliff path. *But not all of us were.*"

"You mean Corky," Billie said. "She could have been making up that bit about being afraid of heights and wanting to visit the shops."

"And let's not forget about Howie," I added.

"Honestly, Chase. Why would Howie want to kill Gretz? Just because the old coot insulted him at lunch?"

"But that is the question, my dear Billie," I said, taking another look at her diagram on the ground. "Why would *any* of us want to kill him?"

We returned to the hotel, and when we reached the door to my room, I bid Billie good night. The exercise of mapping out everyone's place on the cliff path was useful, but it had also made me question again why I hadn't stayed closer to Gretz. Again, the same question plagued me. Could I have saved him?

My guilty conscience caused me to spend more time than I'd planned writing in my journal. I wanted to make sure I noted every detail of Gretz's murder while it was fresh in my mind. Digging deep into my memory, I tried to make sure I got everything down on paper correctly.

When I finished, my self-recriminations for not sufficiently alerting Gretz to the danger he faced had subsided.

Putting everything down in writing supported Billie's belief that there was little I could have done, short of walking directly beside Gretz the entire time, an extreme approach that would have been awkward and, given the capriciousness of the weather, probably would not have been very effective.

I closed my journal and turned off the light, confident that I hadn't been derelict in my duty. There was even a small sense of excitement at being back in an investigation. Yet something was niggling at the edge of my mind. It took a moment's thought to reveal what it was.

Mike. In all the excitement, I had forgotten about him. Had he shown up at the bar that evening, looking for me? If he did, and noticed that I never showed, he might have left, never to return. Discouraged, I stretched out on the left side of bed and waited for sleep to overcome me. Thanks to the stress of the day, it quickly did.

Chapter 16

I awoke in a daze. My sleep had been plagued by a series of dreams in which I was being hunted, fleeing down dark forest paths, hiding behind trees and rocks, trying not to leave footprints by which I could be tracked. Upon awakening, I had to struggle to orient myself, and gradually, reality was reasserted. I was in a comfortable bed, nestled beneath a down-filled comforter, the morning light seeping through the closed curtains. Despite the fact that there had been a brutal murder, the world was more or less normal. My breathing eased.

I considered the dream I'd just had. In it, I wasn't able to identify my pursuer. I hadn't even picked up a helpful clue. So much for my subconscious mind coming to the rescue.

Feeling the need for a jolt of caffeine, I boiled water in the room's electric kettle and made a cup of instant coffee, but the result was too hot and scalded my tongue. I went into the bathroom and found that my electric razor had failed to charge, relegating me to the straight razor I'd brought for such emergencies.

I was not in the best of moods, therefore, when I went to breakfast. Although the prospect of ferreting out Gretz's killer was beginning to dredge up skills I hadn't used for a while, I would much rather have been looking forward to a day of walking, letting that soothing motion take me away from the dark side of human nature, rather than actively seeking to probe it.

When I arrived at the breakfast room, Billie was already there, nibbling on a piece of buttered toast and thumbing through messages on her cell phone. Distracted momentarily by the figures on her sweater—were those ducks or geese?—I grabbed a muffin and joined her.

"Are you ready for the latest?" she said. "Turns out the authorities didn't find any bomb at the surgical center—no surprise there—but because Janice's surgery didn't occur on the date approved by the HMO, the doctors have to resubmit a surgical request."

I filled my coffee cup from the French press on the table. "It's a good thing the insurance companies compensate for their incompetence by charging outrageous premiums."

Billie's eyes narrowed. "If that's supposed to be an attempt at humor, it's not funny."

"Sorry. With everything going on, it's hard not to be paranoid."

"You can say that again. Gretz getting killed is bad enough, but that attempt to frame Brett Nielsen—if that's what it was—has got me thinking that eventually someone might make it look like *I* was the one who killed Gretz."

Her fear was so absurd that I gave a small laugh, but caught myself. Billie had been near me on the trail, there was no doubt of that, yet she wasn't in my view all the time. What is it I always say—never rule anyone out as a suspect? "Don't worry, Billie. I'm sure that won't happen."

She didn't look reassured. "And what about you? Maybe the police will think we teamed up to kill him."

I assured her that the alibis of spouses are often disregarded in such circumstances, but not those of acquaintances with no connection other than occasional walking trips.

Corky appeared, looking a bit less collected than usual. She wore an untucked shirt and scruffy jeans, as opposed to her catalog-perfect walking attire. Her eyes looked groggy as she poured a cup of coffee.

"Hard night?" Billie asked.

Corky nodded. "I couldn't fall asleep, so I came down and started reading one of the mysteries in the hotel library. It was a courtroom drama with a really nasty killer. I couldn't stop until I saw her brought to justice."

"And was she?" I asked.

"Sort of. Her lawyer tried to get her off because she had iron deficiency, but it turned out she was possessed by the devil."

Barker arrived, filled his plate at the buffet, and sat at the table beside us. He gave us a perfunctory nod.

"I trust you were able to get a good night's sleep," I said.

"I slept just fine," he said with a trace of smugness. "You see, I know who killed Gretz."

"You do?" Billie said. "You saw it happen?"

Barker ate a bit of egg and wiped his mouth. "No, I didn't *see* it, but I know who it was." He paused for effect. "Brett Nielsen."

"Brett?" I asked. "Just because the green jacket was found in his luggage? You think he'd be that dim-witted? Someone most likely planted it there."

Barker nibbled a bite of ham before responding. "When we started walking yesterday, Brett was in front of me on the cliff path. But shortly after we started out, he stopped to look out at the sea—as if he were searching for something. I thought it strange at the time but didn't say anything."

"So you walked past him?" I asked.

"That's right. I didn't think anything of it then, of course. But when we learned that Gretz had been killed, that's when I remembered it. He must have been waiting for Gretz to catch up to him."

"But . . ." Billie said, "what about Summer?"

Barker's brow raised slightly. "What about her?"

"Well, she was walking with her husband. How could Brett murder Gretz without her seeing him do it?"

Barker dabbed his mouth again. "Don't you see? She was in on it too! Haven't you noticed how lovey-dovey she and Mr. Nielsen have been? They were planning it so they could be together. It's the only explanation."

I had dealt with plenty of would-be detectives in my career, but Barker was one of the most pathetic. "Do you have any other evidence on which to base your accusation?" I asked.

Barker clearly was not used to being challenged. "*Evidence?* I just told you what I saw. What other evidence do you need?"

"Well, the police may need more than that."

"Speak of the devil," Billie said. Through the window, we saw Inspector Kilbride's black sedan pull up. "Here he is."

I excused myself and was leaving when Brett walked in, also looking bleary-eyed. "I hope there's still food left. My watch alarm didn't go off."

I reached the lobby just as Kilbride and Bright walked in. The inspector spotted me and said, "Good morning, Mr. Chasen. Can you tell us where we might locate your walk leader, Miss Anders?"

We found Sally in the parlor drinking tea and reading the account of Gretz's death in the morning paper. The inspector asked her to assemble the group. I could discern no hidden subtext in his tone. He certainly hadn't spoken with the conviction of someone who'd discovered an incriminating fingerprint.

Most of the others were found on the terrace or in the breakfast room. Summer had not yet left her room, so Sally went to collect her. When the two came down, Summer appeared to still be in a vacant-eyed haze. I wondered if perhaps she had indulged in some of her husband's drug supply.

"So what did you find out?" Brett asked Kilbride once we were gathered. "Were my fingerprints on that jacket?"

"No, they were not," Kilbride said. Brett beamed with self-satisfaction.

"Then whose fingerprints were they?" Corky asked.

"We found no fingerprints at all," Kilbride said. "Either they were too faint to detect—as Mr. Chasen pointed out, lifting prints from that kind of fabric isn't an exact science— or whoever wore that garment must have been wearing gloves. To be honest, that is what I expected."

"Has any other information come to light?" I asked.

Kilbride paused a moment, and said, "As a matter of fact, yes. The body still needs to be examined by the county coroner to verify the cause of death, but the medical examiner who initially examined Gretz was able to determine the *time* of death. It appears that the man had been dead somewhere between fifteen and thirty minutes when his body was recovered."

"I checked the time when Billie and I saw Gretz," I said. "It was two-forty."

Everyone pondered this bit of information. Gretz must have been pushed to his death just minutes before Billie and I found him.

"That doesn't exactly let any of us off the hook, does it?" Justin asked.

Phaedra asked, "So what happens now?"

The inspector took a deep breath. "The fact remains that one of your group has been murdered, and I must do my best—with the help of the constable here—to find out who did it."

"And just how long will that take?" Justin asked.

"That depends, Mr. Meyers, on your cooperation and that of the others. We will be questioning everyone. The more honest and open you are in your responses, the quicker this whole matter can be resolved."

"Well, I have nothing to hide," Justin said.

"Glad to hear it," Kilbride responded. "DC Bright and I will meet with each of you individually. But before we get into that, I want to get a clear understanding about where everyone was yesterday afternoon when the . . . incident occurred."

Sally explained that everyone in the group, with the exception of Corky and Howie, was walking on the cliff path. She didn't elaborate on the order of the walkers.

"The height of the cliff spooked me, so I stayed behind in the village," Corky explained. "I bought an ice cream cone, looked around a bit, then rode in the van with Howie to meet up with the others afterward."

"I see," Kilbride said. "But the rest of you were on the path, correct?"

Everyone affirmed this.

"Did you walk in pairs, groups, or individually?"

"Most of us were walking individually," Billie said. "The path wasn't wide enough for us to walk beside each other. Plus, as you know, it was very foggy, and there was quite a drop down to the sea. We all wanted to keep as far from the edge of the path as possible."

From his questions, Kilbride was able to piece together the order of the walkers, which he noted on a small pad. Everyone agreed that, at times, they were completely out of sight of the others, largely due to the mist and fog. Even Billie and I, as close together as we were on the trail, sometimes couldn't see one another.

"So Mr. Gretz was at the rear of the pack," the inspector confirmed. "Were you walking directly ahead of him, Mrs. Gretz?"

All eyes turned toward Summer. "Of course, I was," she said. Then a light bulb turned on. "Hey, wait a second. That makes it sound like I was the only one who could have killed Ronnie." The light from the bulb grew brighter. "But I didn't do it. *I didn't!*" She wailed the last denial, buried her face in her hands, and began sobbing. Brett went to her side, knelt, and placed his hand on her shoulder. She gave him a small, thankful smile.

Summer's reaction seemed genuine enough—her husband had just died tragically, after all—yet I couldn't dismiss the suspicion that it seemed a bit staged. Perhaps I formed that reaction from seeing Doug prepare for various acting jobs through the years (although he was primarily a voice actor, he took occasional stage and TV roles as well). Regardless, if Summer was faking it, she was doing a damn good job. Everyone else seemed to be buying it.

Brett looked up at Kilbride. "Mrs. Gretz has been through hell and didn't sleep well last night. Can she go to her room and speak with you later?"

Kilbride nodded. "I don't see why not."

"I'll escort her and be right back." Brett helped Summer to her feet and led her up the staircase.

"Speaking of the order of the walkers," Billie said to Kilbride, "Chase and I have been discussing that very topic." She briefly outlined our theories. The inspector listened impatiently, twisting his hat in his hand and shifting from one foot to another.

"Yes, yes," he said before she had a chance to finish.

"We'll get into all of that in time, Miss Mondreau. The fact remains that the nearest person to Mr. Gretz at the time of his murder was his wife."

"Not necessarily," Barker injected.

Kilbride turned toward him. "What do you mean?"

Barker explained how Brett stopped on the trail to look out over the sea, letting him pass. "It struck me as odd at the time, and of course now I know why. He was stalling so he could be walking near the Gretzes and push the old boy to his death. There's no other explanation."

"I heard that, you little worm!" Brett said, standing in the doorway. "What are you getting at? You think I let you pass me on purpose so I could stay behind and kill Gretz?"

"It does contradict the order of walkers we discussed only a few minutes ago, Mr. Nielsen," Kilbride pointed out. "If that order wasn't correct, why didn't you speak up?"

Brett let out a frustrated sigh. "Because I didn't even remember *doing* it until Barker told everyone just now. So, you're saying that I'm again a suspect, just because I stopped to appreciate the view?"

"You're *all* suspects," the inspector reminded us.

This set off a flurry of denials and explanations.

"Everyone, please be silent!" Kilbride said. "You'll each have the opportunity to explain yourselves. At present, I need to find a room in which to conduct our interviews."

After checking with the front desk clerk, Kilbride announced that a small game room near the hotel's side entrance had been secured to conduct the interviews. He turned to Howie. "Let's start with you, Mr. Crane, shall we?"

"Me?" Howie said. "But I don't know nothing. I wasn't even on the bleeding path!"

"Then this will be a quick interview," Kilbride said. Howie reluctantly stood and walked off with him.

"This is so exciting!" Corky said once they left. "I never

thought I would be questioned in a real British murder investigation. It's like a dream come true."

"More like a nightmare," Phaedra murmured.

"That's for sure," her husband said. "I mean, think about it. If someone in our group went off the rails and killed Gretz, who's to say one of us won't be next?"

Faced with what appeared to be a long wait, the group dispersed itself among the parlor's generously sized couches and overstuffed chairs. Everyone fell into an uneasy silence—leafing through magazines, checking cell phones, sipping coffees and teas—while waiting to be summoned by the inspector. It reminded me of my fifth-grade class after a spitball fight had broken out and all the boys waited sullenly outside the school principal's office for a tongue-lashing.

I was surprised when Howie reappeared after only a matter of minutes. He went to Sally and tapped on her mobile phone to get her attention. "Your turn now. You know where to go, right?"

She finished sending a message before nodding and getting to her feet. "Anything I should be aware of?"

"Not really. It was nothing like on the telly."

"No trick questions?" she asked with the trace of a smile.

"No, except . . . well, I told the inspector about Gretz accusing me of mucking up his lunch order and us having a dustup. I said that I coulda killed him."

"Oh, Howie, you didn't."

"It's just what people say, innit? Don't mean nothing. Anyway, watch your tongue."

Sally walked off with an air of stiff self-assurance.

Brett said, "This is all so pointless. What good does it do to interview us?"

"You certainly don't expect him not to speak to us at all," Justin said.

"Yeah, I guess he has to. But it just doesn't make sense that any of us would have killed Gretz. My money is still on some local nutcase. Like that guy Chase and I saw on the trail. That's where he should be looking."

"Where he should be looking is at the grieving widow upstairs," Phaedra said.

"Would you get off that kick?" Brett snapped. "Summer's not a killer."

"Why do you keep defending her? You must be bright enough to realize that any deflection of suspicion away from the wife will only be focused on us."

"I've said it before, and I'll continue saying it. I have nothing to hide. Do you?"

I was expecting Brett's comment to set off fireworks, but Phaedra stood and walked silently away. Brett folded his arms.

"You didn't take my advice about staying away from Mrs. Gretz," I said to him.

Brett squirmed. "Well, can you blame me? It's hard to resist a woman like that. She's got everything in the right place, know what I mean?"

"Including a wedding ring. Not that she's technically married anymore, of course."

Brett gave a nervous smile. "Just because I think she's hot doesn't mean I killed her husband. If I did that with every married woman I've been with, I'd be on Death Row by now for sure."

Sally came back and, after informing Corky that she was next to be interviewed, sat down with an outflow of breath.

"How did it go?" I asked.

Sally turned her palms upward. "I felt so helpless. What could I say? I'm the leader of the walk, and I couldn't even prevent one of my group from falling off a cliff."

"You're being hard on yourself," I said, thinking of my

own guilt feelings. "Don't forget we have a witness, and according to him, Gretz didn't fall; he was pushed. You couldn't have done anything about that." I wondered how many details the police were able to extract from the witness. There was an art to doing that, and I was skeptical the local force was up to it.

Sally ran her fingers through her hair. "I suppose you're right. I just wish I had noticed something helpful. I'm usually very attentive."

I imagined myself in her shoes, leading a group along a precarious cliff path with limited visibility. I knew there was little I could have done to prevent Gretz's murder, and that applied to Sally as well. Still, I had reservations. "I know the mist and fog made it difficult, but did you try to keep the group in sight while we were on the path?"

Sally let out another sigh. "Of course I did. I always try to keep an eye on everyone. But you saw how thick the mist got. It was all I could do to see the Meyerses behind me, and I even lost sight of them once or twice. That's no excuse, though. In retrospect, I should have called the whole thing off."

"I remind you again that Gretz's death was no accident. It was intentional."

She looked down. "I should have insisted he wear proper walking shoes. I should have stayed closer to him, as he was the oldest of our group. I should have—"

"What you should do is knock off that self-reproach."

Sally stood and returned to the table and her papers.

Corky reappeared and said to Brett, "He wants to see you now."

"How was your interview?" her brother asked.

She nodded. "A breeze. Until they brought out the thumb screws."

"What?" Brett said.

"I'm joking! Don't worry. He won't rough you up."

Brett walked off, and Corky lowered herself into an armchair upholstered in a russet color similar to her hair.

"The interview wasn't quite as exciting as you'd hoped?" I asked.

"It was dullsville! 'Had you known the deceased before'? 'Did you see anything unusual?' I kept explaining that I didn't even go on the walk . . . that I was in the village. If I'd gone on the walk . . . if I'd been there . . . I might have seen something. Maybe I even could have prevented it." She looked outside the windows wistfully. "We were supposed to walk over the moors today. Now I'll never get the chance."

"Cheer up. I'm sure you'll get back here someday."

"Yeah," she said with a bitter laugh. " 'Someday.' That's the day after 'never.' " She looked again through the window. "I'm worried about Brett."

"What on earth for?"

"I'm no psychologist, but I know my brother. He doesn't do well with authority figures, especially men. He sees them as father figures. Never actually having had a father, he desperately wants their approval, but feels he can never satisfy them. He gets nervous and stammers. I'm afraid the inspector will think he's as guilty as hell."

"As long as he hasn't done anything to be nervous about, you don't have to worry. The police are fairly good at sticking to evidence and facts."

"If you say so." She didn't sound convinced. "He brought me over here to cheer me up after our mother died, and I wanted this trip to be good for him also. Guess it's too late now."

"I wouldn't go that far. I'm sorry about your mother."

Corky took a deep breath. "It was quite a blow. As I said, our father ran out on us when Brett and I were just babies. Our mom was the only parent we'd ever known. After she passed, Brett suggested this trip, figuring a change of scene would do us good. I was frankly surprised he brought it up—it's awfully expensive—but eventually I gave in."

"I thought he was rolling in dough," I said. "The Lamborghini and the yacht and everything."

"Well . . . that's what he wants people to believe. But actually, he's as broke as a skunk. Wait a minute. That's not right, is it?"

"You're thinking 'drunk as a skunk.' "

"Well, that fits too," she said with a giggle. Then she got serious. "Earlier this year, Brett was persuaded by one of his investor friends to invest practically all of his money into some start-up company. He tried to get me to do the same thing, told me it couldn't fail. Well, I was lucky that I didn't. It went belly-up right out of the starting gate. Seems its patent's claims were exaggerated. The deal pretty much wiped him out."

This was interesting. How desperate was Brett to restore a fortune that had been yanked away from him? Desperate enough to kill?

"But please don't tell him I told you that," Corky said. "He'd absolutely kill me. Well, not actually, of course. That was a slip of the tongue; Brett would never kill anyone. I mean, seriously, he wouldn't. Anyway, we're paying for this tour with the small inheritance we got when my mom died. Do you think we'll get a refund if it's canceled?"

"That will be likely," I said. "Don't worry about it."

I rose, stretched, and eyed the room's remaining occupants. Barker was engrossed on his cell phone. Billie was knitting. The Meyerses were on a sofa, shoes off, reclined at either end. Justin was scanning the morning *Times*, and Phaedra was thumbing through a decorating magazine. She paused and began to slowly look around.

"Is something the matter?" I asked her.

Phaedra paused a moment. "It's this room."

I gave a quick look around. "What's wrong with it?"

"The question should be, what's right with it? Look at that horrible dark wallpaper with its disturbing imagery. What are those things?"

I peered at the wall behind the sofa. "I believe those are horses engaged in a fox hunt."

"Well, there you are! How is that supposed to make you feel?"

"In the mood to hunt a fox?"

"It's a barbaric sport, if you can actually call it a sport. Very unsettling. And that glaring overhead lamp—much too severe. Plus those dreadful damask curtains are so depressing. This sofa is the least comfortable I have ever had the misfortune to sit upon. And don't get me started on the lack of ventilation. This is the kind of room they hold hostages in."

What was she talking about? I thought the room was very comfortable.

"Justin and I could work wonders on this place," Phaedra said.

"That's your line of business, isn't it? Interior decorating?"

Her eyes widened. "Good heavens! We're not *interior decorators*. Where did you get that idea? Our business is enhancing the livability of interior environments. We focus on how they make you *feel*. Do they uplift you, inspire you, nurture you?"

"That's a tall order. What kind of 'interior environments' do you work on?"

Her enthusiasm faltered. She looked back down at her magazine. "All sorts. Business offices. Retail establishments. Entertainment venues."

"Mrs. Meyers?"

She looked up to see Brett. "Your turn in the hot seat," he said.

Pushing herself off the sofa, she slipped on her shoes and said to Justin, "If I'm not back in thirty minutes, contact the American embassy."

As she walked off, I again wondered if she was joking. I'd encountered her type before—the haughty individual critical of nearly everything, but masking their contempt beneath a veneer of forced humor. I realized, however, that I was seeing her under unusual circumstances.

It struck me how little I really knew of my companions. On these trips, I usually made snap assessments about the other walkers and was eventually heartened that, being a good judge of character, my guesses turned out to be mostly correct. As a police detective, I'd honed the knack of seeing beneath the surface, paying attention to speech patterns, body language, and facial movements to peel off the mask of guile that most people wore. Although I suspected that this bunch might be hiding a nest of secrets, there was no indication any had a bearing on Gretz's murder. Nevertheless, I couldn't be sure. The only person I truly trusted was Billie.

I had to admit I was getting a kick out of putting my detecting skills back into gear. I absent-mindedly began whistling "Lovesick Blues."

Phaedra returned and dropped onto the sofa next to her husband. "You're next, darling. It should be painless. He'll ask about why you came here and about our employment. I reminded him that our work has nothing to do with Gretz's operation. You'll remind him of that also, won't you?"

"Well, of course, it doesn't," Justin said as he got up and walked off.

Phaedra turned toward me. "I wonder if there's any significance to the order in which he's interviewing us."

"I wouldn't read anything into it."

She gave me a withering glare.

When Justin returned, Barker was summoned, and then Billie. She returned looking none the worse for wear. "Looks like I'm the grand finale," I said, getting up from my chair. "I hope that isn't significant."

"I wouldn't read anything into it," Phaedra said, her eyes not leaving her magazine.

"Anything I should know?" I asked Billie.

"I told the inspector that you and I have walked in England together many times before. I hoped that convinced him we're regular walkers and not crazed killers."

I gave her a smile and nod of thanks, but a glance at the birds on her sweater made me wonder how sane the inspector might think she really was.

Chapter 17

The door to the small interview room was ajar when I arrived. Kilbride was seated in an upright chair, studying his small notepad with one hand and holding a pipe, smoke curling upward from it, in the other. DC Bright was beside him, checking his mobile phone.

The inspector looked up as I walked in. "Ah, Mr. Chasen." Gesturing to the chair opposite, he said, "Please make yourself comfortable. Although 'comfort' is a relative term with these chairs."

I sat, for some reason feeling anxious. "Please call me Chase. How can I help you?"

The inspector pocketed his notepad. "You mentioned that you had been a police investigator during your working career. A researcher on my staff discovered that you have quite a reputation. It seems you headed up several significant homicide investigations."

"That's true. I was an investigator for many years, and worked on several murder cases."

"Come, come, now. Don't be modest. From what I hear, you single-handedly tracked down the Scorpio serial killer in California. I remember the case well—it was quite famous, even over here—but at first I didn't place your name."

I shifted in my chair. This kind of praise made me uncomfortable, maybe because so much of it seems designed to achieve a hidden agenda. "Thank you. But I wouldn't say I solved the case 'single-handedly.' I had quite a bit of help."

"Nevertheless, your expertise may come in handy." Nodding to Bright, Kilbride said, "The constable here has only been in his position a short time, and as capable as he is, I'm certain he would welcome assistance on this matter, particularly from a seasoned professional with such an esteemed background."

The noncommittal expression on Bright's face told me he perhaps wasn't as wild about this suggestion as the inspector believed. Yet Kilbride's appreciation of my credentials was an interesting development. Perhaps he wouldn't mind if I offered my own opinions on the case.

"Of course, I would be happy to be of any help I can. But . . . might I not be considered a 'person of interest'? After all, I was with the group on the cliff path yesterday when Gretz was killed."

Kilbride took a puff from his pipe. I wondered if Britain's prohibition on indoor smoking applied to country hotels. After savoring it for a few seconds, he exhaled a toxic cloud that made me turn my head.

"Do you smoke, Mr. Chasen?" Kilbride asked.

I waited until the smoke had dissipated and turned back. "Please call me Chase. I did smoke, years ago. Cigarettes—until my . . . until I realized I was threatening my health. But I never smoked a pipe."

The inspector held his up, as if to wishing it to be admired. "I have a cousin who regularly visits Cyprus and sends me packets of Latakia—really the most heavenly blend of pipe tobacco one could ever find. I truly don't be-lieve I could function without it."

Kilbride's accent was still driving me crazy. It sounded close to that of the old British actor James Mason, of whom Doug could do a spot-on impression. Mason, how-ever, was from England's north country—Yorkshire—not Devon.

"If you don't mind my asking," I said, "where are you from originally, Inspector?"

"I was born near York, up north. But I've lived here in Devon for years."

I smiled, thinking how pleased Doug would be at how I'd figured that out. Kilbride took another puff from his pipe.

"I probably shouldn't mention it," I said, "but smoking indoors isn't allowed over here, is it?"

He leaned forward and said in a half whisper, "I won't tell anyone if you won't." His gray-blue eyes took on a mischievous glow before snapping back to the matter at hand. "Yes, you are correct that you are a person of inter-est. But your law enforcement background—not to men-tion the fact that you and Miss Mondreau have participated in walking tours here in England several times before, and were fully in sight of one another during the time in which Gretz was murdered—inclines me to place you rather low on my list of likely suspects. I could be wrong, of course, but let's just say I'm willing, at this point, to assume that risk."

I gave a nod of grateful agreement.

The inspector's face tightened. "However, you are on holiday, isn't that so? I certainly don't want to impose on your leisure time."

"Don't worry. This murder has already done that."

A smile pierced the inspector's businesslike counte-nance. "Quite so. Now that you've joined our team, so to speak, Mr. Chasen, I would like you to be present when we interview the final person on our list, Mrs. Gretz."

"Are you sure? She might think it odd."

"Quite the opposite, I suspect. Yours is a more familiar face to her than mine. It might put her more at ease."

I didn't completely share the inspector's opinion, but I gave my assent. Kilbride sent Bright off to retrieve Summer. As we waited for them to return, Kilbride asked, "Mrs. Gretz regularly administered medication to her husband, did she not?" I wondered where he'd heard this. From Billie, most likely.

"It seems like it," I replied. "I overheard Gretz loudly complaining about having to take so many pills one evening when I passed their room. Still, if he had serious health issues, it stands to reason Summer would insist that he take the medication he needs. And it also makes sense that Gretz would complain about it. He griped about everything."

DC Bright walked in with Summer. She was wearing a more-demure outfit than usual—a loose blue shirt and cotton slacks—with her hair pulled back and her face bearing little makeup. She didn't appear as distraught as she had been earlier. She almost looked like another person.

"Ah, Mrs. Gretz," Kilbride greeted. I could tell by his widened eyes he was surprised by her attractiveness. "Please have a seat. I hope you don't mind that I have asked Mr. Chasen to join us."

Her face remained stoic and semi-mournful, but there was a hint of an acknowledging smile as her eyes turned toward me.

Bright switched on the recorder and stated the time and the subject's name. Kilbride began. "I understand these past twenty-four hours have been very hard on you, Mrs. Gretz. I will try to make my questions as brief as possible."

"Thank you," she said, and after a pause leaned forward. "Please believe me when I say that I want you to catch whoever did this to Ronnie. Except I can't see how I can be of any help." Her voice, which I'd never fully believed was completely natural, sounded different: less breathy, less exaggerated.

"You were walking close by your husband on the cliff path yesterday afternoon, were you not?" the inspector asked.

"Of course I was. Chase here knows that."

"And you were at the rear of the group?"

She nodded. "Ronnie and I always were. He isn't as young as the rest, and he wasn't used to walking very much. He had a hard time keeping up. I didn't pressure him, though. He was making an effort for my sake." She dabbed at her eyes.

"Were you able to see anyone ahead of you on the cliff path?"

She thought for a moment and shook her head. "Not most of the time, no. This huge bank of wet fog came in almost as soon as we started off on the trail. I think Mr. Barker was in front of us, but the fog was really thick. It was also really windy."

"The wind didn't blow off the fog?"

Summer looked momentarily confused. "Well, sometimes—"

"Yes, it did, briefly," I interjected. "But the bank of fog was especially thick. It kept coming at us. As I understand, that was unusual, even for here."

Kilbride nodded, looked down at his notepad, and then up at Summer.

"When you were able to see, however, were you always within view of your husband?"

She gave this some thought. "Most of the time. With the cliff so close, though, I had to keep looking around to make sure I was staying on the path. But I'm sure Ronnie was right behind me. He would have called out if he weren't."

The inspector contemplated her statement. "Yet your husband *was* attacked. You claim you saw or heard nothing, is that correct? No shout or cry?"

"Nothing," she said soberly.

"Don't you think that odd? You just said that your husband would have called out if he didn't see you. Our eyewitness claims that your husband screamed as he fell off the cliff. Why wouldn't you have heard that?"

Summer remained cool. "You don't understand how much noise there was, with the wind and all. If I heard Ronnie yell or something, of course I would have done something. But the wind probably drowned out his voice. I didn't hear a thing, honest."

"She's right about the wind," I said. "It was deafening at times."

The inspector didn't alter his stonelike expression. "Quite. What about his assailant, then? Did you see anyone on the path you didn't recognize? Anyone who may have passed you, walking in the other direction?"

She shook her head slowly. "No. Nobody. But the fog was so thick and all, someone could have slipped past us without my noticing, I suppose."

"You didn't see Mr. Nielsen?"

"Brett? I didn't see him while we were on the path, no."

Kilbride gave a brief nod and looked down at his notepad. "Had you and Mr. Gretz been wed very long?"

"Not really. We met a little under a year ago. It was at a Halloween party a friend of mine's husband was throwing. Everyone had to come as a fairy-tale character. I was dressed like Rapunzel. You know, with a long blond wig? Ronnie came as the Big Bad Wolf from 'Little Red Riding Hood.'" She gave a small smile. "That was always my nickname for him. My Big Bad Wolf." Her smile faded, and she began sniffing.

"And you were married soon after?"

"Almost right away. Ronnie said he was tired of being alone, and so was I." She turned to me. "He wasn't always the way you saw him on this trip, Mr. Chasen. He was so sweet usually. But he'd been under stress recently because of his business."

"What was happening in his business?" Kilbride asked.

She gave a guilty shrug. "Something to do with cash flow or overhead or whatever. Honestly, I didn't understand most of what he talked about. I don't have a head for that stuff."

"Yet he was quite successful, is that not correct?"

"Yes, he was."

"A wealthy man, am I safe in assuming?"

Summer appeared taken aback by the question. "Ronnie did very well for himself, yes."

"What was your profession before marrying your husband?" Kilbride asked.

Summer hesitated. "I was a cocktail waitress. I . . . quit not long after we got engaged."

Kilbride and I exchanged glances. "Quite," he said. "Let me see now. Did . . . did your husband have any other family?"

"A couple of ex-wives, I think. He only mentioned them once or twice. They've been out of the picture for a long time."

"Any children?"

"Not that I know of. Ronnie doesn't . . . didn't like kids. They made him nervous."

"So, as far as you're aware, you are Mr. Gretz's only living relation?" Kilbride asked.

Summer sat back, her eyes widening. "Gee. Now that you mention it, I guess I am."

If this was an act, it was convincing.

"How was your husband's health, Mrs. Gretz?" the inspector asked. "Did he have any ailments for which he needed to take medication?"

"Oh, did he ever," she said with a roll of her eyes. "There were six or seven pills he had to take twice a day. For blood pressure, cholesterol, anxiety—I can't remember them all. He hated taking those pills, let me tell you. I had to practically force them on him. He didn't trust they were doing any good. Ronnie had a tough time with trust."

"I see. Did these medications ever compromise your husband in any way?"

Summer cocked her head. "Compromise?"

"Did they impact his mental acuity or physical coordination?"

She thought a moment. "Did he get high or woozy, do you mean? No, never. But you never could tell with those pills. Sometimes he would tell me he hadn't taken them, so I forced him to, and later he'd remember that yes, he had taken them after all, so he ended up taking too many. I tried to keep it all straight—I really did—but sometimes I may have got it wrong."

The inspector nodded as he gazed at his notepad. "How about the day he was killed? Did he take the correct dosage that day?"

Summer gave a sheepish smile and said, "I don't really know. I think so, but I could never be sure."

Kilbride kept his eyes on Summer and bit the corner of his lip. After a few moments, he said, "Right." Looking at me, he said, "Do you have any questions, Mr. Chasen?"

"Yes." I asked Summer, "Was this trip entirely for pleasure?"

"What do you mean?"

"That is, was your husband conducting any business

over here in England? Meeting with any business associates?"

"Gee, I don't think so. He would have told me if he was."

"What made you choose a walking tour in England?"

Summer reacted as if she'd been asked to explain the Pythagorean theorem. Her brows knitted as she searched for an answer. Finally, she said, "I really don't know. It was Ronnie who brought it up. We'd never had a real honeymoon, you see—just a weekend in Atlantic City. Ronnie was always working. But I kept telling him I wanted an honest-to-goodness honeymoon, one where we had to get on an airplane and fly away somewhere. I was thinking of an island in the Caribbean, but he—wait, now I remember! One night, we were switching TV channels and landed on one of those old movies about a queen who lived in a castle in England. I told him I had always dreamed of going to England, ever since I was a girl and wanted to be a princess. The next thing I knew, he found this walking tour. It includes a visit to a castle, doesn't it?"

"Well, it's supposed to," I replied, knowing the itinerary had most likely been blown to bits by her husband's murder. "Dunster Castle, up the coast a bit."

"You see? My Big Bad Wolf wanted to see his princess in a castle." She smiled, but broke into tears when she realized her dream wouldn't happen.

Kilbride pulled a handkerchief from his pocket and handed it to her. "We didn't mean to upset you. Any more questions, Mr. Chasen?"

"One more. Summer, did your husband mention to you any threats he'd been receiving?"

"Threats?"

The inspector also was intrigued. "What kind of threats?"

I repositioned myself in my chair. "Mr. Gretz got me alone on the first day and asked if I would help him out.

He mentioned he'd been receiving threatening emails. They were very general but menacing. 'You'll be sorry.' 'There's no escape.' That kind of thing."

Summer looked away and then back. "N . . . no. He never told me about anything like that. I guess he didn't want to scare me."

"Do you know of anyone who would wish your husband harm? Someone he had crossed swords with in his business?"

Her expression underwent a transformation, from innocence to awareness to placidity. "I'm afraid I don't," she said. I didn't think she was being completely truthful, but I didn't press the point. "If you don't mind, I'd like to go back to my room." She daintily dabbed at her eyes as she stood. "Is that okay?"

Kilbride looked at me and Bright for our reaction. When we both nodded, he said to Summer, "Very well. You may go."

Before turning to leave, she said, "I really hope you find the guy who killed Ronnie. My husband didn't deserve to die. Especially that way."

Once Summer was gone, Kilbride said to me, "She's a very pretty girl, don't you think?"

I shifted in my chair. Was Summer's attractiveness the main thing Kilbride had taken from this interview? "She seemed different just now," I said. "Of course, her husband has just been killed, but she wasn't quite as . . . artificial as she's been. She wasn't overdoing the sexpot act for once. I always suspected that was mostly for Gretz's benefit anyway."

"She did appear torn up about the old boy."

"Yes, she did," I said, although I'd seen my share of faked emotions, and not all of them concerning murder.

"Those threatening emails you mentioned are certainly intriguing."

"It's even worse than what I told Summer. A couple days ago, Gretz showed me one he'd just received that was much more specific—'Watch your step,' it said. 'The next one could be your last.'"

"My word! Why didn't he bring that to the attention of the authorities?"

"That's exactly what I suggested. But he was dead set against that. I'm guessing he had a few legally questionable skeletons in his closet he didn't want discovered."

Kilbride pondered this for a few moments before turning to the constable. "Bright, would you check in with Sgt. Miller? He must have Mr. Gretz's mobile phone. I'd like to see those messages for myself. Also, he told me he was going to search the cliff path in the morning light to see if he could spot any evidence that may have been left behind."

I noticed the lack of enthusiasm on the constable's face. He stood. "Of course, sir."

When Bright was gone, Kilbride took time to relight his pipe. I was amazed at what an elaborate process it was—the careful opening of the tobacco packet, the slow and measured tapping as the pipe bowl was filled, the tamping down of the tobacco afterward, the striking of the match against the table leg, the positioning of the flame over the bowl as he sucked on the pipe stem, the sudden spout of smoke that indicated success. Kilbride savored his first puff and sat back in his chair.

This ritual was fascinating but also maddening. Something was on his mind, and I needed to know what it was.

"What did you think of Mrs. Gretz's statement?" I asked. "Do you think she did it?"

The inspector exhaled a small stream of smoke. "Oh, she did it, alright. She's as guilty as sin."

Chapter 18

My look of surprise made Kilbride chuckle. "You don't agree? Just think of the incredible tale Mrs. Gretz just told us. There she was, walking beside her husband on the cliff path the entire time, and yet she doesn't notice when someone appears and pushes him to his death? We're supposed to believe that the wind and fog masked all of that? Bosh!"

I took a deep breath and rubbed my eyes. "I know it seems hard to believe. Nevertheless, you weren't there, and I was. The elements were maddening—one minute everything was clear, the next near-total darkness. And the sound . . ."

Kilbride dismissed my explanation with a wave of his pipe.

"At any rate," I said, "don't you think it's much too soon to make such a determination? That is, unless you've learned something in your other interviews that makes you so certain."

Kilbride shook his head. "Not really. All in your group were on their guard, as you might expect—surprised that I might consider any of them a murderer. None claimed to have known Mr. Gretz before coming on this tour. None claimed to have seen anything helpful, or unusual."

"So, based on the unlikelihood of anyone else being the killer, you're convinced it's Summer Gretz?"

The inspector formed a condescending smile. "I have learned from experience, Mr. Chasen, that the most obvious solution is most often the correct one. Look at what we have here. An attractive young woman marries a man old enough to be her father. He's rich and she's not. He has no other apparent heirs. She convinces him to come to England and participate in an activity for which he is obviously not prepared. She compounds this by giving him drugs that dull his senses and reaction time. From the itinerary, she knows that they will be walking along the top of a steep cliff. She makes sure she and her husband are always at the rear of the pack and at a distance from the rest of the group. She waits until the perfect moment comes— and what luck, a bank of fog rolls in! She seizes the moment and gives the old boy a push. He wouldn't be expecting it, and he wasn't in shape to resist anyway."

"Don't forget that she would have had to put on that green jacket," I reminded him. "Which indicates it might not have been quite the fortuitous act you make it sound."

My comment dampened Kilbride's smugness, but only for a moment. "That was a bit of amateur misdirection. Mrs. Gretz must have stowed that jacket in her rucksack, awaiting the right moment. I believe we're dealing with someone who's keener than she comes across. She knew exactly what she was doing and exactly how to go about it. I've had experience with these types before." He sat back in his chair and took a self-satisfied puff on his pipe.

I waited a moment before responding. "Yes, what you say sounds very logical and very damning. But I've had experience in this type of thing as well. And I've learned not only that appearances can be deceiving, but that it can be a mistake to draw ironclad conclusions from circumstances, as convincing as they may seem."

Kilbride's smile faded. "What, then, is giving you pause?"

"Many things. For example, how did she gain access to Mr. Nielsen's room so she could plant the jacket there?"

"Didn't I hear someone say that she had been getting very close to Mr. Nielsen? She could have lifted his room key."

"Possibly, but—"

"The inescapable point, Mr. Chasen, is that no one in this group had any connection whatsoever with Mr. Gretz prior to coming on the journey *except his wife*. Have you ever been involved in a murder case like this where a total stranger was the guilty party?"

"No, I haven't. But we don't know for a fact that all of these people *were* strangers to Gretz."

"If he knew one of them, wouldn't he have acknowledged it?"

"One can be known to someone without ever meeting them face-to-face, particularly in business, where negotiations are conducted through emails and phone calls."

"Yes, but—"

"I mentioned the threats that Gretz had been receiving. I think it's time to be open about all that I know." I told him I had accepted Gretz's offer to act as a quasi-bodyguard and be on the lookout for anyone who might be sending him the threats. I said I had stayed close to Gretz when he choked on the bone placed in his bisque, when he collapsed on the trail, and when the clay wall crumbled beneath him at the lime kiln.

"These could be written off as simple mishaps, of course," I said. "Shit happens, as they say. Nevertheless—"

"Indeed," the inspector said, not as flip and confident as he was a moment before. "The odds of three possible murder attempts occurring before an actual murder are difficult to ignore."

"Exactly. Yes, Summer was near her husband when each of these incidents occurred, but it didn't appear she was the *cause* of them. In fact, when the wall around the kiln collapsed, she fell too."

Kilbride thought a moment. "You said there were 'many things' that cause you to doubt Mrs. Gretz's guilt, Mr. Chasen. What else do you have?"

"Just a general sense of unease. Nothing definite. Nobody liked the man. Barker got quite vocal at dinner when he learned Gretz was in the nursing-home business. It seems Barker's late mother didn't have a good experience in hers."

"Hmm. Did she reside in one of Gretz's properties, do you know?

"No, I don't. It bears looking into."

"Anything else?"

"There were a couple of other ugly scenes." I told him about the spat between Howie and Gretz over the confused lunch order, and Gretz's warning to Brett not to touch his wife.

"My word," Kilbride said.

"Plus, there have been discrepancies here and there. Mrs. Meyers says she first learned of this tour in a brochure. The Wanderers, however, markets online rather than through direct mail. Barker claims he's come over to England to see his mother's homeland and attend some cultural events. Yet I saw him studying a book on estate law in the hotel library with more than just casual interest. He was taking notes."

"I see."

"These are small things, granted, but when there's been a murder, small things can take on a new meaning."

"Quite so."

"And there is still the mystery of the other walker on the path. The jacket he wore and the one found in Brett Nielsen's luggage were of two distinctly different shades of green. Can you check with your eyewitness to be more precise about the color he saw?"

"Good idea," Kilbride said. "I'll have DC Bright look into that. He has a photo of the jacket we found, I believe."

He noticed his pipe was no longer lit, emptied it in an ashtray, slid it back into his coat pocket, and stood. "I'll not take up any more of your time this morning, Mr. Chasen. I will say that I have greatly appreciated your input."

"Have I succeeded in changing your opinion of Mrs. Gretz?"

Kilbride narrowed his eyes and said, "Let's just say you've cracked open the door to other possibilities." He walked off a few steps before pausing and looking back. "A very small crack, but definitely a crack."

The inspector's cell phone buzzed, and soon he was embroiled in a conversation that had nothing to do with Gretz's murder. Feeling like an eavesdropper, I stood to leave. Kilbride briefly looked up and gave me a quick "we'll catch up later" nod.

On my way to the parlor, I thought more about Kilbride's certainty that Summer was the killer. I couldn't help but think of my sister, Allison. We hadn't spoken in years. She never returns my phone calls or emails. She has two daughters—nieces whom I've never met.

Our estrangement began when she was a sophomore in high school. An athletic and buoyantly enthusiastic girl, Allison was one of the school's star cheerleaders. When the team qualified for a statewide competition, she joined her teammates on a three-day trip to San Francisco. She had the misfortune of being assigned a hotel room with the one girl on the cheerleading squad she most despised: a spoiled brat named Francine. The two were always at odds.

Sometime during the first night, Francine's body was found on the sidewalk beneath the eighth-floor hotel room she shared with Allison. Suspicion immediately fell on my sister, who had recently engaged in very heated arguments with Francine, including one at dinner that night. Allison swore she'd fallen asleep within minutes of returning to their room after dinner and hadn't heard Francine come in. Nobody believed her, not even the police, but since they had no proof Francine had been pushed to her death, there was nothing they could do.

Allison's friends began snubbing her, and even our family wasn't convinced of her innocence, including me. Even though she had never given any indication that she could be capable of such an extreme act, I was positive that my sister was guilty. It didn't help that we were in a particularly intense period of sibling rivalry, and I'd heard her bitch about Francine constantly. When she found she couldn't even count on her own family for support, Allison packed her bags and ran off.

A few days after Allison disappeared, Francine's mother came forward and confessed her that daughter had been manic-depressive and had threatened suicide many times. She'd left a note saying she'd intended to kill herself that weekend. Her mother claimed she hadn't discovered the note until after her daughter's death and was reluctant to reveal proof of what she considered to be insanity in her family. It wasn't until she had shown the note to her husband that the truth came out.

Allison returned home shortly after that, but our relationship never recovered, even though I apologized repeatedly. Ultimately, I suffered more than she did. To deal with my guilt, I became obsessed with helping those who believed they'd been wrongfully accused. I flirted with pursuing law as a career, but police work, in which I could remedy such situations before they got to the courtroom, seemed a better fit. In my job, I encountered many Allisons, people whose self-professed innocence was often doubtful; and on many occasions, I was able to prove that it was true. Still, I never felt absolved for the way I had treated my sister.

In my lowest moments, when I became filled with regret over my treatment of Allison, I felt kinship with Bill Buckner. He was the Red Sox first baseman whose tenth-inning error was widely blamed for losing the team the 1986 World Series, even though the team had already blown its lead. It was a slipup that could have happened to anyone, but the incident haunted Buckner for years. When the Sox won the series in 2004, he was finally "forgiven." Maybe, someday, I'd receive such closure with Allison. In the meantime, I was wary of making the same mistake with Summer Gretz.

Passing through the foyer, I found DC Bright playing a game on his mobile phone. He looked up as I arrived, surprised perhaps to see me alone without the inspector. When he made an attempt to hide his phone, I said, "Please don't stop your game on my account. Nothing wrong with a little fun to take the edge off all this business."

He smiled and pulled his phone back up, but then Kilbride walked in.

"I checked in with Sgt. Miller about the crime scene, Inspector," Bright said.

"What did you learn?" Kilbride asked.

"He did find a couple things."

"Indeed?" the inspector said. "Very well. Let's go into the parlor, where we won't be overheard."

We headed to the rear of the room, passing Billie in a small armchair, knitting away. She looked up at me with a glance that conveyed surprise, curiosity, and a slight touch of envy. She doesn't like to be excluded from juicy discussions. When the three of us were seated, Bright fished out his mobile and brought up a photo of a tasseled, scuffed brown loafer.

"That's the kind Gretz wore," I noted.

"Yes," the constable confirmed. "It matches the one that was still on his foot when he was found."

Kilbride waited for Bright to elaborate, but when he didn't, the inspector said, "And what would be the significance of your discovery, Constable?"

"Well, don't you see? That tassel there has unraveled a bit. Mr. Gretz may have tripped on it and fallen."

"Yes, that's a possibility," Kilbride said with a trace of impatience, "except we have witness testimony that Gretz was pushed. What about other shoe prints?"

Momentarily shaken that his theory had been dismissed, Bright took a moment for the question to register. "Shoe prints? I'm afraid not, sir. That part of the trail was almost solid rock, plus the rain would have washed any prints away."

Kilbride nodded. Bright said, "There's more. Miller went to the spot where the chap fell. Right next to it is a bunch of plants—up against the cliff on the other side of the trail. Gorse and bushes that come up about chest high. It would have been a convenient spot for someone to have lain in wait and pounced on Gretz as he walked past."

That was precisely my theory. Kilbride considered it. "I see. Was there evidence of someone's presence at this spot? A discarded handkerchief? An extinguished cigarette?"

"No, sir," Bright said.

"Well then," the inspector said.

"But . . ." the constable ventured. "It is so *convenient,*

sir. That was the perfect place for someone to hide and then leap out and push Gretz. There weren't such places fifty paces before or behind."

"Constable," Kilbride said with forced patience, "you have the makings of a good officer, but you must learn the difference between *convenience* and *evidence*."

Bright looked chastened. Kilbride, I thought, had been too hard on the guy. I searched for something to say that would salvage the man's pride—his discovery was possibly significant, it had to be said—when the inspector's mobile chimed.

Kilbride extracted it from his pocket and checked the incoming message.

"Good heavens."

"What is it, sir?" Bright asked.

"The coroner has completed his preliminary examination of Mr. Gretz."

I said, "That was quick work. Has he discovered anything important?"

"Have no idea," Kilbride said. "Constable, let's go and have a talk with the chap face-to-face. I always prefer to do it that way whenever possible. Would you mind accompanying us, Mr. Chasen? The coroner is at the district hospital in Barnstaple, not far away. It's the closest place where he could carve up the old boy."

"Of course, I'll go with you," I said. As I followed the inspector out of the room, I stopped next to Billie.

"It seems I have become part of the investigation team," I said.

"Good to hear! If I were the killer, I'd be shaking in my boots."

I gave a small laugh. "Well, if the killer wore boots, he left no traces of them on the path. Right now, we're off to speak with the coroner. He's completed his initial examination of Gretz's body."

"But he died from the fall, didn't he? What else would you hope to discover?"

"You'd be surprised. It's not unusual for factors to pop up that lead in other directions."

"You mean that maybe Gretz had a heart attack while he was falling and would have survived otherwise?"

"Very funny. No, I meant something a little more . . . probable."

She gave a small shrug of acknowledgment, although I suspect she wasn't convinced we'd find out much more. As I walked off, I realized I wasn't convinced either. Gretz's death seemed straightforward: a quick push, followed by a tragic fall to a bone-crushing end. Yet I knew the most straightforward-seeming murders often turned out to be the most complex.

I had a suspicion of which type of murder this would be. And it wasn't the straightforward kind.

Chapter 19

The drive to the hospital in Barnstaple took twenty minutes. As I sat in the back seat of the police car, alerts came on the radio, mostly regarding innocuous events such as missing dogs or pub altercations. The inspector and the sergeant ignored them.

The hospital was a modest, two-story structure that looked more like an apartment house than a hospital. No ambulances were parked in front, nor was there much activity at all. Bright parked in a temporary zone. I followed him and the inspector inside.

We were directed by a man at the front desk to the second floor. We took the lift and walked down a long hallway. At the end, we entered an antiseptic room that smelled of chemicals, with the kind of green walls Corky found so objectionable. Behind a partition was a table on which lay a body covered by a white sheet.

"Tibbets?" Kilbride called out.

A slender, middle-aged man promptly emerged from a side room, wearing a white coat. My heart literally skipped a beat. I recognized that handsome boyish face, betrayed slightly by thinning gray hair on the side. It was Mike.

His eyes flashed at me, and we traded surprised smiles. Then he turned toward Kilbride. "Ah, Teddy! I wasn't expecting you to make the trip over here. I would have sent you my report."

"It was a short journey," Kilbride said.

Tibbets turned back to me, his smile broadening. "And I see you brought someone new. Who might this be?"

"Say hello to Rick Chasen, over from America," Kilbride said. "He was on the same walking holiday as the deceased. I've asked him to assist us in our inquiries. He's a retired police detective."

"A Yank, eh?" Mike said. Despite our earlier encounter, he held out his hand as if we were meeting for the first time. "Mike Tibbets, North Devon County Coroner. Pleased to meet you, Mr. Chasen."

I gave his hand a firm shake. "Nice to meet you, Mike. And please call me Chase."

"An ex-cop, are you?" Mike said, raising one of his thick brows. "Yes, you have that look."

"Am I to take that as a compliment?"

"Perhaps I should say you have an air of benevolent authority." I frequently lament my lost youth, but one thing the years have given me is experience, and the look that comes with it. Yet perhaps there was a deeper meaning behind Mike's words.

"See here, Mike," Kilbride said with a trace of impatience, "you said that you have the results from your examination?"

"Yes," he said after taking another glance at me. "That's why we're here, is it not?" He stood and crossed to the table and Gretz's body. "Normally, I would ask that the body be brought to my lab in Exeter for the full autopsy, but this place served the purpose for an initial examination nicely. I will have the body transported to the morgue, of course, prior to the inquest. Then we can have it released to the family."

Kilbride and I approached the table where Gretz's body was laid out, only his head uncovered. It was difficult to reconcile that lifeless form with the very much alive—and irascible—human being it had been only hours earlier.

"What have you learned?" the inspector asked.

Mike stuffed his hands into his pockets and walked to the head of the table. "The first thing I looked for was any bruising or skin abrasions that might indicate a severe blow or physical assault. I found nothing of that nature, other than those caused by his fall. I then took samples of bodily fluids. Tests can be problematic with bodies found in the sea, because of depredation from the seawater and tides. Fortunately, the deceased's body was on the rocks and the tide had not yet reached him by the time his body was retrieved. My toxicology report is preliminary, yet the findings are fairly conclusive. It should come as no surprise that the fall killed the deceased; his neck was fractured, and there are several other traumas related to the impact. But in addition, he had a veritable chemist's shop of medications in his bloodstream. Most of them are drugs designed to address cardiac conditions—betaxolol, principally, used to treat angina and arrhythmia, as well as a few hypertension drugs. We also found large traces of two sleeping medications—zolpidem, which is fairly common, and andorphinol, which is not."

"*Two* sleeping medications?" I asked. "That's unusual, isn't it?"

Mike shrugged. "Yes and no. I would say it's excessive, but then, folks do go overboard on the meds these days, don't they?"

There was an obvious follow-up question to all of this, and I waited for Kilbride to ask it. He didn't disappoint.

"What we need to know, Mike, is how muddled Mr. Gretz would have become by these medications."

Mike thought about this. "That's difficult to say. He was not in the best physical condition, it's true. Yet there is indication that he had been taking these medications for some time, which does allow for a gradual lessening of their effects. I can't say with absolute certainty, but my guess would be his system had largely adapted to the drugs."

"I see," Kilbride said. "I don't know if you're aware, but we got a lucky break and have a witness who saw someone standing on the cliff right above Gretz as he fell. It appears he was pushed. Would the drugs in his system have lessened his defenses—his reaction time—and made it easier for someone to sneak up on him and attack him in that manner?"

Mike gave this more thought. "Possibly, yes. As I said, he wouldn't have had the strength of a younger man. Nevertheless, if he had seen, or heard, someone coming toward him, he might have been able to hold him—or her—off."

"Would he have been aware enough to recognize this person if he saw him?" I asked.

"If it were someone he knew, I would say certainly," Mike replied. "But that wouldn't be the case, of course, if he were pushed from behind. He might only have had a split second to react. The position of his body at the bottom of the cliff gives us no indication of the attitude of his body when the attack occurred."

Kilbride and I accepted this verdict, and Mike chuckled. "I sound like I'm in the witness box, don't I? It's frightening how easy it is to get into my inquest mode."

"That's one of the perils of the profession, as they say,"

I said. "It's like being a doctor, in a way. You need to frame your words so they don't imply something that can be misconstrued."

Mike returned my smile and held it—maybe a beat more than necessary—before responding. "I'm glad you understand me, Chase. But there's little to misconstrue here. My preliminary finding is that the deceased had been under the influence of medications intended to help him sleep and regulate his cardiac functions, but not to the extent that he would have been unaware of a potential danger unless it was thrust upon him unexpectedly."

Kilbride pondered this. "Thank you, Mike. Did you discover anything else significant?"

"As a matter of fact, I did." Crossing to a nearby table, he picked up a small plastic bag. "I found this in the deceased's trousers."

Kilbride took the bag and held it up. It contained a small piece of paper, on which were clearly written the words THE END IS NEAR in large block letters. He handed the bag to DC Bright, who looked it over and handed it to me.

"This is like the other warnings Gretz received," I said, and peered closer. The paper was off-white and slightly textured. It was torn on one side, as if it had been ripped in half. I handed the bag back to Kilbride.

The inspector said, "We already were aware that someone had been threatening Gretz. This doesn't tell us anything new."

"Yes," I said, "but those warnings came via email. Finding this note in Gretz's pocket indicates that this person was close by. It was likely handed to him—or placed in his pocket—that day. So that person is someone in the immediate vicinity, perhaps even a member of my walking group."

Bright gave a small smirk at his boss being upstaged.

Kilbride only said, "Quite so." To Mike he said, "Is that all you discovered?"

"Just that the deceased had just consumed quite a bit of spicy food that might have upset his digestive system. The only other items that aren't here are his wallet and cell phone. They were retained by one of your sergeants. It was somewhat surprising that his phone was still intact and operable. Yet, perhaps not, given how well they're made these days."

The inspector nodded. "Yes, we need to check Mr. Gretz's call and text message history. Anything else?"

Mike shook his head. "Not that I can think of, no."

"Very well. Thank you for being available on such short notice, Mike."

Mike looked at me and smiled. "Part of the job, you know. It often keeps me from having a personal life like everyone else."

"Quite. Please do send me the final report when it's completed."

"No worries, Teddy. Always willing to help."

"Nice meeting you, Mike," I said. I resisted saying more—this was not the time or place—but I gave Mike what I'd hoped was an encouraging smile before I started walking off with the inspector. Mike followed close behind.

"Sorry your walking holiday has been spoiled, Chase. If you need someone to show you around when all this has calmed down, give me a ring."

That's what I wanted to hear. "I will most definitely do that."

Mike waited until Kilbride and Bright had walked a distance away from us before leaning close and saying, "So glad we could catch up again. I feel terrible about not contacting you, but I was called away the last two nights and couldn't get to your hotel. And I didn't have your full name to leave a message."

Should I believe him? Given Mike's offer to play tour guide, I had no cause to think he was being untruthful. I said, "It's funny how this murder has brought us together again."

He reached out and gave my hand a squeeze. "I mean it about my offer. Please give me a ring when you're free. Just call my office."

We exchanged smiles, and I walked off to join the inspector. Perhaps I was reading more into Tibbets's invitation than he intended, but it sounded definitely as if it was offering more than sightseeing.

Chapter 20

Wednesday, late afternoon,
Downsmeade Grange

Thanks to seeing Mike again, my spirits were high on the drive back to the hotel. I looked at the countryside going past with a new sense of wonder. Even the hints of a sunset showing on the far edges of the distant hills—a common sight this time of the day—sent a tingle down my spine. The prospect of spending more time with Mike made me feel like a lovestruck teenager. It was a bit jarring, though, to experience such a rush while investigating something as ugly as homicide.

Kilbride, by contrast, didn't appear to be feeling as lighthearted as I was. Instead of looking at the glorious sky, he grimly studied his notepad. I asked if the medical examiner's findings had led him to any further conclusions.

He looked up at me. "If your theory is correct, Chase, and that note came from someone in your walking group, we're right back at the start. Someone in your group may very well not be who they seem. Or Mrs. Gretz had been playing a devious game with her husband."

I still didn't figure Summer as the culprit, yet I couldn't deny she was leading the pack. Maybe she enjoyed seeing Gretz sweat and decided to write him those notes. He perhaps hadn't been familiar enough with her handwriting—even though the note was in block letters—to recognize it. Another possibility was that her relationship with Brett Nielsen might not be as recently formed as it seemed. Could they have known one another before coming on this walk? That was something to explore.

I added that possibility to the other tidbits straining to connect in my mind. Some were connecting already. Before I pursued those, though, I had a question for Kilbride. "Brett Nielsen suggested that Gretz's killer might be someone totally unconnected with the walking tour—perhaps that man we saw on the trail. Have there been any other murders or attacks of this sort around here?"

DC Bright spoke up. "There's the bra bloke, sir. What about him?"

"Oh, Constable, for heaven's sake."

"Bra bloke?" I asked.

Kilbride gave a sigh. "It's some local chap who grabs young women and forcibly removes their brassiere. He doesn't rape them or molest them further. Once he has their brassiere, he dashes off. He always wears a ski mask, so we haven't the foggiest idea what he looks like. I strongly doubt he was behind what happened to Mr. Gretz."

"But he *is* a local lunatic, sir," Bright said.

Kilbride regarded him with the studied patience of a schoolmaster. "In view of the fact that Mr. Gretz was neither a young lady nor was he wearing a brassiere, Constable, I don't think that's an angle worth pursuing. Plus, Mr. Gretz's attacker wasn't wearing a ski mask." There was also the extremely unlikely possibility, I thought, that a local lunatic would have gained access to Brett Nielsen's hotel room and stashed the green jacket in his suitcase.

Plus, the man I spotted on the trail most definitely wasn't wearing a ski mask.

"The next step I suggest would be to do some digging," I said. "Find out all you can about the folks on the tour, see if there's anything in their past that might connect them to Gretz."

"Precisely," the inspector said. He mentioned that Olea, the research assistant on his staff, might be working on that even as we spoke.

"I was also curious about your interview with Ben, the fisherman who saw Gretz pushed off the cliff."

"What about it?"

"He claims he saw Gretz being pushed, but did he keep watching? The fog might have cleared soon after, and that might have given him a better look at the culprit."

Kilbride paused to think. "Ben seemed a reliable sort. Not the kind to see something shocking and make a snap judgment about it. I imagine he would have told us if he had any additional information to impart."

My approach is not to "imagine" what might have happened but to do my best to verify it. I asked Kilbride if he would mind if I had my own conversation with Ben, and he reluctantly agreed.

When we arrived at the hotel, the inspector promised to contact me if he learned of any new information.

"What should I tell the others?" I asked. "They're bound to have questions—what happens next, when can they go home, that kind of thing."

Kilbride huffed in frustration. "Of course, of course. What a bother. In these situations, I normally deal with local residents, not foreigners on holiday."

"I'll just tell them they'll have to remain here a bit longer. Don't worry, I won't divulge anything of what we've discovered. It's good for them to be on edge. People are more liable to let things slip that way."

"I suppose you're right."

"Cheer up," I said as I stepped out of the car. "It might not seem like it, but I believe we're making progress."

"If you say so." Kilbride gave me a half-hearted "Toodle pip!" as he and DC Bright drove off.

When I entered the lobby, Brett Nielsen was walking toward me, looking chipper in white shorts and a blue polo shirt.

"Did you know they have a tennis court here?" he said. "I've been working on my backhand, but there's no one to play against."

I knew next to nothing about tennis and wasn't about to offer to take him on in a match. I politely excused myself and saw Billie at the entrance to the hotel bar. She beckoned me to join her. I excused myself to Brett and walked over. Billie took my arm and guided me into one of the bar's alcoves.

"I hope you don't mind, but while you've been gone, I've been doing a little sleuthing of my own."

"And?"

"I keep trying to reimagine what precisely took place on the cliff path yesterday, to picture everyone on the path as they were."

"Haven't we already done that?"

"Bear with me, alright? One thing I do remember is that, whenever I saw Justin Meyer, he was almost always taking pictures with that camera of his."

I nodded.

"So why not check out his camera and see if it can tell us anything? I took the liberty of asking him to bring his camera to dinner. We can look over what's on it afterward."

"Good work. Anything else?"

Her shoulders slumped. "Give me a little credit, Chase!

You've only been gone a couple of hours. I thought remembering anything at all was pretty good. What about
you? Any news from the coroner?"

I considered telling Billie about the note found in Gretz's
pocket, but remembered my promise to the inspector. Although I was fairly sure she would keep the information
confidential, I didn't want to risk it. Instead, I said that I'd
found the coroner himself to be more interesting than his
findings. I mentioned our initial encounter in the bar earlier in the week and my surprise at discovering him again
in a professional capacity.

"You old devil!" she said, giving me a wicked smile and
a playful jab to the arm. "You never know where love will
rear its head, do you?"

"*Love?* I think you're jumping ahead of things. I only
just met the man."

"And yet it sounds like there was a definite connection."

For some reason, this discussion was making me uncomfortable. Perhaps I suspected Doug was listening to us.
"What about you? Any new romances in your life?"

Billie grinned sardonically. "Don't try to change the
subject, Chase. Anyway, I'm past all that. I turned seventy-
five last year."

"Didn't I hear someone just say that you're never too
old for love? And seventy-five is the new fifty."

"Well, my legs still walk like they're fifty. But my face
has been losing a lifelong war with gravity."

"You're simply at another stage of your beauty."

She laughed. "You can really dish out the bullshit, can't
you? Seriously, Chase, don't blow this one. If you and this
coroner are on the same wavelength, follow up on it."

"Well, he had offered to take me sightseeing when this
is all over, and I just might take him up on it."

"I'll kill you if you don't. Oops. Guess I shouldn't be

joking about murder, should I? Any other news from Kilbride or his team?"

I smiled and leaned close. "Only this. If you're wearing a bra, guard it with your life."

Billie gave me a puzzled look as Corky entered, clutching a book in her hand. "We're having dinner in here tonight, right?" she asked.

"That's what Sally told us," Billie replied. "What's that you're reading?"

Corky's face lit up. "Another one of the mysteries from the library." She handed the book to Billie. "I've been eating them up like chocolates!"

Billie eyed the book cover. "*Penhallow* by Georgette Heyer. Isn't that the one where the family patriarch is this awful old goat everyone hates?"

Corky took back the book. "That's the one; he's just as nasty as Mr. Gretz! Although the rest of his family is rotten too."

"So who killed him?" I asked.

"Don't know yet. My money's on the lesbian daughter, but it could be one of the evil twin sons."

Not seeing much relevance in that scenario to Gretz's murder, I offered to place everyone's drink orders. I was heading for the bar just as Phaedra and Justin walked in.

"What are they serving us this evening?" Phaedra asked. "Stale bread and water in tin cups?"

"My wife is still bemoaning our incarceration," Justin said with a smile.

"If this is what prison is like, where do I sign up?" Corky said.

Brett Nielsen appeared and went to sit next to Corky. He'd changed clothes from his tennis outfit. Lucien Barker then appeared, followed shortly by Sally. She was dressed in casual slacks and a loose-tailed flowered shirt—a striking difference from her walking attire. Her somber expression suggested she was still haunted by what had happened to Gretz.

I was about to ask if I could get her something from the bar when she said, "I spoke with the Wanderers management. They're willing to reimburse everyone's full fee."

"That's very generous," I said. "They aren't legally obliged to do that."

"That is the *least* they can do!" Phaedra scoffed. "What about our other expenses? Airfare? Insurance? The money we're paying to our house sitter?"

"It wasn't the Wanderers' fault Gretz got pushed off that damned cliff," Justin reminded her.

"How do we know?" Phaedra asked. "We still don't have a clue who *did* do it."

"I don't think the Wanderers will reimburse more than your fee," Sally said, "but you might check with your credit card company to see if they'll cover any of the other expenses."

I collected everyone's drink orders and relayed them to the barkeep. When I returned, Brett turned to me. "Be straight with us, Chase. Are you and that inspector getting any closer to finding out who bumped off Gretz? I'm enjoying the tennis court here, but I'm pretty much knocking balls around on my own."

An off-color joke about Brett knocking his balls with someone else in our group flashed to my mind just as Summer came in and walked to the bar without looking in our direction. The others kept silent.

"I'm sorry, but if the inspector has learned anything new, he hasn't shared it with me," I said. I hate lying, but in certain situations it's unavoidable.

The lack of news only served to further cool an already chilly atmosphere. The barkeep brought over our drinks. Seated beside me, Billie ran her finger around the brim of her ale glass. Corky held her glass in one hand while flipping her drink coaster over and over with the other. Brett nervously twirled the swizzle stick in his cocktail. Barker stared at the table, while Justin tapped away at his cell phone. Phaedra reached over to silence him and turned toward me.

"There must be something you can tell us, Chase. We know you went off with the inspector this afternoon. Is he getting any closer to making an arrest?"

Weighing my words, particularly with Summer standing close by, I said, "He's still trying to get a clearer picture of the circumstances and the people involved. That's about all we can expect at this point."

"What 'circumstances'?" Corky said. "Except for that stupid stunt of planting a jacket in Brett's bag, no evidence connects any of us to the murder." She held up her book. "I know my murder mysteries. Evidence is what they need!"

"Let's not forget a motive," Phaedra said, pointedly looking at Summer, who went to sit by herself at a nearby table. She hadn't yet touched her drink.

"And opportunity," Justin said.

Phaedra's gaze didn't divert from Summer. "Precisely."

"Well, I'm going to contact the American embassy first thing in the morning," Brett said. "They should be able to help light a fire under this thing so we don't have to stay here much longer."

"Why not do that now?" Justin asked, digging for his phone. "I'm going to text them, if I can get a decent signal."

"Don't be a fool," Phaedra snapped. "What do you expect the American embassy to do? Let a pack of potential murderers loose on the streets?"

At that moment, Inspector Kilbride strode in, accompanied by DC Bright. I was surprised to see them again so soon. Had they had enough time to go all the way to the police station and return?

"Well, what do you know?" Brett said. "Scotland Yard is back. What have you discovered now, Inspector? Another clue incriminating me? Did someone find a bottle of poison hidden in my shaving kit?"

"Brett, don't be an ass," Corky admonished.

The inspector seemed strangely confident, a contrast to his despondence in the police car scarcely an hour before. "I think that we are making very good progress. Very good progress indeed. Mr. Chasen? Could I have a word with you in the other room?"

Everyone's eyes were on me as I followed Kilbride and Bright into the study. Nothing was said as we sat at a small table. My curiosity was buzzing at such a high pitch that, when the inspector reached in to retrieve his pipe and light it, I almost grabbed it from his hands.

He went through his usual maddening preparation process, carefully adding the tobacco to the pipe bowl and lighting it carefully, before finally taking a bracing puff and pulling out his trusty notepad. "Our researcher has indeed uncovered some interesting information. It was waiting for us just as we got back. To begin with, she discovered that Mr. and Mrs. Gretz had signed a prenuptial agreement before they married."

"Interesting. But it isn't unusual in that kind of marriage. You could argue that it shows Summer not to be the gold digger everyone thinks she is."

Kilbride nodded. "But the agreement only applies in the event of a divorce or bankruptcy, not a death. Some such agreements prohibit a spouse from claiming an elective share of an inheritance—that is, more than the will stipulates they receive."

Something in his tone suggested he was making a point without coming out and saying it. I decided to say it instead. "So . . . one way to sidestep the prenup is to make sure the spouse kicks the bucket before they file divorce papers, right?"

"I wouldn't put it in such a crass manner, but yes, that's what I was getting at. Of course, that doesn't work so well if the surviving spouse is proven to be a murderer." He looked down at his phone. "We also discovered that Gretz's firm is multinational, with properties here in the UK as well as other countries around the world."

"That too doesn't surprise me," I said.

"Furthermore, regardless of whether Gretz's wife inherits, the firm's line of succession seems firmly in place. There is a senior vice president who is well placed to step in should the chief executive—that is, Gretz—be incapacitated."

"Gretz has been 'incapacitated' alright. Was that senior executive anywhere near the cliff path on Tuesday?" I asked, clearly in jest.

Kilbride seemed to give this serious thought. "I don't know. We can have him checked out. His office is in North Carolina."

Surely, he realized what a long shot it would be to consider that man a suspect. So far, this new information hardly warranted his return visit.

He continued. "DC Bright was also able to speak with Ben, our witness. He said the jacket found in Mr. Nielsen's suitcase looked like it could have been the one he saw. But he admitted that the jacket may have been a darker green, which looked brighter with the sun shining on it."

"That isn't very helpful, is it?"

"I'm afraid not." Kilbride looked down at his phone. "Olea was able to get into Gretz's email account and look into the threatening messages on his phone. They all came from a dummy IP address, incredibly difficult to trace. She'll continue trying, but it looks like the person who did this knew something about encryption."

I nodded. None of this seemed to be working in our favor.

Kilbride said, "Olea also uncovered more on the others in your group."

This was more like it. "Such as?"

"It concerns the Nielsens. I didn't want to let more time pass before speaking directly to them. Unfortunately, it appears that you lot are about to have your dinner."

"Don't worry about dinner," I said. "What did you learn?"

Turning to Bright, the inspector said, "Constable, would you ask the Nielsens to join us in here?" When he left, Kilbride said, "I want you to be present at this interview, but I must ask you not to say anything right away. I want to give them the chance to respond first."

Of course, I agreed. The possibility that new information might crack open the case was so enticing I was practically salivating in anticipation. I was about to say the hell with it and ask Kilbride to tell me what he'd discovered when Bright returned with Corky and Brett, who were looking puzzled and apprehensive.

Chapter 21

Wednesday, evening,
Downsmeade Grange Front Parlor

"What's going on?" Brett snapped. "We've already told you everything we know."

"Brett's right," Corky said. "Everything!"

The inspector motioned for them to sit. "That's just what we want to know—everything. And this time, I suggest that the two of you hold nothing back."

Silent and looking humbled, Corky and Brett sat.

Kilbride pulled out his notepad. "Let's begin with you, Miss Nielsen. You didn't inform us about your previous felony convictions and jail terms for burglary."

Now, this was a surprise. Brett and Corky traded guilty looks. Corky managed an awkward smile and said, as if it were the most logical statement in the world, "Well, you never asked! If you had, I would have been honest with you."

"So, perhaps you try being honest right now," Kilbride said.

"Listen," Corky said, looking down as she smoothed her dress over her knees. "I didn't tell you about my past because I'm ashamed of it. Those . . . things happened years ago. Our mom worked, and I didn't have the supervision I should have had. I got kind of wild and started hanging around with the wrong crowd."

"In high school, Cork was voted 'Most Likely to Be Arrested,' " Brett said.

Corky shot him a dark look. "This is nothing to joke about, Brett." She turned back to us. "As I said, I was messed up. I ended up falling hard for this older man who, I later realized, became a sort of father substitute. Trouble was, he was a crook, and he swept me into his racket— breaking into rich people's homes, stealing jewelry and money. He even gave me a crash course on lock-picking. I could blame all of what happened on him, but I take full responsibility. I was so hungry to please an older man in my life."

"I didn't see what was going on with Cork," Brett said. "If I had, I would have put a stop to it. After her first conviction, I was sure she'd learned her lesson. But she got back into trouble again right away. That's when I convinced her to get into therapy."

I'm no psychologist, but Corky's explanation of searching for a surrogate father figure made sense. I could also see how her opinion of her real father, who deserted their family when she and Brett were infants, might have been darkened further by this experience.

"Anyway," Corky said, "I paid for my mistakes. Believe me when I say that I am a totally different person now. I don't identify at all with the girl I used to be."

"I'll vouch for that," Brett said. "I could have been a better brother, I guess—"

"Please, Brett, stop." Corky turned to the inspector. "I apologize for not coming clean earlier. But my past has nothing to do with what happened to Mr. Gretz, I swear to that. And besides, I was in the village when he was killed. *Someone* must have seen me. I went into those little shops selling T-shirts and figurines and boats with 'Lynmouth' written on them. I'm not into junk like that, but I almost bought a jigsaw puzzle until I realized how much space it would take up in my suitcase. I ate an ice cream cone instead. Then I went to the van, and Howie drove me to meet up with the others."

"Very well," Kilbride said, with resignation. Had he really expected these new facts to coax a confession out of Corky? "We'll check with the proprietors to see if any remember you."

He turned toward Brett. "We've also learned more about you as well, Mr. Nielsen."

Brett's face tightened, and he shifted in his chair. "Well, you won't find anything like that in *my* past. I've never been in trouble with the law."

"It's true that we've found nothing illegal. But you have accumulated some rather steep debts."

Brett's eyes flashed. "How did you find out about that?"

Kilbride looked down at his notepad. "Bank records. They become surprisingly available when a murder is being investigated."

Brett gave an exasperated sigh. "So I made some bad investments. So what? That's one reason I came on this trip, actually—to get away from all of that and clear my head. Not a bit of good it did me, right? Trouble catches up with me even here! Shows you how small the world is."

I leaned forward. "Are you being completely truthful, Brett? If you're hiding anything, it will only make it worse for you."

"What else would I be hiding?" Brett shot back.

Kilbride's eyes focused on the Nielsens. "Mr. Chasen is correct. Now is the time for you to tell us everything."

The siblings looked at each other.

"You'd better come clean, Brett," Corky said. Turning to Kilbride, she said, "My brother's debts aren't only because of 'bad investments.' Well, you could call them that,

I guess. But where he really got in over his head was in high-stakes poker games. The kind run by people who don't like not being paid. They don't like it one bit. Not only did he lose all his money—and most of *mine* as well, I came to discover—but he borrowed a lot more."

"And you thought coming over here might get you away from those people?" I asked Brett.

He hung his head and, in a more penitent tone, said, "Something like that. Or at least I thought it might give it all time to cool down. Who knows? Maybe one of my worthless stocks might turn around. Whatever . . . you can see it has nothing to do with Gretz, can't you?"

Kilbride's eyes went to his notepad. "Gretz was, as I understand it, a wealthy man. That most likely makes his wife a wealthy widow. A widow who might very well be able to pay off a new boyfriend's debts."

Brett shot to his feet. "There you go again! You think this was all part of some master plan for me to kill Gretz and marry his wife? Give me a break!" I remembered thinking that Brett and Summer could have met back in the States and planned all of this, just as the inspector had said. But it didn't make sense. Why would Brett have brought his sister along? And wouldn't Corky have remembered Summer, if she indeed had been seeing her brother? They were very close, after all.

The inspector held up his hand. "Please calm down, Mr. Nielsen . . ."

"How can I calm down? I fly thousands of miles to get away from a bunch of goons who want to waterboard me, and now I'm a murder suspect! I have half a mind to leave this godforsaken place tonight. You don't have any authority to stop me. I'm an American citizen, you know."

"I wouldn't recommend that, Mr. Nielsen," Kilbride responded calmly. Brett reluctantly sat back down.

Corky gave a small smile. "Trust me, Inspector. Nothing

against my brother, but . . . that idea about him planning to murder Gretz so he can marry his wife? Frankly, if you knew Brett, you'd know he isn't . . . well, smart enough to pull off something like that."

"Cork!" Brett yelled, glaring at his sister.

"You know you're not," she said softly.

Corky's opinion of Brett's intellect notwithstanding, I suspected that Gretz's murder could have been more the result of an opportunity presenting itself rather than one of careful planning.

"You *have* been focusing a lot of your attention on Mrs. Gretz, Mr. Nielsen," the inspector pointed out.

Corky brushed this away with a wave of her hand. "That's just Brett. I know him like the back of my hand, and I always meet the girls he dates. He's a pushover for a pretty face and a big bustline. It's gotten him into trouble before, and it will get him into trouble again. But that certainly isn't a reason for him to kill Gretz, for goodness' sake!"

I said, "Don't forget, Mrs. Gretz's breasts are no longer her only assets. Nor, perhaps, are they even her largest."

"You're being absurd," Brett said. "And also crude."

"It's absurd, alright," Corky said to me. "There is something else Brett finds more appealing about Mrs. Gretz than just her cup size."

"Cork!" Brett said.

"It's her *name*," Corky said. "Don't ask me why, but Brett has a thing for women with seasons for names. He dated an Autumn for years, and then there was someone named Spring. I hope he meets Winter before global warming takes over."

"Just a coincidence," Brett mumbled.

The inspector said, "Nevertheless, it does seem odd that you traveled halfway around the world just to get away from paying debts that you will still owe when you return to America."

"He also did it for me, don't you see?" Corky said. "Brett knew I always wanted to see England. We got some money from our mother's estate. We can use some of it to help pay off Brett's debts, but he wanted to make his big sister's dream come true. So he agreed to bring me over here."

"That was very thoughtful," Kilbride said with a trace of skepticism.

"I try to be there for Cork," Brett said. "I've played the role of father more than I have the brother."

"You never did find your real father, did you?" I asked.

"No, but we've tried," Brett said. "We even hired a professional detective to look into it, but he wasn't able to find anything. Corky won't let it go. She's been out for revenge for years."

"Brett, please," Corky said. "That's all water under the bridge."

"She wants to track the man down and make his life miserable," Brett continued. "I keep telling her to give it up. Our mom did a good enough job raising us. Even with Corky's problems, we've turned out okay. What's the point in muddying everything up?"

"Very sound advice," Kilbride said.

"But she won't listen. She keeps checking out people online—"

"Brett, knock it off!" Corky snapped. "I've let it go. Please believe me."

Her piercing glare shut him up.

Kilbride smiled uncomfortably. "Very well. Any further questions, Constable? Mr. Chasen?"

DC Bright replied in the negative. I paused before responding. Threads were beginning to connect, and the picture they were forming was almost too ludicrous to be be-lieved. I needed to be sure, which meant I had to force my hand.

I turned toward the Nielsens. "You seem like nice kids, but you don't realize what you've gotten yourselves into. Murders in books are a lot of fun and games, Miss Niel-sen, but in the real world, they're not. Unless everyone involved—and that includes you two—is completely hon-est, and I mean *completely*, the murderer remains at large and might—just might—kill again."

The two looked appropriately sobered at my words.

"You've already been found to have been, shall we say, less than honest with Inspector Kilbride here," I contin-ued. "He's been gracious enough to write it off as an inno-cent mistake, but I have a feeling he won't be as forgiving if he discovers further deception."

Corky and Brett looked at one another, but remained silent.

"For example," I said to Corky, "the inspector might be interested to learn that you, Miss Nielsen, were aware the stone ledge circling the mouth of the lime kiln at Heddon's Mouth was, in fact, ready to crumble apart. You knew it could very well collapse when you encouraged Mr. Gretz to go sit there."

Corky's eyes widened slightly. It was a look that didn't reflect surprise I had suggested such a thing but that I had figured it out. Her eyes darted to her brother and then back to me.

"I saw you standing at the top of the kiln just moments before," I continued. "You placed your foot on the ledge and looked down at it, probably because you expected it to be sturdier than it was. When you were able to easily chip some of it off with your walking boot, you got an idea."

My accusation hung in the air and nobody spoke. Corky twitched slightly as she felt everyone's eyes on her.

After a moment, she said, "Alright! So what if I did? I was ticked off at the old guy! He was ruining my dream vacation and deserved to be shaken up a little. So I played an innocent practical joke. I honestly didn't think I was putting him in danger."

"Not in danger?" Kilbride said, aghast. "That pit was a good ten or fifteen meters deep, Miss Nielsen. Mr. Gretz could have fallen into it and *died*, or at least be gravely injured!"

"But he *didn't* die, did he?" Brett said. "Cork told me what she was up to, so I made sure I was there to grab him and pull him to safety if that ledge gave way."

"He didn't even end up with a scratch," Corky said. "He just got spooked, which is what I wanted. I'm not a murderer! I swear that I'm not!"

She dissolved into tears. Brett put his arm around her.

This show of remorse seemed to have no effect on Kilbride. "Suffice it to say that I will think twice before trusting anything the pair of you say," he said with undisguised contempt. "For the last time, is there anything else the two of you need to confess?"

Now contrite, Brett and Corky looked down and shook their heads. Kilbride studied his notepad and waved them off. He couldn't bring himself to thank them for coming clean.

The Nielsens stood and silently left the room. DC Bright switched off the recorder.

The inspector looked up at me. "The question now is, did Miss Nielsen make another attempt at 'scaring' Mr. Gretz? One that was more successful?"

"You're not thinking this through, Inspector. Yes, the Nielsens have skeletons in their closet, but Corky got it right; they're not killers. Brett was right there to keep Gretz from falling into the kiln pit, wasn't he? Why would he have done that if their goal was to kill him?"

Kilbride nodded. "You may be right. All that burglary and gambling debt business looks dodgy, no mistake, but it seems a long chalk to connect it with our murder. All signs still point to Mrs. Gretz."

"Don't get me wrong; I'm not dismissing the Nielsens entirely. Didn't it strike you as odd how Corky tried to quiet Brett when he carried on about her search for their missing father?"

"Seemed right strange to me, it did," Bright chimed in. "Like he was about to let slip with something juicy."

Kilbride nodded. "What are you getting at, Mr. Chasen?"

"Has it crossed your mind Gretz was old enough to have children of Corky and Brett's ages? That he could be the lost father they've finally tracked down?"

The inspector lifted his eyebrows. "The Nielsens' father ran off when they were children, didn't he? Would they really carry a murderous grudge all these years? And there's another angle to this we're not seeing. If Mr. Gretz was really the Nielsens' father, murdering him may have benefited Brett in another way."

I saw where he was heading. "You mean they could reveal Gretz was their father and make a claim for part of his estate?"

Kilbride smiled. "Precisely. Now that we've learned he's skint, that makes it all the more likely."

It was tempting to pursue that angle, but I saw an immediate flaw. "That doesn't make sense, though, for the same reason as before. Brett pulled Gretz out of the pit, so it's unlikely that he would have turned around and killed him on the cliff path. Although, if it turns out he benefits from Gretz's death through his bloodline, that would place him back on top of the list of suspects."

The inspector relit his pipe, took a puff, and stared into the distance before replying. "What you say is logical, unless Mr. Nielsen performed that first rescue to disguise what he intended to do later. It's all pure speculation at this point anyway. For the present, let's focus on what we know."

I stood. "I'll tell you what *I* know—my dinner is growing cold. Care to join me?"

Kilbride shook his head. "It's late, and we still have to finish our report. The constable and I will find something to eat back at the station."

I was getting accustomed to the sidelong glare Bright directed at the inspector. I bid them good night and headed for the bar. On the way, I heard someone call my name. I turned to see Corky hidden in the shadows of a corner. She motioned me over.

"There's something I should mention," she said in a whisper. "I hate being a tattletale, but since now I'm a murder suspect, what have I got to lose?"

"What do you know?"

She looked around. "That afternoon Gretz was killed? I did what I told you I did; I returned to the town, looked around the shops, and had an ice cream cone. Then I went back to the van so Howie could drive me to meet up with you guys at the Valley of the Rocks."

"Right," I said, waiting for the punch line. "And . . . ?"

"Howie wasn't in the van when I got there."

Chapter 22

"Howie wasn't in the van? Why didn't you tell us this before?"

Corky held up her hands. "Okay, okay, don't get on my case again. I just figured it didn't mean anything. Why would *Howie* want to kill Gretz?"

I shut my eyes and tried not to give Corky another lecture on the danger of hiding secrets in a murder investigation.

"He showed up and got to the van almost right after I did, anyway," she said.

"Did he tell you where he'd been?"

"No. But why should he explain anything? We didn't know Gretz had been killed at that point."

What bothered me more than Corky not sharing this piece of information earlier was that Howie hadn't either. I took a deep breath, thanked Corky, and told her not to mention what she'd told me to anyone else.

When I rejoined the group, everyone was halfway through dinner. I was about to join Billie when Justin Meyers approached me, carrying his camera. He motioned me over to an empty alcove.

"Billie suggested I review the photos I took on the cliff path," he said. "And it's a good thing I did. Look here."

He held up the camera's display. It showed the cliff path stretching in the distance, the choppy sea to the left, the rocky cliff wall to the right, and in the distance, barely visible through the mist, a lone figure on the path.

"I shot this with a telephoto lens at one point where the sun came out and the fog seemed to have momentarily thinned out. I wanted to take advantage of that, since I figured it wouldn't last long. What you see here is the section of path we had already covered. All of our group were closer, out of range."

"So, this person, whoever it is, was walking at quite a distance behind us."

"Correct," Justin said. "Now look." He enlarged the image on his viewfinder. What was only a small, indeterminate form before was shown to be a tall woman with long, russet-colored hair, wearing dark trousers.

"Is that our Miss Corky, do you think?" Justin asked.

I examined the photo more closely. Along with her other lies and omissions, had Corky misstated her whereabouts and indeed had returned to the cliff path—to murder Gretz? Upon further study, however, my hopes of finding the answer faded.

"Unfortunately, this person isn't quite clear enough to make a positive identification. And look there—some of the mist was still there, and it obscures most of her upper half. You can't really make out what she's wearing. It certainly doesn't look like a green jacket, though. Can you enlarge it further?"

Justin tried, but his attempts only made the figure less

distinct. "I admit it's not too clear," he said, "but this woman's the same height, with the same hair as Corky."

I took another look. "Wasn't Corky wearing a scarf? Bright yellow, I think."

"She could have taken it off."

Further inspection only added to my frustration. The figure was so distant, with the weather making her even more indistinct, it was difficult to tell if she was even wearing a backpack.

Justin couldn't help but note my frustration. "Chase, I know this wouldn't exactly be admissible in court as evidence, but it does at least raise the question."

"Don't feel bad. I'm glad you brought this to my attention. Please show it to the inspector the next time you see him. Maybe one of their staff knows how to make the image sharper. I'll remind him to check with the shop owners in the village to see if any remember Corky as a customer. Even if she isn't the person in this photo, she still must be considered a suspect."

There was another thing I noted from Justin's photo. Where was Doug's look-alike at the time it was taken? He'd been walking in the opposite direction and should have been well past us. Yet this woman was the only one to be seen.

Rather than again question whether I had seen a ghost— I could just hear Kilbride saying, "Poor old Chase. He's really gone off his onion"—I figured the phantom walker had been on another section of the path out of view of the camera when this picture was taken.

When Justin and I rejoined the others, everyone was curious about my discussion with the inspector and the sudden meeting with the Nielsens. I said it was just a false lead that meant nothing. Corky looked at me appreciatively.

"So, what you're telling us is that the inspector has made

no progress whatsoever," Phaedra said. "Which means we're stuck here until God knows when."

"I wouldn't put it quite that way," I said. "Inspector Kilbride is gathering information, pursuing leads . . . these things take time."

"What on earth does he need to gather or pursue?" she said. "We all know who killed Gretz, for God's sake. There's only one of us who had a personal relationship with him."

Everyone's eyes turned toward Summer, whose solemn, grief-stricken expression was now one of cold steeliness. She glared at us.

"You've all got your minds made up that I did it, don't you? Pretty little wife, all she's got is her looks, married the old man for his money. And when she sees the opportunity— a steep cliff, lots of fog, no one around—how can she resist? Just one little shove, and bingo! She's a free woman—and rich! Who else could have done it, right?" Her eyes widened in a mock display of innocence. She was surprising me, showing more spunk, and more eloquence, than I thought she was capable of.

Justin said, "My wife, I'm afraid, put it more bluntly than necessary, but—"

"Bluntly?" Phaedra retorted.

"Well, you did, dear." To Summer, Justin said, "You certainly must see our point, Mrs. Gretz. You're the only one here who knew your husband. You were walking right beside him on the cliff path. If someone else had tried to kill him, wouldn't you have seen who it was?"

"Or heard them?" Corky asked. "That seemed weird to me too."

"We're not trying to be unreasonable," said Barker. "If you did kill him, we don't blame you. The man treated you like a slave. Anyone would understand you wanting to do away someone like that."

"*I didn't kill my husband!*" Summer declared in a

stronger tone than any I'd yet heard from her. "But if one of *you* did, you're not going to get away with it!" She stood, swept up her coat, and marched off. Brett dashed after her.

I turned to the others. "Well, that went well, didn't it? Let me remind you of a saying that is sometimes used back in our country: 'innocent until proven guilty.' If anyone here has *evidence*—real, true-to-life evidence, not conjecture—that Summer, or anyone else, pushed Mr. Gretz to his death, then speak up. If not, then please keep your thoughts to yourselves." Painful memories of my own condemnation of Allison flared up.

"I'm sorry, but I can't remain quiet," Phaedra said. "If Mrs. Gretz didn't bump off her husband, who did? There is simply no one else!"

I cleared my throat and was prepared to patiently outline objections that could be raised in a court of law if Summer were put on trial before a jury—the thickness of the fog, the deafening wind, the mystery of the green jacket, and the phantom walker. There were also far more suspicious factors, such as the threatening notes and suspicious "accidents" that had befallen Gretz, the culprits behind one we already knew.

But I didn't go into any of that. Instead, I said, "One lesson I've learned in my career is that one should never rush to judgment without the facts. All of them."

My little lecture accomplished its purpose. The group looked chagrined and fell silent. Corky said, "The trouble is, I've tried to feel bad about what happened, but I just can't. We all could see that Mr. Gretz was not a nice person. That doesn't mean I think he deserved to be killed, but I can't be sorry that he was."

"Even blowhards like Gretz can have a decent side that others may not see," Billie said.

"You mean like Doctor Jekyll and Mr. Hyde?" Corky said.

"Or Norman Bates in *Psycho*?" Justin asked.

Billie smiled. "Well, I wasn't thinking of such extreme examples. Someone more like Edmond Dantès in *The Count of Monte Christo*. He became bitterly vengeful when he was framed for a crime he didn't commit. Yet he actually was a very intelligent, honest, and loving man."

"That doesn't sound like Gretz," Phaedra said. She was correct, but Billie's analogy struck a chord. Had Gretz turned bitter because of the threats he'd been receiving? Had he lashed out because he was being accused of something he didn't do? Again, I was reminded of Allison.

"What about his nursing homes?" Barker asked. "I can guarantee you that 'decent' people don't run places like that. For them, it's all about money."

" 'Nursing homes,' " Sally said, spitting out the term as if it were a bitter piece of fruit. "What a ridiculous name. There's nothing 'nursing' about them. That word implies that people interned there have a chance to improve, when that's almost always not the case, not unless resources are directed toward actually helping them. And that rarely happens. You're correct, Mr. Barker, most nursing homes are just holding pens for the elderly."

What triggered that diatribe? Perhaps Sally had lost a family member in such a facility, just as Barker had. That was becoming common these days, as more people live past the point where they can adequately take care of themselves.

Sally shifted nervously, as if aware of the effect her words had on the others. "I'm sorry. I spoke out of turn."

"I did too," Phaedra said to me. "I apologize for being so hasty."

Everyone began discussing their plans once we were free

again. Some (Billie and Corky) were eager to stay on in the UK, while the Meyerses said they'd had all the British hospitality they could take and couldn't wait to get home. Barker mentioned he would be visiting his aunt in Bideford.

"What a coincidence," Sally said. "That's where I grew up. What's her name?"

Barker paused. "Tawney. Carole Tawney."

Sally thought a moment. "That name sounds familiar, but I can't quite place it. Bideford is a large town."

Once the dessert plates were cleared, the group began heading off to their rooms. I told Billie I wasn't yet ready to turn in.

"Something on your mind?" she asked.

"Something *in* my mind is more like it—like a piece of grit in my eye. I'm not going to be able to sleep until I get to it."

"Maybe it will come to you in a dream."

I chuckled. "My mind doesn't work that way. If any brainstorms are to come, I need to be fully awake."

"Good luck, then," she said, giving me a hug. "If your piece of grit finds its way into my mind, I'll let you know."

I said good night and, once I reached the hotel foyer, pulled out my cell phone. I texted Inspector Kilbride:

Check Lucien Barker's relationship with his aunt, Carole Tawney in Bideford. Also check with shops in Lynmouth for confirmations of sightings of Corky.

I debated asking him to check with Howie again on his alibi, but thought it best to save that tidbit and share it in person. I pressed SEND and was pleased to see that the message went through, given the iffy cell reception.

Now what? I could go to my room, but I didn't feel like watching television or reading, and there was nobody back home I wanted to call. A walk outside sounded tempting, but as I stepped out the door, I realized I wasn't dressed for the cool night air. I stayed inside and strolled past the bar—still busy, with mostly locals getting rowdy and drinking too much. I continued walking down a hallway leading to the far side of the hotel toward the health spa. At some point, it became clear—perhaps because of the institutional lighting or the faux William Morris wallpaper—that this part of the hotel was a recent addition.

Whistling "I'm So Lonesome I Could Cry," I wandered up a corridor lined with small meeting rooms. The mournful tone of the Hank Williams song wasn't exactly lifting my spirits. I tried switching to "Hey, Good Lookin' " when I heard a feminine giggle coming from a small nook nearby, positioned between two of the meeting rooms. I froze in my steps.

"Don't be silly!" the woman's familiar voice said.

"Who's being silly?" an equally familiar man's voice said. "You need someone to look after your husband's business interests. And I'm as qualified as they come."

It was Summer and Brett. I ducked into one of the side rooms and continued listening.

"Right now, I have other interests you can look after," she said seductively.

"Won't you get serious for once?"

"Why are you getting so nasty? Are you going to turn on me like everyone else?"

"Don't play coy with me," Brett said. "You're good at putting on the empty-headed bimbo act, but there's a working brain in there somewhere. You know I would be a valuable addition to your husband's firm. Yet you just want me for sex."

"Oh, honey-babe," Summer cooed. "Why do you say things like that? Why can't we just have fun?"

"Because your husband has just been murdered!" Brett railed. "And you don't seem to care."

As Summer let forth a few petite sobs, I again thought

of the possibility I had considered earlier. Could Brett and Summer have known each other back in the States? Rather than the result of a chance encounter, could their affair be the continuation of a carefully laid out plan that had been in place for some time?

Whatever the explanation, Brett seemed to have had enough. "Go ahead and cry. I can't figure you out. When you want to have a discussion like a grown adult, let me know."

He strode off, but I remained hidden, waiting for Summer's next move. For a minute or so, I saw nothing, and just when I was certain she'd slunk off without my noticing, she sauntered past.

Even from the shadows, I was able to get a good look at her face. She didn't look hurt at Brett's departure. In fact, her mouth was set in a self-satisfied grin, as if everything was working out according to plan.

Chapter 23

Wednesday, late evening,
Downsmeade Grange

I followed Summer at a distance, careful not to make my presence known. She walked steadily, her bag swinging from her shoulder. A book dangled from a side pocket before slipping out and thudding onto the wood floor.

"Crap!" she said. As she turned to pick it up, she saw me and froze.

I stepped forward and retrieved the book. *The Essays of Michel de Montaigne.* What an unexpected find. Billie had turned me on to Montaigne many years before when I was trying to come to terms with the death of my father, a man I never felt I really knew.

"My, my," I said. "Montaigne! The renowned sixteenth-century French essayist who pondered the roles of sexuality and social position, far ahead of his time."

She gave a nervous laugh and held out her hand to take the book. "Ronnie was always after me to improve my mind. But silly me. I just can't understand this egghead stuff."

Her bubbleheaded façade was weakening and more transparent than ever. "I think you understand it just fine.

Just as I hope you understand that pretense doesn't wear too well during a murder investigation."

Summer's face underwent several stages of transformation, from vacuous innocence to indecision to acknowledgment of being found out. She gave me a smile, reached out and took the book. "Very astute, Mr. Chasen," she said in a voice an octave lower than the one she'd been using. "Montaigne's writings say a lot about the world we're living in now. He was an advocate for women's rights more than five hundred years ago."

It was as if she had become someone else. "Yes, equal rights for women is a problem," I said. After a pause, I added, "So is murder."

"I couldn't agree more. That's why you must believe me when I say I'm truly saddened at the murder of my husband and would like nothing better than to see his killer come to justice."

It was difficult to tell if this was another act. If so, I had to admit, she was quite a good actress.

Summer added, "Which is not to say, however, that I didn't want Ronald dead. I most certainly did. But I didn't want it to happen that way."

Not only did her new voice make her seem more assured; her face began to look different as well—more mature, with an air of wisdom born from hard experience. Was it, though, a face to be trusted? I didn't want to repeat the mistake I had made with Allison, and yet, with this new revelation, Summer's likelihood of guilt had gone up a few notches in my mind. The old, air-headed Summer wouldn't have had the smarts to pull off her husband's murder. This new, savvier Summer certainly would.

"Listen," she said. "Let's go the bar, where we can talk more comfortably. I have nothing to hide anymore. It's too tiring. It will be a relief to be myself for once."

The bar had emptied except for one grizzled local, bending the barman's ear about the theft of one of his sheep. I ordered a beer for myself and a White Russian for Summer, at her request, and joined her at a small table.

"Here's to being ourselves," I said, raising my beer. She clicked her glass against mine, took a sip, and reached out to feel the edges of my beard.

"How often do you need to trim that?" she asked.

Was she flirting? "Every once in a while," I said. "But I have a question for you. Why have you been putting on the vacant-headed bimbo act?'

She propped her elbow on the table and tilted her head against her hand. "Why do you think?"

"I could state the obvious. You felt the best way to reel in a man like Gretz was to become his ideal woman: attractive in a flashy way, carnal, and not too bright."

Summer gave a small nod. "I knew you'd figure it out. Truth is, I didn't meet Ronald Gretz at a Halloween party; that was a story I felt better suited my Summer persona. I actually met him when I was a night manager at a happy-hour bar in Charlotte's business district. He'd come in with a gang of his yes-men around six o'clock and start chatting up anything in a skirt. It was clear he loved women with a big bosom and no brains. I also quickly picked up on the fact he was loaded, and he was single."

"Why would that be of interest to you?" I asked.

She sighed. "Because I was six years out of college with nothing to show for my philosophy degree except the ability to discuss Descartes with old academics who didn't have two dimes to rub together. I certainly wasn't going anywhere working at that bar. I needed a rich husband."

"And . . . ?"

"And I got a full makeover. I bought this silly blond wig and some push-up bras. I adopted a new personality. I'd done some acting in college and played Billie Dawn in a production of *Born Yesterday*. I decided to mimic her. I even gave myself a new name."

"What's the old one?"

"My middle name *is* actually Summer, but before meeting Ronald I went by my first name, Karen." She reached out her hand. "Karen Arnhalt. Pleased to meet you." We shook.

"So, you changed your name and zeroed in on Gretz."

She gave an acknowledging laugh. "It didn't take long. He saw his 'golden sunset' years coming on fast and didn't want to die alone like the 'clients' in his zombie warehouses. I auditioned for the role of his wife. And I got it."

"That must have been exhausting, having to keep up that act. Unless . . . unless you knew you wouldn't have to be doing it for very long."

She raised her brows. "There you go again, being perceptive. You're absolutely right. Ronald was a walking catalog of ailments. Not only was his heart in terrible shape; he ate all the wrong foods and did nothing to take care of himself. I knew it wouldn't be long before he'd kick the bucket."

I was surprised at her candor. "And did you do anything to . . . speed that process along?"

She weighed my question. "Perhaps a little. Oh, not in any criminal way, I assure you. I'm no killer. Mostly, I just looked the other way when he'd order a double cheeseburger and a large order of fries. But when he became concerned about his properties over here in the UK and talked about paying a visit, I got a brain flash. We were still at the stage where he would humor me and give in to my whims. What about a walking trip? I suggested. A chance to take a real honeymoon. With Ron's gamey heart and poor constitution, I'd hoped he might not survive the experience. To my surprise, he agreed."

She had been explaining all of this matter-of-factly, without any portent of the tragedy to come. Now her face began to cloud. "Don't you see? I wanted Ron to go as naturally—or close to it—as possible. He wasn't long for this world anyway. What better way for him to meet his maker than by collapsing in the beautiful English countryside? But once we got over here, I started thinking differently. I took a vow to be his wife—for better or worse, all that stuff. Even if he hadn't much more time left on this planet, his wife shouldn't be the one to hurry it along. So I made up my mind to make sure he took his meds."

I remembered where I'd heard Summer break character—when I was passing their room and overheard her strongly exhort her husband to take his medications.

"You must imagine how horrified I was when he died the way he did. It was violent and ugly and much too sudden. I didn't want that to happen, not at all."

With Summer's book on the table before us, the words of Montaigne came to mind: *We do not know where death awaits us: so let us wait for it everywhere.* Still, I couldn't help but suspect that this coming-clean performance was all a put-on to win my confidence.

Summer looked down. "I know I'm taking a big chance in telling you all of this. The others at dinner tonight were right—I'm the perfect suspect. Who wouldn't think I killed Ron? But I ask you to believe me. I could never bring myself to kill anyone, not directly. It pains me to think that anyone would believe otherwise."

I took a swallow of ale, hoping it would help my gut determine if I was hearing the truth or a blast of bullshit. There were undeniable echoes of Allison in Summer's account, the same soul-deep belief of her personal sense of honor under attack. Yet the circumstances in this situation were much more damning.

"You were right about how exhausting it's been to keep up the Summer act," she continued. "It made me realize that there's no need to pretend any longer. So what if everyone finds out I'm a conniving gold digger? They already think so anyway."

"Inspector Kilbride understands you signed a prenuptial agreement with your husband," I said.

"There are no secrets anywhere, are there? Yes, I willingly agreed to that. Why wouldn't I? As long as I kept Ron happy, he wouldn't think of divorcing me. I figured his health issues would do him in eventually. His doctors were optimistic, it's true, but only if Ron would agree to a strict diet and exercise program, which he never would. I figured it was my wifely duty to keep him happy in whatever time he had left."

I cocked my head, trying to figure out this new persona. Summer seemed to be telling me that, rather than being a ruthless fortune hunter, she deserved praise for acting selflessly in providing comfort in her husband's final days. I'd overheard her trying to get Gretz to take his medications, after all. And yet, she admitted to suggesting the walking trip in hopes of taxing his weak heart. So, which was she: saint or slayer? It was an enigma, alright.

She formed a slight smile, aware of my scrutiny. "I know this is a lot to take in, Chase. You're wondering if this is just another act. Believe me, that act is over. It served its purpose and is no longer needed."

"Your impersonation had another benefit, you know," I said. "You certainly caught Brett Nielsen's eye."

She gave a small laugh and waved her hand. "Oh, him. He's so transparent; he thinks he can win me over and insinuate himself into Ronald's business. I mean, as if. Although I must admit he's good in the sack."

"Are you going to be honest about your true identity with him as well?"

"Trust me. You've seen my last performance as Summer Gretz, and so has everyone else."

Part of me was still resisting the impulse to trust her. "What I have a hard time understanding is why didn't you come clean about your true self as soon as your husband was killed? Why give us that silly story about a Halloween Party and wanting to be a princess in a castle?"

She blurted out a laugh. "If I was up front about everything at that point, I might as well have held my wrists out to be handcuffed. No, I needed to keep the pretense up for a while longer. If I showed a sudden transformation, it would have been too much."

"The police over here are the same as police everywhere. They don't like to be lied to."

"You're right," she said with a nod. "Maybe what I did was dumb. But I was in a situation I had never imagined being in. I was prepared for Ron to die from a strain on his heart. That wouldn't seem suspicious. But *murder?*"

She leaned forward and displayed an emotion I had never seen on her face—genuine terror. "That stuffy police inspector thinks I did it, doesn't he? As do all the others. And now when they find out I've been deceiving them, it will look even worse. Do they still hang murderers over here?"

"Well, I don't know if I'd go that far—"

She grasped my hand. "If anyone can find who really killed Ronnie, it's you, Chase. You didn't go along with everyone else when they were accusing me. That means you have your doubts. You've got to help me." Her grip on my hand tightened. "You've *got* to."

Allison again flashed to mind. So did Ronald Gretz, beseeching me across the table in the bar to help him. The man had clearly been terrified, but he was no dummy. If he'd suspected his own wife of plotting against him, wouldn't he have told me?

"I can afford to make it worth your while," Summer said. "I'm very rich now, don't forget."

I pulled my hand away. "I'm assisting the police in tracking down the murderer. If you're truly innocent, that means I'm already helping you as well. Rest assured, I don't make up my mind strictly based on circumstantial evidence. But tell me. If you didn't kill your husband, who do you think did?"

She steepled her fingers. "Don't you think I've thought about that, over and over? The thing is—and I'm no expert, mind you—none of them strikes me as the murdering type. None. Except . . ."

She paused too long.

"Except?" I prodded.

"Um . . . I shouldn't say. It's just a silly feeling anyway—nothing to base it on."

"Those feelings sometimes can be the most accurate."

"It's that little worm of a man, Barker. I can see him murdering someone without batting an eye."

I was tempted to agree. But based on what? That grit of an idea lurking somewhere in my head?

"You know what?" said Summer, as I still thought of her, with an upwardly curled lip. "I'm asking you to trust me, so I'll reciprocate and place my trust in you. With your experience, I firmly believe you're going to figure this one out."

"Ah, but you must know what Montaigne says about experience," I countered. " 'Without sound judgment, experience is about as useful as being a fool.' "

Summer finished her drink and stood. "I know I'm right. Your judgment is sounder than any of the others."

"You do know, of course, that I'll need to let the inspector know of your true identity."

"I'll tell him myself." She walked a few steps and turned back. "Right now, I'm going up to my room to burn this wig. Don't freak out if you hear the smoke alarm."

As I watched her walk off, my thoughts darted to Allison, to her roommate, Francine, to Gretz, and finally to the lurking shadow, genderless and diffused, of Gretz's still unidentified killer.

Writing an account of my discussion with Summer that night in my journal, I couldn't help but thumb back and review the earlier misgivings I'd had about her ditzy persona. I had doubted its validity and was tempted to congratulate myself on my intuition, but I knew that skill came from years of listening to Doug practice different accents and dialects.

Oh no. There I went, thinking of Doug again. I considered doing a Flip it, Vanna! but instead pulled out my wallet. I withdrew a photo, taken years before, of him and me enjoying a summer party at a friend's house in Laguna Beach. We were both newly in love, as our smiling faces clearly displayed, and happier than ever seemed possible. I took a long, painful look at it. How could we ever have been so young, and so carefree?

I slowly slid the photo back into the wallet, and sat on the bed. The room, so cheerful at first with its Ellsworth Kelly print and geometrically patterned carpeting, had grown dark and gloomy. Even the daylight outside, diminished but still lingering at 10:00 p.m., seemed oppressive. I hadn't seen a truly dark night sky since I arrived.

I reclined on the bed and stared at the ceiling. Would I ever again find the kind of happiness I had with Doug? Each day, I felt older and more useless. If the San Diego Police hadn't imposed a mandatory retirement age for officers, I might still have been on the job, helping, even in a minuscule way, to combat evil in the world. Instead, my life had become a meaningless succession of Red Sox games, walks in Southwest canyons, unanswered dinner invitations from well-meaning friends, and far too much time spent sitting in my cookie-cutter "villa" inside a well-intentioned but vapid over-55 "senior community."

Billie was right; coming to England had been the jolt I needed to begin to see things differently. Furthermore, Gretz's request for help had given me a sense of purpose. Yet I had failed to save his life. Now I felt equally helpless in finding his killer. I had to face it; my time had passed. There was no Flip it, Vanna! that could fix this. It was time to get back home and try to repair my life there.

It was with a heavy heart that I got under the covers. Billie always suggested forming a mental image before sleep of something that brings you joy; it will give you pleasant dreams, she said. I pictured Mike Tibbets's face, smiling and handsome. A lightness flared inside, radiating hope. He'd seemed genuinely pleased to see me that day. The thought of being with him again made that spark of hope glow brighter. It was all very well to pursue justice and seek punishment of the guilty, but that wasn't enough to make life worthwhile. Only the love of someone else could do that. Thinking of Mike helped me fall asleep and want to face the morning.

Chapter 24

Thursday, 5:00 a.m.,
Downsmeade Grange

Even though I was getting used to the early English sunrises, I awakened earlier than usual the next morning. My talk with Summer was still weighing on my mind. Although learning her true identity was an intriguing development, it hadn't revealed anything new regarding Gretz's murder.

Or had it? Again, there was the unmistakable sense that a valuable clue was kicking around the corners of my mind, struggling to make itself known. Perhaps a hearty breakfast would provide the fuel I needed to make a breakthrough. I dressed, headed outside, and was about to enter the main house when I spotted Billie standing not far off, her arms wrapped around her torso, looking at the gardens and the morning sky.

"Communing with nature?" I called out.

She turned and smiled when she saw me. "Seeing as we're not walking anymore, I have to get outside every once in a while or I'll go stir-crazy."

I walked over to her. "I know what you mean. But a

cup of coffee and hot food sound better right now. Care to join me?"

She took my arm, and we were about to head back to the main house just as a small truck pulled up to the kitchen entrance. One of the cooks, a large woman in a hairnet, stepped outside to greet it. "What d'ya have for me this mornin', Ben?" she called out.

A weathered-looking older man in a heavy woolen sweater emerged from the truck. "Mornin', Hazel. Got mussels and monkfish from yesterday's catch, fresh as you please."

"Ben," I said to Billie. "Wasn't that the name of the fisherman who saw Gretz fall from the cliff?" She nodded.

As the man began unloading iced boxes of fish from his truck, I approached and introduced myself. "I'm helping Inspector Kilbride with his inquiries regarding the death that occurred on the coastal path yesterday. Are you the man who saw it happen?"

"Aye, that was a horrible thing, wasn't it? I still can't believe it." He noticed Billie at my side and broke into a wide—and possibly seductive?—smile. "Good morning, you pretty thing! Are you and this gentleman together?"

It was difficult to tell in the dim morning light, but I could have sworn that I saw Billie blush. She smiled demurely and said, "We're just friends."

This made Ben smile even wider. I needed to nip this flirtation in the bud while I still could. "I hope you don't mind, but I have a couple of questions about that day. I'm sure you told the inspector everything, but I have to ask again. Have any other details about that day come to mind? Something you may have remembered since you first spoke with the police?"

Ben reluctantly withdrew his attention from Billie and turned to me. He huffed out a breath and slowly shook his head. "Nay, I told him everything. I didn'a see much, y'know. There was so much fog. It only cleared for a moment after I heard the bloke scream."

"But did you keep your eye on the spot where it happened?"

"Aye, I did, because I could hardly believe what I'd seen. Yet I couldn't . . ." He paused, and his eyes widened slightly. "Y'know, now that I think of it, there *was* something else. It's probably nothin', but I did, as you say, keep lookin' up at the cliff path. I was just about to turn away and go look for the man's body, when the fog cleared again."

"It did? And what did you see?"

"Well, that's just it—I didn't see *anything*. The fog was gone in a flash, and I could see that whole section of the path. There wasn't a soul on it."

"You didn't see anyone?"

"No, and it didn'a make sense! How could that person I'd seen just a moment before have gotten away so quickly? It was like he vanished!"

"Yet you're certain you saw someone?"

"Aye, absolutely sure. Fella was up there, plain as anything."

"Tall? Short?"

"Nay, about average. Like yourself."

It seemed strange that he saw no other walkers on the path, particularly Summer and Brett, who would have been the ones nearest to Gretz. They most likely continued walking when the attack was occurring, but there was also that other walker I'd spotted heading in the other direction. Ben didn't see him either—unless he was the killer.

"You said it was like 'he' vanished," I said. "Do you remember more clearly if the person you saw was a man?"

He paused to think and shook his head. "I'm sorry, but I don't. It looked like a bloke, but it could have been a lassie as well."

I thanked him and asked him to give the inspector a call should he remember anything more. He again smiled at Billie, revealing the crooked, discolored teeth for which the British have, perhaps undeservedly, gotten a reputation. "I will, but might I call this pretty lady first?"

This brought on another blush from Billie. "I'm afraid I won't be here much longer. I'll be going back to America soon."

The cook stepped up. "Ben, stop your chin-wagging and help me get this fish in the freezer."

He gave Billie a reluctant wink and went back to his work. I took her arm and led her into the main house. When we got inside, I nudged her playfully. "What's this about it being too late for love?"

She nudged me back. "Chase, honestly. You really think I'd take up with an old salt like that?"

"He wasn't bad-looking—sort of like the fellow on the Gorton's frozen fish packages."

"Except when he showed his teeth," Billie said.

Laughing, we entered the breakfast room, where Lucien Barker hovered over a bowl of porridge and a slice of toast. I put a muffin and jam on a plate and went over to him.

"How are you bearing up?" I asked.

Barker swallowed a spoonful of porridge. "I'm alright. This walk wasn't my main reason for coming to England, so I'm not too concerned about it being put on hold."

It seemed odd, but not entirely out of character, that he wouldn't be bothered about a murder having been committed.

"What else do you have planned?" I asked, remembering Summer's suspicion of him from the night before.

His face was its usual expressionless mask. "As I've mentioned, I'm scheduled to visit my aunt here in Devon. She contacted me shortly after my mother passed. I promised I would visit when I came over. I also decided to see some of the Devon countryside while I was here, and that's when I found this tour. Mother often spoke of the moors and valleys when she was a small child. She had very happy memories of her years here, and her stories are so vivid in my mind. I thought seeing those places for myself would honor her legacy."

"I'm sorry about your mother," I said. "I lost mine a few years ago myself. I know how hard it can be."

Barker paused and said calmly, "I know what you're trying to do, Chase—get me to give you some reason why I might have murdered Gretz. Yes, it's true that my mother was in a senior-care facility similar to those he owned. I disliked it intensely. It was cold and impersonal, not the type of place in which I wanted my mother to spend her final days. It was, however, the only option I could afford."

I was surprised when a small sob escaped from Barker's throat. "Being in such a place shortened her life, I'm certain of it. The management could have made it a better experience for her, but they didn't. So I know, indeed I do, how anger can stir up the urge to kill. It is frightening how easily that can happen."

There was something he wasn't saying. Was he reluctant to incriminate someone else, someone who had abruptly succumbed to the "urge to kill"? "Those are strong words," I said.

Barker took a deep breath. "I didn't kill Gretz. I wouldn't have minded if he'd sprained an ankle and spent the rest of the time in bed, but that's the extent of my ill will." He wiped his mouth and stood. "Forgive me if I take my leave. I've become interested in some of the books in the hotel library and want to finish one in particular."

I recalled the large volume on British estate law. I was going to ask about it, but didn't want to let on that I'd been snooping. Heading toward the door, Barker paused and turned back. "Do you think we might be free to leave by the weekend? I need to be in London on Saturday for a concert."

"That's up to the inspector, I'm afraid."

Barker left, and I joined Billie at her table.

"Have a productive conversation with Mr. Bowling Pin?" she asked.

I smiled. "I did. He's quite an unusual man."

"Is he ever. But, apart from all of that, he's short."

That made me laugh. "Surely that's no crime, is it?"

"What I mean is, he doesn't match the physical description of the person seen pushing Gretz off the cliff. Ben said he—or she—was of normal height."

I took a bite of muffin. "Yes, but bear in mind that Ben was quite a distance away. And Barker normally slouches. I wager that if he straightened up to strike someone, he might look like a different man."

"Maybe," Billie replied. As she buttered her toast, I asked if she'd heard anything new about her sister's surgery.

She put down her butter knife and took a deep breath. "Are you ready for Profiles in Bureaucracy, Chapter Twenty? The good news is the doctors submitted the new surgery request, and it was approved. The bad news is that, because so many surgeries had to be rescheduled as a result of the bomb scare, they can't operate until tomorrow. I don't know what's better—being a thousand miles away or right at her bedside. Either way, it's a waiting game."

She was also waiting, as were the rest of us, to learn the identity of Gretz's murderer, and one of those working on that problem—yours truly—was seated across from her. I didn't want to betray Inspector Kilbride's confidence, but Billie was practically part of the team. Looking around—we were practically alone, the Meyerses having taken their breakfasts out to the terrace—I related the discovery of Corky's burglary arrests.

"Interesting," Billie said. "I don't know what her sordid past would have to do with Gretz's murder, but I've always had a strange feeling about that girl. Her Anglophile routine seems a bit put on to me."

"It is curious," I admitted. "She thought Walt Whitman was a British poet. Not many Anglophiles would make that mistake. And then there's that brother of hers."

"Yes," Billie said. "He seems curious too. Comes across as a wealthy go-getter. But I wonder."

"Apparently, he isn't as rich as he seems. The inspector discovered that Brett lost most of his fortune—and Corky's too, as it turns out—gambling, and loan sharks are demanding payment."

"Well, that explains his interest in the recently widowed Mrs. Gretz. Even before she was widowed."

"He denied that his interest was anything more than physical," I said, although I had overheard him ask Summer to let him help direct her late husband's firm. "He's a healthy young male, and she's a healthy young female. The attraction is most likely purely sexual, a story as old as time. Still, I learned something else also." I told Billie about Corky admitting to directing Gretz to sit on the lime kiln wall, knowing it would likely collapse beneath him.

"Good heavens! If that wasn't an attempt at murder, what on earth was it?"

"Corky claims she just wanted to frighten Gretz, get him to bail on the rest of the walk. She didn't think he would get seriously hurt because she arranged for her brother to catch him when he fell."

Billie looked skeptical. "I think she knew exactly what she was doing. She might be in league with her brother. We can't be sure where he was on the cliff path when Gretz was killed. He let Lucien Barker walk past him and could easily have made his way back to the Gretzes, maybe even passing Summer in the mist without her noticing. And don't forget, that green jacket was found in his suitcase."

"He's not that dim, Billie. If he put on the jacket to protect his identity in the event someone spotted him pushing Gretz off the cliff, why wouldn't he have just thrown it away afterward? His fingerprints weren't on it. Why keep the jacket as evidence?"

Billie gave a grudging nod. "Okay then, but what about his sister? One of her skills is lock-picking, isn't that what you said? She could have snuck back onto the cliff path, given Gretz the fatal push, and picked the lock to her brother's room in order to plant the jacket in his suitcase."

I mentioned the photo Justin Meyers took of the woman on the trail, and while it was too indistinct to identify as Corky, it couldn't be dismissed.

"You see? Maybe I'm right!"

"But why would Corky implicate her own brother?" I asked.

"Didn't you just tell me he'd gambled away her money? Maybe she wanted to get back at him for that."

I considered this for a moment, but too many facts stood in the way. "If Corky wanted Gretz out of the way, why did she arrange for Brett to grab onto him when he began to fall into the lime kiln? Only to kill him later herself so she could frame her brother? That just doesn't add up."

Billie accepted this with visible disappointment. "So we come back to the same question. Why would anyone other than Summer want to kill Gretz?"

I was about to tell her about the new development in that department as well when an elegant brown-haired woman appeared in the doorway. It took me a moment to realize it was Summer herself, looking exotically chic rather than comically cheap. Her eyes passed over us as she walked toward a table in the corner.

I could tell from Billie's astonishment that she had figured it out. "Good Lord, is that who I think it is?"

"It's the new Mrs. Gretz."

"You know something!" Billie said. "Come on now, Chase, tell, tell!"

I gave a brief summary of Summer's masquerade as a bimbo and her decision to revert to her true identity.

"But if she was lying about who she really was," Billie asked, "why should we believe her now when she claims she didn't kill her husband?"

"Yes, that bothered me too. She could have kept up the pretense if she'd wanted; it's probable that none of us would have caught on. But still, I count it a point in her favor that she came clean. It's a risky decision that I doubt she'd make if she was Gretz's killer."

Billie took a bite of toast. "She's still our likeliest suspect, regardless."

"Don't forget those threats Gretz received. Yes, you could make the case for Summer killing her husband to inherit his fortune, but why would she advertise that by sending him threats? Not to mention how cruel that is— and Summer doesn't seem a cruel sort. She was very diligent about making sure he took his pills, remember. She might have had reason to be angry with him because of the way he treated her, but not to the point where she would torture him that way." I mentioned the note Mike Tibbets found in Gretz's pocket.

"Someone must have given that note to him that very day," Billie reasoned. "Which makes it look like his killer is either one of our group or somebody lurking nearby."

"My thoughts as well. Unless, that is, the person making the threats isn't the killer."

Billie stood and stretched her arms. "This is all so frustrating! Who would have thought murder could be so complicated? Between this and the fate of my sister hanging in the hands of bureaucrats, I need to go outside and breathe some more fresh air. Perhaps that will clear my mind."

"Please be careful, Billie. We know there's a killer around here somewhere. My experience has been that when someone kills once they're less hesitant to kill again. Our killer might suspect you've been trying to figure out his—or her—identity."

"Don't worry about me," she said, hefting up her bag. "I've always got my knitting needles close at hand. And I can't wander very far. We're not allowed to."

"We're permitted to walk around the grounds. Have you tried the garden maze?"

"Those things frighten me. I always feel I'll get hopelessly lost."

"You've got your knitting yarn, don't you? Just leave a trail of it behind you."

She flashed me a smirk and walked away, passing Corky, who gave me an acknowledging nod and scanned the room. Summer Gretz did not catch her attention. Corky went to survey the breakfast offerings.

Within minutes, Brett, Justin, and Phaedra came in as well, and even though they too cast a cursory glance around, none recognized Summer.

I was amazed at how unobservant people could be. During my career, I'd questioned hundreds of eyewitnesses to crimes, and most hadn't noticed even the most obvious details. Summer's new look was different, yes, but Billie had seen through it. Why hadn't any of the others? Moreover, what other details had they overlooked on the day Gretz died?

More important, what might *I* have overlooked?

Chapter 25

Thursday, late morning,
Downsmeade Grange

After finishing my breakfast, I found myself in a similar dilemma as Billie. Where to go? What to do? I wasn't accustomed to having unscheduled blocks of free time on my England visits. When I wasn't walking, every other minute was usually filled visiting manor homes or gardens or soaking up the local color at pubs and tea shops. Those were no longer options.

I went into the hotel bar, quiet with no barman in sight. Though the weather had turned warm, a small fire still burned in the grate, more to provide atmosphere, I figured, than warmth.

The coziness of the room was inviting. I decided to sit and gaze into the flames; maybe they would thaw whatever might be separating those stray thoughts in my head. I headed for one of the semi-private alcoves that lined the bar's inner wall and was surprised to find Inspector Kilbride seated there. He held his pipe in one hand, smoke curling upward, and in the other was his omnipresent notepad, at which he was looking intently.

"Inspector!" I greeted. "I wasn't expecting to find you here so early. Don't you ever go home?"

He looked up and smiled. "Good morning, Mr. Chasen. Of course, I spent the night at home; I can't afford the rates in this place. But they don't charge to sit in the bar, and I felt my time could be more productive here than in my dreary office. Please have a seat."

Joining him, I said, "I was having the same thoughts. Maybe pubs make you as reflective as they do me. Or is it that you want to be close at hand in case one of the suspects . . . what's the term . . . scarpers?"

Kilbride chuckled. "I wouldn't put it past Mrs. Gretz to make a run for it. I've asked the hotel staff to keep their eyes on her, but I suppose it never hurts to handle something yourself if you want it done good and proper."

I decided not to inform the inspector of Summer's new—or recovered—identity quite yet. I did, however, mention Corky's confession about Howie not being in the van when she returned after her circuit of the village shops.

Kilbride raised his brow. "That doesn't sound good, does it? We'll need to question him again. Is he about, do you know?"

"I haven't seen much of him since the afternoon Gretz was killed. There hasn't been any need for him to drive us anywhere. But he shouldn't be far. I'll check with Sally."

"Very good," Kilbride said. "Crane doesn't seem a likely killer, but we shouldn't rule him out."

I wondered how many unlikely killers the inspector had encountered. "May I ask when was your last murder case?"

Kilbride paused, took a long draw from his pipe, and released the smoke pensively. "The last was just this past February. A small-time racketeer in Torquay had knifed an accomplice, who, it turns out, had stolen quite a bit of money from him. No honor among thieves, as they say. It was very straightforward and uncomplicated, and didn't require much brain power to get the killer to confess. He hadn't even bothered to dispose of his knife."

I laughed. Besides the unobservant eyewitnesses I had come across, I never ceased to be astonished at how careless some criminals could be.

"As far as the last case that required actual deduction, well, that's been a while," Kilbride said. "I am proud to say, however, that in my unit we always find the culprit. I've had no cold cases on my watch."

"A one hundred percent clear-up rate is something to be proud of," I said.

"Thank you. And I don't intend this case to be the first."

"I'll do my best to help ensure that it won't." Did that sound presumptive? My own record hadn't been as stellar, but my cases had likely been more demanding. I often looked at my success rate through the lens of baseball, where batters typically fail to get a base hit seven out of ten pitches. And yet even those players can become All-Stars.

"Your help will certainly be useful," he said. "Because we've discovered that another one of your group has been less than truthful with us."

Had he discovered Corky actually *had* returned to the cliff path? Or had he found out about the newly transformed Summer Gretz?

"It's that Lucien Barker chap," Kilbride said. "Olea found out that his mother was, indeed, quartered in one of Mr. Gretz's senior-care facilities."

"Interesting. But that doesn't necessarily mean he's been lying to us. Gretz's properties have different names. Barker might not have realized his mother's facility was part of Golden Sunset."

Kilbride acknowledged that as a possibility. He reached into his coat pocket, pulled out his notepad, and flipped it open. "Far more interesting, however, was what Olea learned about Carole Tawney, Barker's aunt. You asked us to check her out."

"I'm all ears."

"When I contacted her, she was quite surprised to learn that her nephew was in this country and was part of a murder investigation."

"She didn't know Barker was here? He said he was planning to visit her."

"She was alarmed because she claims he has been threatening her."

"Threatening her? How?"

Kilbride eyed his notepad. "Mostly through emails. 'You won't get away with this' was one of the threats. 'You're going to pay' was another."

"Those sound very much like the threats Gretz received."

The inspector nodded. "Indeed. I asked Miss Tawney why her nephew should be upset with her. It turns out he's angry because she is claiming her right to some of his late mother's estate. She says it is all perfectly aboveboard, but Barker is convinced she's stealing his share."

I told Kilbride about the book on British estate law Barker had been perusing in the hotel library. "This gives Barker motives to kill both his aunt and Ronald Gretz. One is to secure some of his mother's estate, and the other is for revenge."

"Possibly so."

"But I'm not inclined to believe he did either." I related my cryptic conversation with Barker that morning, which, in light of the new information, seemed to exonerate him. "It was as if he had considered murder, but didn't go forward with it."

Kilbride stroked his hand across his notepad. "That's as it may be. It still remains that the chap, along with the Meyerses, has not been completely open with us."

With Barker looming more likely as a suspect, I could see no benefit in delaying the news about Summer. "I'm afraid there's another piece of deception," I said, and shared my discovery of her real identity.

"Good Lord, how did Olea miss that?" the inspector said, clearly disturbed.

"Don't be too hard on her. Summer did a good job of covering her tracks. She's a pretty smart cookie."

"Smart enough to get away with murder? This charade of hers seems to place her right back at the top of the suspect list."

"Yes, there is good reason to think that. But she could have kept up the pretense if she wanted to. She came clean, even knowing the facts show her to be deceitful. We still must consider her a suspect, of course, but I'm inclined to move her lower on our list."

Kilbride sighed. "Our list, I'm afraid, is a complete muddle. How nice it was when we only had one obvious suspect. Now we have at least four, not to mention the mystery chap you spotted on the trail. And in view of the inescapable fact that so many of the bunch are hiding secrets, there may be even more."

"Inspector Kilbride?"

A trim, middle-aged man with dark-grayish hair stood before us. He wore a crisp business shirt with no necktie.

"I am he," replied the inspector.

"The lass at the front desk told me I might find you in here. My name is David Chambers. I think you might want to speak with me."

"And why is that?"

"Because I was scheduled to meet today with a man I've just learned has been murdered."

Chapter 26

Dumbstruck by this announcement, Kilbride and I could do nothing but look at each other.

"May I sit?" Chambers asked, and Kilbride gestured to the seat beside us.

After sitting, the man said, "I just heard the news about Ronald Gretz. It was quite a shock, to put it mildly."

"You were scheduled to meet with him?" Kilbride asked. "What for?"

Chambers hesitated and then said, "To keep him from making the biggest mistake of his life."

"A mistake?" Kilbride asked. Nodding toward me, he said, "This is Rick Chasen, a colleague of mine. Would you mind if he listens to what you have to say?"

"Not at all," Chambers replied before clearing his throat. "I probably should start at the beginning. I am . . . that is, I was . . . an employee of Mr. Gretz's. I manage three of his elder-care facilities here in the UK. I oversee their day-to-day operations."

"Yes, we're aware that Mr. Gretz's business extends to the UK."

"Has for several years," Chambers said. "Although the US office keeps a hands-off policy as long as we make our numbers. That, however, changed recently."

"Indeed? And why is that?" Kilbride asked.

Chambers took a breath. "We've been under increased pressure to cut costs. That is to be expected from time to time, of course—it never hurts to periodically audit expenses and see what fat can be trimmed—but we'd already been cutting nearly everything to the proverbial bone. We couldn't make any further cuts without severely damaging the quality of our care."

I thought of Lucien Barker's mother. Could this have had something to do with her death? But she'd been back in the States, hadn't she?

"This issue came to a head, though, over the beta test of a special program we had been conducting at our facilities," Chambers said.

"Special program?" Kilbride asked.

"It is an innovative new regimen designed to keep our guests—we don't call them patients—more alert and active. The program is difficult to explain, but essentially it encompasses improving our guests' well-being by making changes to the environment—décor, diet, activity, music. I know it sounds all my eye and Betty Martin, but it was surprisingly effective. Several of our more compromised guests behaved as if they'd sipped from the fountain of youth; they became more social, more independent, more interested in life."

What he was describing reminded me very much of the Meyerses' program.

"That sounds awfully good," the inspector said. "Wouldn't mind trying it myself. So, what is the problem?"

Chambers paused. "The problem is that when our guests reacted positively to this treatment, they became more . . . costly to accommodate."

"In what way?" I asked.

"To put it plainly, they were more demanding," Chambers said. "Rather than spend the day in bed, sedated and ignored, they had greater interests. They wanted better food at their meals. They wanted high-speed Internet access and computers. They wanted books to read, more activities. And all of this cost money and was stretching our budget."

"Couldn't you simply raise your rates?" I asked.

"Not easily, no. The elder-care market is very competitive, so our rates need to be competitive. The fees we charge for our services are subject to regulations as well, which limit what we can charge."

"Of course," Kilbride replied, "but what does this have to do with Gretz?"

Chambers paused. "Well, he was always after us to cut costs. Recently, he issued a blanket order that we cease providing this new treatment . . . entirely."

"Could he do that?" I asked. "Aren't the patients . . . aren't the *guests* able to decide which treatments they choose to engage in for themselves?"

"The ones who are able to think clearly can do so, yes," Chambers said. "But for those with less sharp minds, we need to get a signed release from their families or estate attorney. Gretz wanted that to no longer be an option?"

Could this be what Gretz was reluctant to share with me?

"So, you see," Chambers continued, "it was a twofold problem. Gretz wanted costs trimmed precisely at the time when this trial program was showing results. We had no alternative but to cut it off. But the problem went deeper than that."

Chambers looked down, struggling with how to continue. "Some of our guests took the cancelation of the program very hard. Almost all began regressing to their previous state. A few . . . well, a few went downhill to the point where they . . ."

"Passed on?" Kilbride asked.

Chambers nodded. "Keep in mind that many were elderly folks who weren't in the best of shape to begin with, but still . . ." He gave a small laugh. "You think I must be crazy, right? I've just given you a first-class reason why I would want Gretz out of the way! But honestly, I just heard about his death a few minutes ago, at the front desk. It was quite a jolt. If he were still alive, I would be meeting with him right now."

"What were you two going to discuss?" I asked.

Chambers cleared his throat. "Mr. Gretz could get very unreasonable where expenses were concerned, but I don't think he realized how serious this was. I have already heard rumors of lawsuits about negligence in regard to the guests who have died. If any more pass on, Golden Sunset could have serious legal problems on its hands. It might even threaten the existence of the company altogether."

Chambers paused to calm himself before continuing. "I was going to propose an alternative plan. My staff and I have found a way to reallocate costs without severely affecting our quality of care and reintroduce the Enviro-Plus program at the same time."

"Enviro-Plus?" Turning to Kilbride, I said, "That's the name of the Meyerses' firm, isn't it?"

"I believe it is," the inspector said.

"Meyers? Justin Meyers?" Chambers asked.

"Do you know him?" I asked.

"Absolutely. We've worked closely together in getting the program up and running. We've worked remotely, that is, mostly through phone and online connections." The inspector and I exchanged looks. "What is it? How do you know Mr. Meyers?"

Kilbride began rolling his pipe between his fingers. "We . . . we're familiar with these individuals." Looking at Chambers, he asked, "Were you in this vicinity on Tuesday, Mr. Chambers?"

"No," he said. "I was in my office all day."

"And where is your office?"

"Manchester."

Kilbride turned to me. "Four or so hours by train or car." Turning to Chambers, he said, "It looks like you're in the clear, unless it comes to the point where we need to check on your whereabouts."

"I'm not worried," Chambers said. "I may be many things, but I'm not a murderer. My staff can vouch for me." He slid a business card toward the inspector, who thanked him and told him he'd keep him informed.

"I'd like to ask you one thing," I said. "Did you speak with Mr. Gretz a few days ago? Did he tell you about any threats he'd received?"

Chambers looked surprised. "Why, yes. To be honest, we spoke often and he . . . well, let's just say that he could be what you might call paranoid. He was always imagining supposed enemies. When he told me of these threats, I'm afraid I didn't give them much credence. Do you suppose they might have been sent by his killer?"

I traded glances with Kilbride. "We're still investigating," he responded.

I explained I'd overheard part of Chambers's conversation with Gretz. "And you have no idea who that person may have been that he was referring to?"

Chambers shook his head. "Absolutely no clue."

I thanked him. He said he was going to explore the grounds a bit—"I've heard such good things about this place"—and eat lunch in the hotel restaurant before heading back to his office.

After Chambers left, Kilbride slowly rose to his feet. "It looks like we need to have another conversation with Mr. and Mrs. Meyers, wouldn't you say?"

Chapter 27

We found Phaedra on the terrace, flipping through a magazine. The day had turned warm, so she had taken off her coat and kicked off her shoes. She looked up as we approached.

"Wait, let me guess," Phaedra said. "You've found out whodunit. Colonel Mustard in the library with the rope."

We pulled up chairs and sat. "I'm afraid not, Mrs. Meyers," the inspector said. "But we do have more questions for you and your husband. Is he about?"

Phaedra looked out onto the croquet lawn. "Justin told me he was going to take a stroll." She checked her watch. "It's almost lunchtime, so he should be back soon. But what else can we possibly tell you?"

Kilbride took out his notepad. "The truth might be nice."

Phaedra closed her magazine. "And what makes you think we haven't been telling you the truth?"

"You told me, Mrs. Meyers, that you learned of this walking tour from a mailed catalog. The problem is, the Wanderers does no direct-mail advertising."

A patient smile formed as she gave a small sigh. "Oh, honestly, do you expect me to remember something like that? What does that have to do with anything?"

"More significantly," Kilbride said, "we have learned that your firm—Enviro-Plus—has been in a partnership with one of Mr. Gretz's nursing homes in the UK to test a new program. Yet when we asked each of you, separately, if you had ever encountered Gretz, you both denied it."

Phaedra's jaw dropped. Her eyes flared and her mouth gaped. "*What?* The facility we've been dealing with is *Gretz's?*"

"You didn't know?" I asked. This didn't seem credible.

"I can't believe it! I'm going to kill my husband! I'll absolutely *kill* him!"

"Do you mean to tell us that you were unaware of your firm's connection to Gretz?" Kilbride asked.

"No! I mean . . . yes. This is the first time I'd heard of it." Sensing our skepticism, she said, "Listen. I know it sounds crazy, but Justin handles the business side of things. He knows that those kind of details bore me silly. I prefer to focus on the creative part without worrying about mundane things like money."

Her explanation hung in the air like a fragile balloon about to pop.

"If you'll pardon me, Mrs. Meyers, that's hard for me to accept," the inspector said. "You expect us to believe that you just happened to be on a walking tour with the man who canceled your firm's primary program, which was being tested in a facility in this country, and you were unaware of it?"

I recalled Phaedra's cryptic comment to Justin when he went off for his interview with Kilbride. *I reminded him that our work has nothing to do with Gretz's operation. You'll tell him that also, won't you?*

Phaedra's cool façade was shattered. "Okay, yes, I know

it sounds absolutely unbelievable. I'm trying to make sense of it myself. I can't imagine why Justin wouldn't have told me . . ."

I had already formulated an answer to that question, and Phaedra realized it. "Oh, no. Absolutely not. If you think Justin came over here to kill Gretz, you're out of your mind. He could no more murder someone than he could . . . win an Olympic gold medal for downhill skiing! There must be another explanation. There simply must."

The inspector let out a sigh. "Perhaps. But where is your husband?"

"As I said, he must be on the grounds somewhere. He should be back any minute."

Kilbride turned to me. "We need to find him. I'll look around the property. You check inside the hotel."

"Right," I said. Standing, I told Kilbride, "This case keeps getting weirder and weirder. I'm beginning to wonder if any of this bunch has told us the truth."

"Truth," the inspector replied, "can be a surprisingly elusive concept. I doubt if one ever knows it completely."

That kind of thinking would get us nowhere. "Nevertheless, the truth is out there, and we have to try to find it," I said before walking off.

It didn't take long for me to complete a tour of the hotel's common areas. Guests were beginning to fill up the bar and dining room for lunch, but Justin Meyers was not among them. I asked the front-desk clerk to phone the Meyerses' room—no response. I then headed off to find Billie and ask her to help me search, but she wasn't around either. Recalling that she'd expressed an interest in exploring the grounds, I went outside.

The day had turned pleasant and warm. I walked across the croquet lawn on a path leading through the gardens to the lake. On the other side of the garden, a sign pointed toward the hedge maze. I had suggested that Billie try her luck with it. It had been ages since I'd walked through a maze myself. They appeal to my puzzle-loving mind, despite the fact that I had absolutely no sense of direction. I headed toward the maze as Lucien Barker rounded a corner. He didn't acknowledge me and kept walking past.

"Did you try the maze?" I asked.

Surprised, he stopped and turned. "I don't engage in silly activities like that," he said, and resumed walking.

Silly or not, I felt an urge to attempt it in hopes of locating Billie or Justin. The maze was on the other side of a gate and looked formidable. Its hedges, neatly trimmed dwarf box shrubs with thick, leathery leaves, were nearly seven feet high, so I couldn't peer over them to get a sense of the maze's size or see the top of anyone's head.

I decided to plunge right in. It was slow going. One promising turn would lead to a dead end, and another would send me back where I'd started. After several minutes, I began to wonder if I would ever find my way. Nevertheless, I plugged on and, after a few minutes, began to feel that I was making progress. If all else failed, I could use my cell phone to call for help.

Someone once told me a strategy for conquering garden mazes. Was it always to stay to the left? Or to the right? I tried the left-hand approach, which seemed to move me into passages I hadn't yet explored.

Something on the ground beneath me caught my eye: a dark red blotch. Blood? I bent and dabbed at it with my finger. It was still moist. Taking a sniff confirmed my guess; it was blood alright, but whether animal or human I couldn't tell. Ahead of me the path was clear and unsullied. Turning back, I saw further red streaks I hadn't noticed before. The bottom of my shoe was wet with blood as well. I began retracing my steps. Around a bend, I encountered a larger pool of blood, its dampness gleaming in the midday sun. How had I overlooked that?

I followed more blood traces into a side passage, one I hadn't yet taken. It was a dead end in more ways than one. Halfway in, a man was splayed on the ground, his head soaked with blood.

It was David Chambers.

Chapter 28

Thursday, midday,
Downsmeade Grange Garden Maze

I knelt, lifted Chambers's arm, and felt for a pulse. Nothing. I pried open an eyelid and saw no flicker of life. The man was dead.

I stood and examined the ground around the body. There was no sign of a murder weapon. The air was still, and the only sound was a distant wren twittering to its mate. I detected a faint scent of lavender.

Scanning the maze corridor, I spotted a carved stone peeking out from beneath the hedge behind Chambers's body. One side of the stone was dark red and wet—more blood.

I considered yelling for help, but should the killer be nearby, I didn't want to announce my presence. Instead, I pulled out my cell phone and called the front desk. Fortunately, the connection went through, and the desk clerk answered.

"This is Mr. Chasen, one of your guests. I'm in your garden maze, and I've discovered a dead body. I don't want to leave it unattended. Could you find Chief Inspector Kilbride? He might still be in the bar."

Within a minute, the inspector came on. "Did I hear right, Mr. Chasen? You found another body?"

I confirmed this and told him I was in one of the maze's inner rings.

"Good Lord. It will take me forever to find you."

I told him that hotels often had maze maps available for guests. Kilbride checked with the desk clerk and obtained one. I went to what seemed to be a main passage and waited for him. A minute or so later, map clutched in hand, he appeared, accompanied by DC Bright. I cautioned them against stepping on the blood on the ground and led them to the side passage where Chambers's body lay.

"My word," the inspector said. Bright knelt and performed the same life-detecting procedure as I had.

"He's dead alright, sir," Bright reported.

"When did you discover him?" Kilbride asked me.

"Just a few minutes ago. I was looking for Billie and Justin Meyers, and decided to try the maze. I saw traces of blood on the ground and followed them here. I also saw that." I pointed to the stone.

Bright put on a pair of plastic gloves and delicately pulled the stone from beneath the hedge. It was sizable; Bright had to use both of his hands to move it.

"That is likely the murder weapon," Kilbride said as he looked it over. "But where did it come from?"

I stood. "I have a guess. Can you give me your map?"

Kilbride handed it to me, and I studied it for a moment.

"Let's go to the center of the maze," I suggested. "Before we do, however, isn't there some business to take care of?"

Kilbride looked puzzled.

"I think Mr. Chasen means contacting the local crime investigation team," Bright said. "You know. To come and remove the body, snap photos, secure the scene, all of that."

The inspector looked as if he'd just snapped out of a trance. "Yes, quite so, quite so." He pulled out his cell phone and made a quick call.

My confidence in Kilbride's expertise dropped a few notches. Apparently, seeing Chambers's blood-soaked body had shaken him. To be fair, though, not many people can handle such sights.

Taking careful strides so as not to disturb the crime scene further, the three of us, using the map as a guide, made our way to the center of the maze—a small square of loamy earth dominated by a feeble dogwood tree, designed most likely to provide a point of reference for maze-solvers if it grew higher. A ring of carved stones surrounded it.

"See? One is missing," I said, kneeling before a small gap in the stone circle. "Our murder weapon could have come from here."

Kilbride ran his fingers over the remaining stones. "Yes, it seems as if the stone was taken from here. Very well then. Let's go meet the unit coming for the body." He asked Bright to stay with the body while we headed back to the hotel. As we walked, he asked, "Did you pass anyone on your way into the maze?"

"I saw no one in the maze itself. But Lucien Barker was coming around the outside as I was going in. He seemed a bit agitated."

"No one else?"

"Not that I recall."

An emergency-response van pulled up to the hotel entrance just as we arrived, followed by a police car. Two men stepped out of the van, one of whom—I was very pleased to see—was Mike Tibbets, wearing street clothes rather than his laboratory coat and carrying a black body bag.

He saw me and broke into a smile. "They keep dropping like flies around you, don't they?"

I was tempted to laugh, but the situation was too grim. "Good to see you, Mike."

One of the policemen stepped up and asked where they could find the body. Kilbride handed him the maze map.

"A body in a maze!" the policeman exclaimed. "What'll they think of next?"

Mike said, "My tour-guide offer still stands, Chase. Although I'm afraid this second death might extend your stay out here a bit longer."

"I hope not." I believed it might actually shorten it; two murders are harder to cover up than one. The thought of running off with Mike was tempting, but so was the prospect of proving my mettle by finding the killer.

"I'm not suggesting we scurry off now, you understand," Mike continued. "When this nasty business is settled, that's what I'm talking about."

"Of course. I understand."

He studied me for a moment, as if trying to look into my heart. A small smile indicated that he sensed something encouraging. "Very good, then. I'd better go see about this new corpse of yours." He headed off toward the maze with his assistant. Kilbride remained with me as Bright returned.

"The victim's car is right over there, sir," he said, pointing to a gleaming burgundy 330e BMW parked not far away. "I'll arrange to have it taken care of." He went off just as Sally appeared from around the corner of the main house, her hands stuffed into her jacket pockets. She cast a troubled glance at the van and the stretcher.

"What's happened?" she asked.

"Miss Anders," Kilbride said, "can you help us locate the others in your group? I need everyone in the parlor. Immediately."

She hesitated for a moment, her eyes twisted with curiosity, and went into the hotel.

I followed, and soon most of the group were assembled in the drawing room. Howie, Justin, and Summer were the only ones unaccounted for.

"Summer's up in her room," Kilbride said. "The front desk just notified her, and she'll be right down."

"Howie wasn't needed here today, so he's probably back home in Ilfracombe," Sally said.

"I can't understand why Justin hasn't returned," Phaedra said. "Maybe he's lost in the garden maze. Can someone go look for him?"

"Why would he be in there?" Kilbride asked.

"He mentioned that he'd like to have a go at it."

The inspector called DC Bright on his phone and asked if he'd seen Justin in the maze.

Corky asked, "My God. Don't tell me. There's been another murder, hasn't there? There's always more than one. Is it . . . is it Mr. Meyers?"

"Please, no!" Phaedra cried.

This set the others into a furious chatter.

"Quiet, everyone, please!" the inspector said, pushing his thin voice to the limit.

The group fell into a shocked hush as Summer came in. She coolly pretended to be unaware of their stares at her new look and sat in an armchair.

Brett went over to her, mouth agape. "What on earth have you done to yourself?"

She didn't respond.

Kilbride cleared his throat. "The answer to your first question, Miss Nielsen, is yes. There has been another killing. The answer to your second question is no, it was not Mr. Meyers, but a gentleman some of you"—he flashed a glance at Phaedra—"may know. A Mr. David Chambers."

Phaedra gasped. A rumble of puzzled murmurs indicated the name meant nothing to the rest of the group.

"We still don't have an exact time of death," the inspector continued, "but the desk clerk tells me a couple of tourists went through the garden maze approximately forty-five minutes ago and saw nothing out of the ordinary. They were the only visitors of whom she was aware. I need to know where all of you were during that time and since. I'll begin with you, Miss Nielsen."

Corky pointed to a chair in the corner beside a lamp. "I ate an egg salad sandwich in the bar and came back here. I've been reading *Original Sin* by P. D. James."

"Was anyone else here with you?"

She paused. "The whole time? I don't know. Brett was with me for a while."

Turning to Brett, Kilbride said, "Where were you in the past hour, Mr. Nielsen?"

His eyes darted back and forth around the room. "Here and there, I can't remember. I don't keep track of all my movements. We've all been so squirrelly since Gretz was bumped off. I find myself wandering around without even paying attention as to where I am or what time it is."

"Answer my question, please."

Brett let out a sigh. "I guess I was in here for a while, checking my email and text messages. Corky was eating her sandwich, but I'd had a big breakfast and wasn't hungry. I went into the game room and hit a few balls around the pool table. I probably did a couple of other things. It's hard to remember. We're all stir-crazy, being cooped up in this creepy place."

"Did you go outside?"

"I may have stepped outside for a minute or two. I checked if the weather was good enough for tennis."

"What time would that have been?"

"How the hell should I know?"

I couldn't resist commenting. "Perhaps you could have looked at your wristwatch. Isn't your Breguet Guilloché precise to the tenth of a second?"

Brett flushed. "What good is all this talk going to do? Any one of us could have gone off to the maze and come back here before anyone noticed we were missing."

The inspector turned to Summer. He was trying to reconcile her new look with the woman he remembered. "How about you, Mrs. Gretz?"

She was calm and unflustered. In her new, deeper, and more sophisticated voice, she said, "I was in my room watching TV. I found a channel that's playing all the episodes of *I, Claudius*. I did come down to the bar to get one of their croissant sandwiches, but I went right back up."

"*I, Claudius?*" Brett asked incredulously. It seemed he was unable to put together the Summer he knew with the woman he saw before him.

"You didn't go outside?" the inspector asked Summer.

"No."

Kilbride turned to Phaedra. "You told us you were on the terrace the entire time, Mrs. Meyers."

"That's right," she replied. "Reading and enjoying the sunny day. And you were with me most of that time, remember."

"Quite so. As I recall, the terrace provides a good view of the grounds. Did you see any of this group while you were out there?"

She looked upward to dredge her memory, and then turned back to the inspector. "Well, I was mostly thumbing through my magazines. But I did see Chase at one point, walking across the lawn. And, of course, my husband was with me for a bit. I believe I also spotted Mr. Barker. And Sally too, I think. It's so hard to be sure."

Barker spoke up. "Yes, I went out. I was restless and needed some fresh air. I didn't go far. Just around the edge of the property, past the fishpond, and along the border of the forest."

"Did you see anyone on this stroll of yours?" Kilbride asked.

"A few people I didn't know," he drawled. "There wasn't anyone from our group—well, no, let me correct that, I did see Chase."

"When did you return to the hotel?"

"I wasn't out long," Barker replied. "Perhaps ten minutes. I came back and went to my room for a nap."

"Just so," the inspector said. Turning toward Billie, he asked, "And you, Miss Mondreau?"

"Yes, I went outside too. Chase suggested I try the garden maze, and it sounded like a good idea."

I wondered how I'd missed her.

"Not only that," Billie continued, "but I met Mr. Chambers there."

The group began buzzing again.

"Did you indeed?" Kilbride asked. "Can you tell us about that encounter?"

"Certainly. I didn't know who he was at the time, of course. I ran into him not long after I entered the maze and began the trial-and-error process of getting to the center. I bumped into him, we introduced ourselves, and because we were both frustrated at all the wrong turns we were making, we decided to team up. It was a lot of fun; he was such a nice man." Her voice caught in her throat. "I can't believe he was killed just afterward."

"At what point did you and Mr. Chambers part company?" Kilbride asked.

"Well, we reached the center, where there's a little tree and a bench. I was relieved to have solved the puzzle and went to head back to the hotel, but he wanted to stay there for a while. So I came back alone. And no, I didn't see anyone else. That is, not in the maze."

Kilbride asked, "Did you see anyone outside of the maze?"

"Yes, I saw Mr. Barker on his way to the pond. And Miss Anders was walking toward the hotel, but coming from the front."

If I'd been a disinterested third party, I couldn't have failed to notice that here we had someone who had been very close by when two men had been murdered, within days of one another. How could that not look suspicious? Of course, this was Billie, my dear walking companion, but I can't pretend that it didn't give me pause.

The inspector turned toward Sally, perched on a divan.

"She's right," Sally said. "I'm an outdoors type and can't stand being confined inside too long, so I went out. I didn't really have a route in mind. I just wandered."

"And did you see anyone as you . . . wandered?" Kilbride asked.

She thought a moment and shook her head. "Not anyone from our group, no."

"Did your wanderings take you into the maze?"

Sally's lips pursed. "No. I walked toward the coastal path. But I didn't get far. I stopped at the hotel property line, where the path is less maintained. I'd suddenly become confused about direction. As you can imagine, this whole experience has been overwhelming to me. I decided to return to the hotel."

"When did you arrive back here?"

Sally thought. "Well, you saw me. I returned just as the . . . police van pulled up."

The inspector paused and tapped his thumbs together. "I trust all of you are telling me the truth this time. As you know, some of you have had difficulty doing that."

He paused to let this comment sink in.

"But this is even crazier than Gretz's murder," Brett said. "Sure, one of us may have been nuts enough to kill Gretz because he was such a jerk, but how could any of us have known this Chambers guy?"

"Mr. Chambers happened to manage some of Mr. Gretz's nursing homes here in the UK," the inspector divulged.

Brett gave a whistle. "Wow. So there *is* a connection. Probably the same guy killed them both."

"Or woman," Billie added.

"Let's not jump to conclusions," Kilbride said. "But it does make me ask if any of you knew Mr. Chambers. Such as you, Mrs. Gretz."

Summer assumed a look of shocked innocence. "Me? How would I know him?"

"He did, as I just mentioned, work for your husband."

"I never met any of my husband's business associates. I told you that the other day. And I certainly wouldn't have met any who work outside the US."

"Pardon me for being insolent," Phaedra said, "but why are you standing here grilling us like this? A man has just been murdered, and my husband is missing. Why aren't you out looking for him? For all we know, he may have been killed as well!"

"I share your concern," Kilbride said. "The constable is organizing a search of the grounds as we speak. But your husband's disappearance is concerning in another way as well. When someone disappears after a murder, it raises suspicions."

"Please be serious," Phaedra scoffed. "You think Justin could murder someone? I would tell you he wouldn't hurt a fly, but in Justin's case, it's more than a cliché. Whenever there's a fly around, he always asks me to kill it. He can't work up the nerve."

"It's not a question of nerve, my dear," a voice said from across the room.

We all turned to see Justin Meyers in the doorway.

"It's a question of killing a living thing," he said. "I just can't bring myself to do it."

Chapter 29

"Where in God's name have you been?" Phaedra raged at her husband. "Don't you know people are getting killed around here left and right?"

"Has there been another murder?" Justin asked, wide-eyed. He removed his knapsack and went to sit beside his wife. "That must explain the police van outside."

"Brilliant deduction, sweetie," Phaedra said. "And because you were out running around God knows where, you're now suspect number one!"

"That is not necessarily the case, Mrs. Meyers," Kilbride said. "But I do need to learn where you have been these past few hours, Mr. Meyers."

"Well, I certainly wasn't *murdering* anyone," Justin protested. "I just took a walk into town."

"That's four miles away!" Sally said.

Justin shrugged. "I didn't know how far it was. I had a mission to perform."

"What sort of mission, Mr. Meyers?" the inspector asked.

Justin noticed all eyes were on him. He pulled a gift-wrapped box from his knapsack and held it out to Phaedra.

"This is for you, dear," he said. "It's our anniversary, you know."

A smile formed as she took the box. "Well, it's actually tomorrow. But this is the closest you've ever come. How sweet. Should I open it now?"

"Just go on and open it!" Corky said. "I'm dying to see what it is."

"Please don't mention the word 'dying,'" Phaedra said as she untied the ribbon, tore off the wrapping paper, and opened the box. "Darling, this is gorgeous," she said as she held a small crystal otter figurine up to the light. "It's perfect for my collection." She leaned and gave Justin a kiss.

"That was very thoughtful of you, Mr. Meyers," Kilbride said. "But I have questions to ask beyond your walk into town—which we will verify, by the way, from the shop where you claim you purchased your wife's gift. Would you join us in the interview room, please?"

With a questioning look to his wife, he stood.

Phaedra also got to her feet. "I'm coming too. Whatever you say to my husband, you say to me."

Her demand could have easily been overridden, but Kilbride nodded and led the Meyerses off, followed by DC Bright and me.

Once in the game room, Justin asked, "So who got murdered this time? It couldn't have been another one of our group. I just saw them all in the parlor."

"Please be seated," Kilbride said calmly. After Bright rummaged to find another chair for Phaedra, all five of us sat.

The inspector said, "Constable, would you turn on the recorder?" He announced the date and who he was questioning, and to Justin he said, "The murdered man was David Chambers. I believe you're acquainted with him?"

Justin's mouth flew open. "*Chambers?* Of course, I know him! He's been killed? You can't be serious!"

"I'm very serious. Why didn't you tell us about your business association with Mr. Gretz's firm when we questioned you earlier?"

Justin saw Phaedra's glare and took a deep breath. "Okay, you've got me. I should have come clean about the whole thing. Here's the story. When my wife and I developed our Enviro-Plus program a couple of years ago, I began making inquiries at various venues, including large senior-care organizations, to see if they would consider running it as a trial. It was tough going at first—the program is unorthodox, pretty costly, and many think it's a scam—but eventually I found two firms willing to take the plunge."

"These firms included Gretz's?" Kilbride asked.

"Well, that's it, you see," Justin said, shifting in his chair. "One of the firms backed out of the deal, and the other— Gretz's—agreed to test Enviro-Plus, but at only one facility, Starling House, here in England."

He took a breath. "It was disappointing, yet not exactly the end of the world. All we needed was just one facility to run the program for a year. We were confident that the results would be impressive enough for us to take it forward and obtain other clients. And the results were not just good; they were fantastic. Beyond our wildest dreams, as a matter of fact."

Kilbride studied his ever-present notepad. "Then you discovered that Gretz was planning on terminating the program before the year was out, because it was too expensive."

"Insane, right?" Justin said. "Just as it was showing results! The test phase had only one month to go . . . and if it didn't run its entire course, we wouldn't be able to adequately document its effect. Essentially, that would ruin us." He looked plaintively at the inspector. "Well, I couldn't just sit quietly by and let that happen, could I? Trouble is, I'd never dealt with Mr. Gretz directly, just with his go-betweens. Gretz was the one calling the shots. I knew I would have to plead our case with him directly, face-to-face."

"And you never discussed this with your wife?" Kilbride asked.

Justin looked contrite. "It sounds cowardly to say I didn't want to worry her, but that's the truth of it. As you may have noticed, she's easily excitable." Phaedra's nostrils flared, but she remained silent.

Relieved that he wasn't going to get another tongue-lashing, Justin continued. "So I made inquiries with Gretz's office to set up a meeting. But his secretary kept putting me off. Then I learned that he was going to be out of the office for a stretch, on this walking tour. Well, my wife and I have taken walking trips before, so I thought . . ."

"You thought you would come over and catch Gretz unawares?" Kilbride asked.

Justin looked down. "Something like that, yes. But I just wanted to talk with the man! Wait until he was relaxed after dinner or a drink and sit down with him and make him listen to reason. Honestly! I would never consider *killing* the guy."

"Not even if he could . . . as you just put it . . . ruin you?"

Justin held out his hands. "I know it looks fishy, but I'm not a murderer, Inspector."

The inspector raised his eyebrows. I had seen Kilbride undertake this ploy enough times to understand its intended effect—intimidation. Justin could see that the inspector wasn't buying his denial.

I asked, "Were you also planning to meet with Mr. Chambers while you were here?"

Justin gave a nod. "Yes, but only after I had a chance to

speak with Gretz. Chambers said he was trying to come up with his own solution, but I honestly believed that if I showed Gretz how the success of Enviro-Plus would be the best publicity Golden Sunset could ever have, he would change his mind in a flash. Of course, this was before I actually met the guy and saw what an ass he was. There was no way in hell appealing to his higher nature—reminding him of the lives we were turning around—was going to change his mind. But again, I have to say this. *I didn't kill him.*"

"Nevertheless, you agree that his death makes things . . . better for you?" Kilbride said.

"I won't deny that. When I heard that Gretz was dead, I could barely keep from jumping for joy. I thought that maybe whoever takes his place will be willing to listen to reason. But why would I want to kill Chambers? He was trying to *help* us."

Kilbride maintained a poker face. "Two murders within three days—and both victims associated with the same business venture—is more of a coincidence than I'm willing to accept, Mr. Meyers."

Justin fished a small slip of paper from his pocket and held it out to the inspector. "Here's the receipt for the otter. It shows I bought it about an hour and half ago. It's proof I couldn't have been anywhere near here when Chambers was killed."

Kilbride took the receipt. "Thank you, but we'll still need to check it out."

"There's also something you've overlooked, all of you," Phaedra said. "If it was either my husband's intent—or mine—to kill Gretz, why would I have gone out of my way to save his life?"

Justin's face lit up. "That's right! Phaedra performed the Heimlich maneuver on Gretz that first night, after he'd choked on that bone at dinner. If our plan was to murder him, why didn't she simply let him die at the hands of bad luck?"

Here was my opportunity. "Was it really 'bad luck' that Gretz swallowed that bone, Mr. Meyers?"

Justin's eyes darted to me. "What do you mean?"

"It struck me at the time your wife was a little too quick to rescue Gretz. I was sitting right beside him, yet she was on her feet even before I realized he was choking. It was as if *she knew what was going to happen.*"

"That's preposterous!" Phaedra bellowed. "I . . . I saw him spoon up the bone and was afraid he might choke to death."

"Yes, you were afraid, perhaps, but not because you saw Gretz spoon up the bone. You see, you were seated at my other side. You couldn't have seen him. I was blocking your line of vision."

Her outrage faded. "But . . . but—"

"So you kept your ears peeled. You may even have turned your chair so you could make a quick dash at the first sign Gretz was in trouble. It was as if *you had put the bone in his bisque yourself.*"

Phaedra looked at Justin. He returned her look with as much incredulity as she had shown him. For once, she was at a loss for words. After closing her eyes briefly, she turned toward me and nodded. "Yes, what you say is correct."

Both the inspector's and Justin's mouth dropped open.

"Darling?" Justin said. "Please tell me this isn't true!"

"I only wanted to give the old bastard a fright!" Phaedra said. "But *only* a fright. Why would I have saved him if my intention was to kill him?"

"But the man held the key to our future!" Justin said.

Phaedra turned on him. "Well, how was I to know that? You didn't confide in your own wife that you knew the man! I thought he was just some schmuck who deserved to suffer like he was making us suffer. I hoped he would get scared off and leave the rest of us to enjoy the week in peace."

As absurd as the story sounded, it made as much sense as Corky encouraging Gretz to sit on the crumbling ledge. And it had worked. Gretz got scared alright.

Phaedra saw our astonishment. "Crazy, right? I'll admit I didn't think it through; I saw the bone sitting on a plate and just seized the opportunity. Of course, if it had scared Gretz enough to go home, he wouldn't have been around to be pushed off a cliff, would he? I would have saved his life *twice*."

Leave it to Phaedra to turn a potential assault charge into a reason to be congratulated. I had one more question to ask and turned toward Justin. "Had you corresponded directly with Mr. Gretz, Mr. Meyers?"

"Corresponded? No way. My only contact with his firm was through Mr. Chambers."

"Then you hadn't been sending Gretz any emails or texts?"

Justin shook his head.

The five of us sat silent. The inspector pocketed his notepad. "Very well, then, Mr. Meyers, Mrs. Meyers. I think we're finished for now. Even in view of what you have just shared, you should still consider yourselves under suspicion."

"We understand," Justin said.

"Is there any other information you've been keeping from us?"

"Nothing else, Inspector," Phaedra said. "I'm sorry my husband and I haven't been completely on the up-and-up."

After the Meyerses left, Kilbride said, "This is the looniest investigation I've ever seen. We have two suspects who staged 'accidents' that could well have killed Gretz, yet who claim they only wanted to frighten him. Incredible."

"It does buck the odds." I didn't add that a third such suspect was waiting in the wings.

"Don't forget we now have two *actual* murders, Inspector," Bright said.

Kilbride withdrew his pipe and began rolling the stem between his fingers. "Yes. We have two intentional accidents and two homicides, all possibly committed by different people. Before today, I would have said such a thing was impossible. Now I'm not so sure."

I couldn't blame him for being incredulous. The odds that two murders, committed within days of each other, in a remote part of the country, were the work of two different killers did seem highly unlikely. To solve that riddle, however, I needed to settle another matter. "Shouldn't we speak with Lucien Barker?" I asked. "He also wasn't honest with us about his motivation for coming on this tour."

Kilbride pocketed his pipe and withdrew his notepad. "Good Lord, I'd forgotten about that bloke. Bright, could you locate Mr. Barker and bring him to us?"

Within minutes, Bright came in with Barker, bearing the same why-do-you-need-to-speak-with-me-again look we had seen on the Nielsens and the Meyerses. He lowered himself onto a chair. "I've told you everything I know. I resent being treated like a criminal."

"And I resent being misled," the inspector replied.

"Misled?" Barker asked indignantly.

"We've discovered that you are engaged in a legal battle with a relation here in Devon. Therefore, the purpose of your visit is not entirely recreational after all, is it?"

Barker's eyes traveled to me and back. "I suppose Mr. Chasen told you of our conversation this morning. Very well, then. I admit I was wrong to withhold that information. But it has nothing to do with Mr. Gretz or this other gentleman who was killed today."

"When a suspect tells us one lie, it's logical to assume that he may have told us another," Kilbride said. "We have learned that you have made threats against your aunt. That suggests that violence is not alien to your nature."

His eyes lit up with fire. "Did she tell you that? The witch!" He took a moment to compose himself. "Sorry. I was letting my emotions get the better of me. But my aunt is trying to steal my mother's estate by pitting British estate law against US law. The unfairness of it all makes me lose my self-control sometimes."

"Such as the other day, on the cliff path?"

"I was nowhere near Mr. Gretz on the cliff path."

His words that morning came back to me. *I know how losing a family member can stir up the urge to kill. It is frightening how easily that can happen.*

I said, "This morning you spoke of murder in very personal terms, as though it has crossed your mind."

"I don't deny it," Barker said. "I was sickened at how my mother was treated at that rat's nest of a nursing home. But the only other facilities available were too expensive. I continued to complain, and although the staff never did anything actually prosecutable, I'm convinced that their incompetence directly led to her death."

"I imagine that would be upsetting," I said.

"Go ahead and imagine. You wouldn't even come close to how incensed I was. I wanted to buy a gun and mow them all down." He paused for a moment. "I'm saying that figuratively, of course. I would never do any such thing."

"Even if you discovered your mother's nursing home was, in fact, one of Mr. Gretz's?" I asked.

Barker's eyes flashed. "That's not true, is it?"

"You honestly didn't know?" the inspector asked.

"I had no idea! Now I'm even happier someone did him in. I'd like to shake that person's hand."

"All the same, you seemed very angry just to learn Mr. Gretz was in the nursing home business," I noted.

"It's a sore point with me, as I said."

"Did that make you 'lose it' with Gretz?" I asked. "That first day on the trail?"

Barker stiffened. "What do you mean?"

I leaned forward. "When we paused for the midmorning refreshments that day, I saw you hand Gretz a cup of the blueberry water. That struck me as a somewhat strange gesture to make for someone you consider 'detestable.' "

Barker's eyes narrowed.

I continued. "It was only minutes later that Gretz collapsed on the trail. You ran over and handed him your water bottle. That too seemed out of character."

Barker began taking short, nervous breaths.

"That morning you told me you had brought with you a powerful sleep medication to help with your insomnia. You said it put you right out. What was it called, Mr. Barker? Andorphinol, by any chance?"

Barker paused before giving a short, jerky nod.

"It was interesting, therefore, that traces of andorphinol were found in Gretz's system by the county coroner."

Barker raised a trembling hand to his face, which was dampening and reddening. He was silent for several moments before saying, "Gretz was a genuinely nasty individual, mean-spirited and selfish. The prospect of spending a whole week with him was intolerable."

Kilbride and I traded glances.

"So, I thought, what if he discovered that he wasn't physically up to this walk? He might call the whole thing off and go home. That's when I came up with a plan. I know what andorphinol can do—slow down responses, cause sluggishness. I slipped just enough into Gretz's drink to knock him out. When I saw him fall on the trail, I rushed over to give him water, quick hydration to bring him around."

I looked at Kilbride. His jaw had dropped again.

"But I didn't want to *kill* him, for Christ's sake!" Barker continued. "He had a harmless fall onto the trail. So what? He wasn't hurt. And it certainly doesn't mean I pushed him off that cliff. If I really had intended to kill him, I would have increased the dose of sleeping medication. That would have been much easier to pass off as an accident. The old coot must have been taking a lot of drugs anyway."

Kilbride threw his notepad on the floor and shot to his feet. "This really takes the biscuit! Now there are *three* of you!"

"I'm sorry?" Barker asked.

The inspector looked like he might burst a blood vessel. "What in the blazes is going on here? Was Gretz the sort of chap everyone met and said, 'What a rotter, I think I'll have a go at him!?' Is this some new American craze? We have three people, in the same bunch, all of whom claim not to be murderers, yet who've all done a bloody good job of trying to be just that. It's insane!"

I had to agree it sounded nuts. "But someone *did* kill Gretz," I reminded Kilbride. "If we accept that there have been three separate attempts to merely spook him, made by three separate individuals, then, as impossible as it seems, we have to allow for the possibility of a fourth. Maybe someone whose goal was more sinister."

Bright reached down, picked up Kilbride's notepad, and handed it to the inspector. He took it, studied it for a few moments, then looked up. "Very well, Mr. Barker. Thank you for your input. We will let you know if we need to question you further."

Barker rose and left the room. DC Bright switched off the recorder. "So that's it for now, sir, isn't it?"

"Almost," Kilbride said. "I still need to have a word with Mr. Crane."

In the whirlwind of these revelations, I'd forgotten about Howie.

"Mr. Crane?" Bright said. "Dunno if he's still about."

"Well, find him if you can," Kilbride said.

Within minutes, he returned with Howie.

"You wanted to see me?" he asked, clearly puzzled. "I just made arrangements for the group's dinner and was about to leave."

"This will only take a second, Mr. Crane. I have one additional question to ask you about your whereabouts the afternoon of the murder."

Howie gave a quick shrug. "But I've already told you, haven't I? I was in the van listening to the football game."

"Indeed? Then why were you not in the van when Miss Nielsen came to join you?"

Howie's eyes widened in surprise. "*What?*" His features abruptly eased, and a small smile formed. "Oh, right, right. I remember now. I needed to dash off to the loo. I always like to enjoy a beer when I'm listening to a game. I completely forgot."

I eyed the inspector to see if he was buying this. Howie's excuse seemed plausible, but his failure to mention it before was suspicious.

"I see," the inspector said. "Is there anything else you may have . . . forgotten?"

"Now, listen here. Other than for a run to the loo, I was in that van the entire time. If you don't believe me, find someone who can prove different."

The inspector paused before saying, "That will be all for now, Mr. Crane." Howie marched away with no further comment.

Kilbride sat. "What a muddle this whole situation is. I've never felt more at sea."

I refused to be discouraged. "I'm not sure if this applies to cricket over here, but one of the reasons that baseball is America's national pastime is that it's eternally hopeful. Each team always has a chance to make a comeback. And that's what we'll do."

"I wish I had your optimism," the inspector grumbled. "But if one of those three didn't kill Mr. Gretz, who in the blazes did?"

I walked to the window and looked out at the waning rays of sunlight playing upon the lawn. "It took courage for all three to confess to their attack, especially during a murder investigation. Would they have done that, though, even when provoked, if any *were* Gretz's killer? Or Chambers's?"

"You may be correct," Kilbride said resignedly. "Truth be told, none seem like the type who could crack open someone's skull with a heavy stone. But, mostly, I'm exhausted by all this deception. The next thing we'll discover is that Mr. Gretz was suspect number one in one of your past cases, Mr. Chasen, and you've come over here to finally nab him yourself."

I smiled. "I don't believe in meting out justice myself. I prefer that the courts take on that role."

Kilbride stood, stretched, and turned to DC Bright. "Let's be off, Constable. We still need to check with the coroner's office and see if he's learned anything new after examining Mr. Chambers's body, as unlikely as that might be. We will confer again in the morning, Mr. Chasen. Toodle pip!"

I was about to leave as well when I saw that the inspector had left Justin's store receipt on his chair. I picked it up and shut off the light as I left the room.

Chapter 30

When I returned to the parlor, it seemed as if no one had moved. Each member of the group was seated in the same place as when I had left, engaged in the same activity, and bearing the same expression—anxiety, boredom, aloofness. It was if I was viewing a painting entitled *Suspects in Repose.*

"We feel like inmates," Phaedra said when she saw me. "How much longer are we going to be cooped up here? What if they never find the murderer?"

I understood her frustration. "I can't answer that for sure. This second murder has made everything tougher. And there have been other complications."

"That's ridiculous," Brett said. "What 'complications'?"

I lasered my eyes into his. "Go on, hazard a guess. Unless you don't consider lying and making misleading statements 'complications.' "

Brett turned away. The others fell into a nervous silence.

Corky walked to the window and looked out on the evening shadows lengthening over the lawn and gardens. "This is all so wrong. Today would have been our last day, walking over the Quantock Hills. It would have been beautiful."

Brett checked his watch and mentioned that dinner service at the restaurant would soon begin and he wanted to try its nightly special. As the group began to stand and disperse, Billie approached me.

"Have time for a chat over dinner in the bar? Bar food sounds more comforting to me tonight than another Michelin-star meal."

"If it involves a beer, I do."

In the bar, I ordered steak and ale pies for us, and we carried our drinks to a table near the fire. Billie took a large gulp of ale, paused to enjoy its soothing taste. "I felt bad about Gretz's murder, even though he was disagreeable, to put it mildly. But this second murder feels worse. I didn't really know this Chambers fellow either, but he struck me as a good sort."

"He did seem to genuinely care about the 'guests' in his facilities," I acknowledged.

"I suppose I shouldn't judge murder victims. Nobody deserves to be killed, regardless of how objectionable they are. I'm sure Gretz had redeeming qualities buried *somewhere* inside."

The server brought our orders. I pensively ate a forkful of pie. "There's one thing this second murder gives us, though—a chance to compare motives and see where they might overlap."

Billie nodded.

"And here's additional information for you to chew on," I added, proceeding to tell her about the "accidents" concocted by the Nielsens, Barker, and the Meyerses to "scare" Gretz. I also told her about the Meyerses' connection with Gretz's business and that Barker's mother had been housed at one of Gretz's facilities.

Her forkful of pie froze halfway to her face. "For goodness' sake, Chase, what a bunch! And they did all of that just to scare Gretz? I didn't care for him, but I never considered *hurting* him."

"And if you had, you wouldn't have lied about it. The thing about lies is that they're like potato chips. People rarely stop at just one. They keep lying to cover up the previous lie."

"And that makes lying about a murder only that much easier," Billie said.

"Very true. Let's cut through the lies and look at motives for killing Gretz. We already know about Summer's; she inherits a pile from him. I'm not as sold on her as the others are, but money is a time-tested motive. Let's look at the rest of our group again. What about Brett Nielsen?"

Billie waved her fork. "Simple. He wanted to get Gretz out of the way so he could marry Summer, get her money, and pay off his debts."

"Possible, but Summer told me that while she's willing to share her bed with him, his appeal doesn't seem to extend much further."

"That doesn't surprise me."

I took a swig of ale. "Another possible motive for Brett is that he discovered Gretz was actually his long-lost father and he would be in line for an inheritance when the old guy kicked the bucket."

"That also makes him even more of a prime suspect than he is now. What about his sister?"

"Corky? Well, she's wanted to enact revenge on her long-lost father, who deserted her when she was little."

Billie nodded. "It could also be another motive for Brett to kill him as well."

"Then there's Lucien Barker," I said. "He may have been harboring a grudge against Gretz because his company ran the nursing home he blames for his mother's death. Although he claims not to have known that."

"Let's not forget the Meyerses," Billie said. "One of them—or both together—might have wanted Gretz out of the way because he pulled the plug on the program that might be their ticket to success."

"Agreed," I said. "But there's one big problem with looking at them as murder suspects."

"Yes, I know. Each of them directly or indirectly also saved Gretz's life, which is not something a murderer would do for their intended victim."

I narrowed my eyes. "What if the killer is someone we haven't suspected at all?"

"You mean like Howie? Or Sally? They're Brits; how would they have any connection with Gretz? And, as employees of the Wanderers, why would they put their job in danger by bumping off a client?"

I nibbled on a bite of pie. "Howie had that scuffle with Gretz on the second day, and he wasn't in the van when Corky arrived after doing the shops. He strikes me as someone who's quick to anger, and who definitely holds a grudge. And what do we really know about Sally? She joined the Wanderers only a few weeks ago. She was looking to have a big success with her first assignment, and what happens? She gets stuck with this grumpy old coot intent on spoiling everyone's fun."

"Yes, but then there's Chambers," Billie said. "That changes everything. Why would any of these people want *him* out of the way? The Meyerses certainly wouldn't, given that he was an advocate of their program. The Nielsens have no connection to him, and neither does Barker. It's possible, I suppose, that Sally or Howie may have encountered the man at some point; he was British and one of his facilities was nearby. But why kill him?"

"Good point. Plus, we always come back to the mystery man on the trail. Since we know absolutely nothing about him, it's possible that he had some connection with both Gretz and Chambers."

"Except he, whoever he is, wasn't seen anywhere near the garden maze when Chambers was killed," Billie pointed out.

The wheels in my mind were spinning. "Let's go back to Gretz's murder. Howie could have snuck back on the trail, caught up with Gretz, given him that fatal shove. It was just bad luck that he didn't get back to the van before Corky."

Billie nodded. "But what about Sally?"

I paused to think. "She could have snared this job precisely in order to kill him. She's familiar with the countryside. She would know the perfect spot to give the old man a push."

"But why? And how?" Billie asked. "We know she was at the front of the pack. If she's the killer, how did she get back to Gretz? She never walked past us."

"That's the big question, isn't it? How could anyone have pushed Gretz without passing someone else on the trail?"

Billie looked slightly deflated. "Besides, Sally was at the Valley of the Rocks when we got there."

I took a swig of ale and thought a moment. "Kilbride's team still has to dig deeper into her history. She mentioned the name of the seaside guesthouse where she worked before joining the Wanderers. I don't know whether Kilbride has followed up on that."

A raucous group entered the bar, discussing the day's World Cup football game. The noise made it difficult for Billie and me to continue our discussion. We finished our meal and went into the foyer.

"Where does our analysis leave us?" Billie asked.

"Not much further along, if you ask me. In the meantime, we should be cautious. There's very likely a killer within our group." I looked around. "I need to move my legs. Would you excuse me?"

Billie gave me a sideways glance. "I know you—that's Chase-speak for needing time to think. But you just admitted there's a killer nearby. Are you sure it's smart to go walking around by yourself?"

I assured her I would be careful. She bid me good night, and I set off down the passageway where I'd come upon Summer and Brett. I began whistling slowly and was well into the second verse when I realized the song was "I'll Never Get Out of This World Alive," which Hank Williams wrote and recorded just a few months before his premature death at age twenty-nine. Small wonder the man drank himself to death; he wrote such dreary songs. I switched to "My Bucket's Got a Hole in It" and continued on, eventually reaching the hotel spa. Inside, I spotted guests pounding away on treadmills and puffing on rowing machines, trying to work off the hotel's rich cuisine. I debated joining them but decided against it. I hadn't brought any workout clothes, in any event.

When I turned to go back to my room, I heard shouting coming from outside the hotel. Through the window, I saw Howie Crane standing face-to-face with a young man I recognized from the hotel staff. I couldn't hear the argument, but Howie was doing most of the shouting. It ended with him giving the young man a rough shove and storming in through the door.

He was startled to see me. "Crikey! It's you, Chase! Standing in the shadows there you look like Hagrid from those Harry Potter films."

Hagrid? Maybe I should work off a few pounds on the treadmill after all. "What was all that fuss about?" I asked, nodding outside.

He seemed momentarily puzzled. "That? Just a spot of bother. The bleedin' valet chap told me I couldn't leave the van in the staff zone. Can you believe it? With all the business the Wanderers bring to this place? I told him to sod off."

I knew he'd done more than that. "What brings you here at this time of night, anyway?"

"I need to make sure arrangements are in order for you lot to stay another day. That's best handled in the flesh with the forgetful nits at this place, I can tell you. Arrange it face-to-face and get everything in writing, that's my rule."

It appeared Howie hadn't spent the day at home, as Sally had suggested. I asked if he'd heard about the second murder.

He nodded. "It's bleedin' awful, isn't it? If you ask me, that second bloke getting killed is all the proof anyone needs that this was the work of a local. None of your group ever could have met that Mr. Chambers." Howie bid me good night and began to walk off.

"Wait a minute," I said. "How did you know his name?"

Howie shrugged. "Must have heard someone mention it. It's the talk of the town, as you might expect. We don't get many murders out here, let alone two in one week." He continued on his way.

I pondered Howie's explanation, which didn't sound wholly convincing, and decided to go outside, where the lad he'd lambasted was leaning against a planter, smoking a cigarette.

"Good evening," I greeted. He barely acknowledged me, possibly still brooding over his encounter with Howie. Did being denied a parking place warrant such a nasty shove? A shove that could have sent the young man tumbling off a cliff, if the setting had been different?

"Looks like you had a nasty dustup with Mr. Crane."

"Filthy bugger," he said. "He always thinks he can park

that blasted van of his wherever he wants. Doesn't seem to realize he's not our only bleedin' customer."

"This happen a lot?"

The lad took a puff of his cigarette and nodded. "All the bloody time. And not just with me, either. The other day he and some bloke almost came to blows when he nosed into a parking space, nearly clipping the front of the man's BMW."

"BMW? Burgundy red?" Chambers was driving such a car.

"That's the one. The bloke yelled at him, and I thought Crane was going to kill the chap."

Howie told me our killer was probably a local . . . like himself. Plus, he must have been near Downsmeade at the time Chambers was killed, not back home in Ilfracombe, as Sally had suggested, if he earlier had had an argument with the man himself. I bid the young man good night and turned to go back inside. I happened to gaze up at the Grange's rooftop, where a CCTV camera was mounted. Looking where it was directed, I saw the path leading to the rear of the property . . . and the garden maze.

Might the CCTV recordings show something useful about the movements of our group right before Chambers's murder? It was worth finding out—but not at that moment. A quick glance at my watch told me that it was later than I'd thought; checking the camera records could wait until the morning.

The hotel was quieter than usual. Passing through the foyer, I spotted the stack of maps on the chair where the group had left them two nights before. I went and thumbed through them, finding mine. I tucked it into my back pocket and continued to my room, but when I stepped outside into the small courtyard, I could hear music and the faint cacophony of voices coming from the Gables restaurant up the hill. Such a gathering seemed rather unusual for a Thursday evening. I walked out onto the main path to get a clearer view; the restaurant was ablaze with lights. Turning to go back to my room, I spotted a directional sign someone had planted beside the path. On it was an arrow pointing ahead beside an image of a crowing rooster.

It was the same rooster I'd seen on the jacket of the man I'd encountered on the path two days before—the day Gretz was killed.

Chapter 31

Thursday, early evening,
Gables Restaurant

Although I'd been looking forward to relaxing in my room, my curiosity about the significance of the rooster—and the chance of discovering the identity of the mystery man on the trail—spurred me to climb up to the restaurant. Once inside, I followed the voices and laughter I'd heard from below and saw they were coming from a group, nearly all men, in the lounge beside the main dining room.

A placard with the rooster image was positioned at the lounge entrance. Above it, lettering read: WELCOME LE COQ SPORTIF SALES STAFF.

So that explained it. Le Coq Sportif is a French firm specializing in sportswear and athletic shoes. I didn't know much beyond that, other than that their products always seemed overpriced to me. I'd certainly forgotten about their rooster logo.

One of the restaurant staff, a young male server I'd seen the first night at dinner, came up to me with a smile. "May I help you, sir?"

I looked beyond him to a group of men, some standing and some seated, all looking well-oiled after a couple hours of drinking. Four in particular were talking and laughing the loudest. The man I sought was on the left.

Again, his resemblance to Doug was undeniable. Thick, jet-black hair; eyebrows that looked as if they had been drawn with a rugged chunk of charcoal; blue eyes that would freeze anyone in their tracks; prominent cheekbones and a firm jawline. As I walked toward him, however, differences became apparent. His face was pitted with blemish scars, his ears were a size too large, and his nose had a barely noticeable bump. Like the other men, he wore a name badge hanging on a lanyard. It identified him as Jacques Fermi.

As I approached, he looked up at me. His smile faded, but a trace remained. "Yes? Do I know you?"

The last connection with Doug was demolished completely by his voice, high-pitched and sibilant, delivered in a French accent, nothing like Doug's commanding baritone.

"You could say we've met," I said. "The other day on the walking path."

He maintained his half smile while he tried to place me. "Ah, yes! On the high cliff! In that awful vapor, no? *C'etait terrible!* And so very dangerous. How do you do? I am Jacques."

"My name is Rick," I said, shaking his hand. I couldn't help but think his accent had to be a put-on, like Summer's old Betty Boop voice.

"You are American, *n'est-ce pas?* Oh, excuse me, these are my associates." He nodded to the men beside him. "Zis is Reek."

The others introduced themselves—they all seemed to be Brits—and were clearly not happy that I'd intruded on their fun. "I hate to intrude," I said, "but would you mind if I borrowed Jacques for a moment? There are a few questions I want to ask. It shouldn't take long."

Jacques gave a perplexed shrug to his workmates and followed me to a quieter corner of the room. "Thank you for the rescue!" he said with a smile. "I love these guys but—*ooof!*—they drink and drink and talk, talk, talk of all the women they will be bringing to their bedrooms tonight, and all the things they will do to satisfy them! *C'est pathetique*, no? I ask you. Where are all these women? There are no women here! But I listen and laugh and laugh because . . . well, it ees my job and, *bien sur*, tonight is the full moon. It turns all men into the wolves, no?"

I gave an accommodating smile, but I needed to bring up the matter at hand. "Have you heard anything about the man who was killed on the cliff path the other day?"

The joviality drained from Jacques's face in an instant. "Ah, *oui*, I hear of this! *C'est tragique, no?* Was this man your friend?"

"Not exactly, no. But I wondered . . . since you were on the path that day around the time he was killed . . ."

"Are you with the police?"

"I . . . I'm helping them in their inquiries."

This seemed to satisfy him. "But, of course, I understand. Well, let me think. I walk on the path that day to get the fresh air, no? I am here to visit the UK sales team; we meet every year, but one can only be in the meeting rooms looking at the sales figures for so long before one . . . how do you say it? 'Flips the lid'?"

I laughed despite myself. "Yes, that's how you say it."

"So I take the afternoon off and go for the walk. Walking is good, no, in the open air? It cleans *les poumons* . . . the lungs." He patted his chest. "But *c'est dommage*! That day, all the vapor, the heavy clouds. On the path, I like to see *les chevres*, the goats. Such comical creatures! But there was so much vapor I could not see *anything*."

Unfortunately, this was what I expected. "And yet the fog did come in patches," I said, "blowing in and then clearing before it came in again. During those periods, did you see anything . . . suspicious?"

"Suspeeshus?" he repeated, looking up in thought. As he continued to ponder, my hopes of learning anything new at this point faded. Then his eyes widened. "*Oui*, I did see something strange. I just remember! The vapor, it went away for a moment, and I look up on the hillside. Eet was very steep, but there was someone coming down; eet was like they were crawling backward. I couldn't believe what I was seeing. And then the vapor, it comes back, and I see no more."

"You definitely saw a person? Not an animal?"

"No, eet was a human being. Most definitely. Wearing a bright green jacket. And not one of ours."

"Could you tell if it was a man or a woman? Big or small?"

Jacques thought some more. "I'm sorry, but I don't remember any more. It happened so quickly. Could it have been the murderer?"

"That's very possible," I said, processing what he'd just told me. "Did you see anything else? Or hear anything?"

He shook his head. "No, I am sorry. My only wish was to get out of the vapor. I kept on walking with much care until I came to the town. What a relief! I treat myself and order a large beer at the next tavern I saw."

I smiled in appreciation. "Thank you for indulging me, Jacques. I won't keep you any longer."

"Have I been a help?"

"I think so, yes."

"That is good. This killer, is he still at large, do you think? Should I be afraid?"

"Just be careful."

Jacques gave me an acknowledging smile that, with his deep blue eyes, nearly convinced me again that I was looking at Doug. It was both eerie and comforting. Even with the differences between the two, Jacques was an attractive man, but not someone with whom I had any interest in cultivating a relationship. I needed to move on to a new chapter in my life. Whether it included Mike remained to be seen.

After getting Jacques's contact information, should the inspector wish to interview him, I left the restaurant and started down the hill to the hotel. The full moon was shining through the trees and bathing the grounds in an ethereal glow. The ruckus from the sales group had died down, replaced by the murmur of a gentle breeze, cool against my face. Despite the tendrils of the investigation still struggling to connect in my mind, the net effect was one of reassurance: all was right with the world, and the right outcome would prevail.

Back in my room, however, doubts renewed themselves. I suspected the end of the investigation was nearing, but whether it would be brought about by Kilbride or myself I couldn't say. Perhaps jotting the day's events down in my journal would lift my spirits. As I did, I realized I still wasn't connecting all the dots, but Jacques's observations on the trail—and a few other pieces of input—suggested new avenues to explore. Knowing a good night's sleep would be the best preparation for a fresh perspective in the morning, I lay down and was out within minutes.

Chapter 32

A crash of thunder jolted me awake. The view from my window revealed a landscape in tumult. Trees were straining in the strong wind, their branches flinging every which way; ink-black clouds roiled in the early-morning sky.

Even with the dismal weather, I felt refreshed and prepared for the day with the same cautious optimism I'd felt the night before. I dressed quickly, grabbed my ordnance map, and headed for the breakfast room. As I crossed the small courtyard to the main building, lightning flashed, and rain began to fall. Normally, I enjoyed storms for their novelty—they're a rarity in the Southern California coastal hills—but here, half a world away, they seemed like a special effect created to underscore the dark turn the week had taken.

In the main house, I spotted Sally coming down the stairs. She was wearing a sports halter and running shorts. "On my way to the spa," she said. "If I can't walk, I need to get my exercise somehow. I'll grab a bite to eat later."

At first, I thought the breakfast room was deserted—it

was still early—and then noticed Corky curled up in a chair at a corner table, engrossed in a book.

"Good morning," I greeted. Startled, she looked up, but her face eased when she saw me. "Morning, Chase! They haven't brought the food out yet. I came out early to finish this book. I started it last night and can't put it down!"

"Those are the best kind."

She held up the cover. "Margery Allingham. Ever read her? This one's great. Her detective just figured it all out."

"Ah, yes. Albert Campion, isn't it? What tipped the old boy off?"

"It's one of those cases where the answer was right under everyone's nose all the time! The murderer had written her daily schedule on a blackboard, and it didn't match up with her alibi. Nobody noticed, even though it was hidden in plain sight. It would be weird if our murderer did anything that dumb, wouldn't it?"

Hidden in plain sight.

"Excuse me." I spun around and returned to the stack of maps on the chair in the foyer. Each was marked with the name of a walking group member—all but one. An idea flashed into my mind. Returning to the breakfast room, I said to Corky, "Hate to bother you again. But I need you to help me with a . . . rather indelicate favor."

Her mouth curved upward in a sly smile. "Ooh, that sounds juicy!"

"Would you still know how to pick the door of a locked room?"

Her smile disappeared. "Why would you ask that? I told you. My life of crime is well behind me."

"Yes, I know. But I need you to resurrect your skills at the moment. Can you come with me?"

She paused to weigh my request. Finally, she sighed, put down her book, and got to her feet. "Okay then. But this had better be good. I was just about to start *Trent's Own Case*."

"I'm afraid I don't know that one."

"From the description on the cover, the detective reminds me of you, actually. Urbane yet down-to-earth."

Her comment intrigued me, but the matter at hand was more pressing. "Please follow me," I said.

Grabbing her purse, she followed me upstairs and down a hallway. "This is the one," I said, stopping in front of a door.

"This is Sally's room, isn't it? You mean you want me to pick this lock?"

"That's right. Sally's at the health spa and should be away for a while. Can you do it?"

She bent and examined the lock. "Locks like this are as easy as pie. But . . . is this some sort of trap? Are you trying to get me into trouble?"

"Not at all, I swear. You'll be helping a police investigation."

After a pause, she said resignedly, "Alright." She pulled a nail file from her purse and crouched down before the lock. After examining it for a few seconds, she inserted the file and began manipulating it. I eyed the end of the hall in the event that Sally should return prematurely from her workout. I was about to ask Corky to speed things up when the lock clicked and the door opened.

"Voilà!" she said.

We entered, and I switched on the light. The room had been attended to by housekeeping: the bed was made, and most surfaces had been cleaned. Sally's open suitcase was resting on a stand, her other effects placed here and there. I quickly spotted what I was after: Sally's folded map on the desk.

I turned to Corky and asked her to position herself near

the door and keep an eye on the hallway in case Sally returned. She peered through the cracked door while I spread
open Sally's map. There it was—exactly what I'd hoped to
find. I placed the map on the bed, pulled out my phone,
and snapped a couple photos. I refolded the map, and after
I'd put it back where I'd found it, Corky called out in a
loud whisper, "She's coming!"

Holy hell! I motioned for her to shut the door and turn
off the light, then took her arm and led her into the clothes
closet just as we heard Sally's key in the door. We'd no
sooner shut the closet door when the room light came on.

It was a tight fit in the closet. Corky and I were wedged
uncomfortably between an ironing board and one of those
room safes that anyone with Corky's skills could break
into in a flash. Its hard edge pressed painfully against my
jaw. I placed my finger to Corky's lips to make sure she
stayed quiet. From the light leaking into the closet, I could
see her eyes were wild with fear. I wasn't hopeful either.
How long would it be before Sally found us? How would
we talk our way out of this?

I was about to panic myself when the room light went
out, and we heard the door shut. Both Corky and I exhaled.

"She must have forgotten something," she said.

"Let's get out of here before she comes back again."

We went into the hallway, shut the door, and made our
way downstairs. Corky's curiosity was at full throttle.
"What did you see on that map?" she asked.

"I can't tell you yet. But it won't be much longer." I
needed to notify Kilbride. What I'd found was telling, but
there were other pieces of the puzzle that hadn't fallen into
place. Think, Chase, *think*!

Corky said, "You're just like the detectives in the mysteries I read. They love to keep everyone in suspense."

When we returned to the breakfast room, the buffet had been filled with the morning's entrees, but no hotel guests had yet appeared.

"Don't tell anyone about our little adventure, okay?" I said.

She took her fingers and zipped them across her closed lips. The breakfast selections looked tempting, but I wanted to send a message to Kilbride. I stepped into the hallway, pulled out my phone, and tried to send off a text, but saw no reception bars on my phone. Near the front desk, I encountered the Meyerses as they came down the staircase.

"Good day," I greeted.

"It'll be a good day if we're finally released from this hoosegow," Phaedra said. "I don't think I can stand being cooped up with that elephant too much longer. Does it look like you and the police are any closer to the solution?"

I paused before responding. "Let me answer that with a qualified yes."

Justin grinned. "Atta boy, Chase! Qualified or unqualified, we knew you'll pull it off."

At the front desk, the clerk noticed me. "Mr. Chasen? Inspector Kilbride called and left this message for you." She handed me a small piece of paper.

> *Heard from Tibbets. Chambers died from a cerebral hemorrhage as a result of a blow to the head.*

No surprise there. I was about to pocket the note when I took another look at it. What did it remind me of?

Of course! Another puzzle piece clicked into place.

I hurried to my room and found my walking jacket in the closet. In one of the pockets, I found the note Sally had given me earlier in the week with the name of the pub-finding app. The writing was in block letters, but they were precisely formed—just like the writing on the threatening note found in Gretz's pocket.

I pulled out my phone, but there was still no signal. I hurried back to the front desk and scribbled out a note:

Just saw an example of Sally Anders's handwriting. It matches that on the note Mike Tibbets found in Gretz's pocket. Also, check on Howie Crane. His temper has got him into trouble before, it seems. Have other info to share too. When can you get here?

I asked the desk clerk to get the message to the inspector somehow.

Now it was just a waiting game.

Chapter 33

Friday, 7:30 a.m.,
Downsmeade Grange Breakfast Room

A steaming cup of coffee had never sounded so appealing. In the breakfast room, I found Billie, absorbed in her knitting, and Phaedra and Justin Meyers huddled over their breakfast plates.

"Try the sausage quiche, Chase," Phaedra said. "It's remarkable—worth a star of its own. Which makes me wonder. Does Michelin take away an establishment's star if two of its customers have been killed?"

"Only if one is the chef," I said, pouring my coffee. I went to sit with Billie. She wore a brown-and-white sweater with a pattern of deer and elk and was steadily working on what looked like a pair of socks. She held up her work for me to see.

"Size twelve, I believe you said?"

I eyed the thick green wool stockings and thought they were hideous. I smiled neutrally and said, "Have you eaten?"

"I wasn't hungry. Just toast and jam. There's too much tension in the air. Don't you feel it? Like the buildup to a crescendo at the end of a symphony."

"I do feel it."

"And today was supposed to be the final day of the walk." She gazed out the window. "I'd been looking forward to the ride on the steam train."

The itinerary had called for us to walk that day over the Quantock Hills, where a restored steam train would have taken us to the coastal town of Dunster near the Devon-Somerset border. Given the nasty turn the weather had taken, it might have been just as well that we were sequestered indoors.

"You'll have another opportunity to take the train," I said, taking a sip of coffee. My eyes closed with pleasure as the warmth spread through me.

Billie eyed me suspiciously. "You're being unusually enigmatic. Do you know more than you're letting on?"

Thunder boomed as I gave a confident smirk. "Let's just say the pieces are coming together."

Her eyes widened. "So you *do* know something!"

I remained silent.

"Give me a clue at least."

"I'll give you four," I said. "Consider these items: mountain goats, room keys, monogrammed luggage, and ordnance maps."

Billie gave a sigh of exasperation. "Goats? Room keys? How am I going to make any sense of that?"

I reached out and tapped her forehead. "It's called deduction, my dear Miss Mondreau."

Through the window came another flash of lightning, followed by a crack of thunder.

Billie's eyes focused on the doorway. "Look who's here."

I was surprised to see Kilbride, his overcoat wet and dripping, standing there. His pipe protruded precariously from his front pocket, and his hair was soaked and stringy. He saw me and Billie and walked over to us.

"Good morning, Inspector," I said with a smile. "Care for

some breakfast? The sausage is particularly tasty this morning. And you look like you could use some warming up."

"No, thanks," he said, eyeing me curiously as he took a seat. "You're awfully chipper this morning. Care to share your secret with me?"

"What's the matter?" I asked. "Did you have a rough night?"

"This case is keeping me up. And then I had to drive here in that blasted storm."

"So you didn't receive the message I just sent?"

"Message? Oh!" Kilbride said, and pulled from his pocket the note I'd given to the desk clerk. "You must mean this. It was handed to me as I came inside. Haven't read it yet. Is it from you?"

"Now that you're here, I can elaborate," I said. "I saw Howie Crane arguing with one of the hotel's valets in the parking area last night, and it seems that's a habit of his. The valet claimed he saw him earlier yesterday in a heated argument with David Chambers."

Kilbride picked up a napkin and attempted to dry off his pipe. "Indeed? Well, I'm one step ahead of you on this one, Chase. I asked our researcher to look into Mr. Crane, and it confirms he is quite the hothead. He's been in trouble with the law many times for letting his temper get the best of him. Nearly bashed some chap's head in once."

"It's always the ones you don't suspect, isn't it?" Billie said.

"And yet he's never actually been convicted of anything," Kilbride added. "Technically speaking, that is."

"He still bears further investigation," I said.

"Don't forget there's still the chance Howie snuck back on the cliff path the day Gretz was killed," Billie pointed out.

"I'm also concerned about Sally," I said, and told of finding her note in my walking jacket. "Her handwriting was in block letters, and looked an awful lot like the writing we found on the note in Gretz's pocket."

"More coincidences," Billie observed. "Or are they?"

"It's hard to think so," I said.

Kilbride held up his pipe to see if there were any places left that needed to be dried. Satisfied there weren't, he placed it back in his pocket and turned back to Billie and me. "Olea did some checking on Miss Anders as well. She spoke with a member of Wanderers management about the circumstances of her hire. The outfit was rather desperate, as you know; the guide who'd been assigned to your walking tour had quit suddenly when a close friend had become ill. As a result, they needed a replacement, and when Miss Anders applied, they didn't dig very deep into her job history. She said she had quit her most recent post because she had lost some close family members and needed to get her mind off of it. Not much to go on, I'm afraid."

Families can be dangerous, Mr. Chasen. It's best not to grow too close to them.

"Well, besides the note I found, here's something else," I said, opening my ordnance map. "This is a map of this area. Right here is the cliff path we walked on Tuesday."

As Billie and the inspector looked at the map, I pulled out my phone and brought up the photo I'd snapped in Sally's room. "And here is the same area shown on Miss Anders's map," I said, pointing to the corner of the image. "Notice anything unusual?"

The inspector peered close. "A section of the path is highlighted on her map."

I nodded. "That section just happens to be the spot where Gretz was pushed to his death."

Kilbride looked at me. "She could have marked this after Gretz's murder, of course. Although I don't see the point. Where did you take this photo?"

I hesitated. "We can talk about that later. But it was Miss Nielsen who made me think of it."

Billie said, "Corky?"

I nodded. "She was reading a mystery in which the murderer was careless; she'd written down an appointment that conflicted with her alibi and left it out in the open for everyone to see. Yet nobody did. That made me wonder if there was something I had seen in plain sight that could shed light on this puzzle—maybe even more than one thing. That's when I remembered our maps. In the confusion over Gretz's death, Sally had left them on a chair in the dining room. That didn't mean much to me at the time, but last night I remembered that she told me how she liked to make notes on her map before a walk. That's why she preferred printed maps to the ones on her mobile. I knew I needed to find hers."

"And where did you find it?" Billie asked.

I was going to have to come clean. I explained how I'd coerced Corky to pick the lock to Sally's room.

Kilbride frowned. "Really, Chase. You could have just asked the front desk clerk for a key."

"On what basis? To her, I'm just another guest. But thinking of locks and keys brought something else to mind. Remember that green jacket in Mr. Nielsen's suitcase? On our first day, Sally offered to help Howie take the suitcases to everyone's room after we arrived. She had access to the room keys because of her role as walk leader. Putting the jacket in his suitcase would have been quick work for her."

Billie whistled. "You're right! Wow. Talk about evidence piling up."

"There's more," I said. "Remember the mystery fellow whom Brett Nielsen and I spotted on the cliff path? Well, he's no longer a mystery. Last night, I ran into him up at the restaurant. He's a somewhat odd Frenchman who's here in England for a business meeting. I asked if he'd noticed anything unusual on the path that day, and he recalled he saw something—or somebody—edging down the rocky slope on the landward side of the trail. At first, he thought it was one of the goats common to the area, but a closer look revealed it was a person. He couldn't tell if it was a man or woman, but they were wearing a bright green jacket."

"Are you serious?" Billie said, her eyes wide. "Then that means—"

I held up my hand for her to let me finish. "When I was talking with her on the first day, Sally said that she applied for the Wanderers job because she'd had experience walking in the countryside and . . . *rock climbing*."

Kilbride mulled this over. "Did she indeed?"

"Billie and I figured that our killer could have hidden in the bushes beside the trail and leapt out when Gretz approached. But if it was Sally, we were stumped how she got to the Valley of the Rocks before us without passing us on the trail."

"Now we know!" Billie said. "I'm a map enthusiast, and I noticed the contour lines on the map in the photograph from Sally's room. The hill beside the trail was steep, but someone with rock-climbing experience could have scurried over it."

I nodded. "And it's a shorter distance to the valley that way than by taking the path."

Kilbride angled his head. "Yes. Well, I grant you that this does not look good for Miss Anders. Yet we still haven't come up with a connection between her and Gretz, not to mention poor Mr. Chambers."

I gave a grudging nod. "True."

Kilbride grunted. "Plus there's still Howie Crane. We

caught him in a lie about being in the van when Corky arrived, and we have heard how his temper frequently goes out of control. There were three in your group who confessed to wanting to make things difficult for Mr. Gretz, don't forget. At this point, I wouldn't be surprised if we have two murderers."

Despite the revelations that had come to light, that still sounded like a stretch.

"We must proceed carefully and thoroughly," Kilbride said. "This looks grim for both Miss Anders and Mr. Crane, but what we have discovered is, nevertheless, circumstantial evidence. I've sent DC Bright to locate the two of them. Oh, here he is now."

The constable approached, sheep-faced. "Haven't been able to find either, sir. Miss Anders is not in her room, nor anywhere downstairs. The Wanderers van is outside, but Mr. Crane is nowhere to be seen."

Billie said, "Sally often stops by the hotel spa before she comes to breakfast."

Bright headed off for the health club and quickly returned. Sally wasn't there either.

"The constable and I will take the car and search the nearby roads," Kilbride said. "Could you remain here, Mr. Chasen, in case either of them returns?"

I agreed, although I knew Sally wasn't the type to walk along paved roads. Wooded trails and hillside paths—or rocky hillsides—were more her style. As for Howie, he was not a walker at all. When Kilbride and Bright left, Billie said, "Do you think Sally or Howie suspected you were on to them, Chase? If so, I'll bet they're a hundred miles away by now."

I chewed my lip, thinking. "I don't believe they're far. Howie would have taken the van if he wanted to get away.

And Sally might have simply walked off somewhere to gather her wits."

"Really?" Billie asked. "In this weather?"

"She's got the gear for it, and once she mentioned to me that she actually likes walking in the rain. In fact—"

Zing! Another thread connected. "I believe I know exactly where she is." I opened my map again. "See that?" I said, pointing out a small bump on the coastline just off the path we had walked the first day.

Billie peered down. "Did we walk there?"

"No, but we weren't far from it. It's a small promontory with a brace of alder trees. It is one of Sally's favorite places. She said she goes there sometimes to . . . how did she put it? . . . look out at the sea and 'have a think,' I believe it was."

"You believe that's where she's gone?"

"I'd bet money on it."

"Phone the inspector then, and tell him before he wastes time driving all over creation."

I folded the map and stuffed it back into my pocket. "No, I'm going to go find her myself."

"Chase, that's crazy! If your suspicions are correct, Sally is dangerous. She may have killed once, and wouldn't hesitate doing the same to you."

Standing, I said, "I know how to take care of myself. And there's no telling what she'd do if she saw a whole gang of police coming after her. No, I'm going to my room to grab my coat. If I'm not back within two hours, please inform the inspector."

Billie grabbed my arm. "I wish you'd rethink this. Are you sure you're not just trying to recapture your past glory? If so, let it go. You don't need to prove anything."

I was about to protest, but her words struck close to

home. Was I doing this for that reason? Doug had often accused me of taking unnecessary chances. And yet, what was wrong with wanting to make a difference? I gave Billie a reassuring smile and walked off.

In my room, I donned my walking jacket and, as I headed outside, reached into the pocket. Sally's note was still there. I took it out and looked at what she'd written. This time, however, I flipped it over.

There was something written there also.

Chapter 34

Friday, midmorning,
North Devon Coast

When our group had walked the coastal path on Monday, Howie had dropped us at the trailhead. Now I had to make it there on my own, and in dicey weather as well. I had just tightened the zipper clasp on my walking jacket and started off toward the path I suspected would take me to the coast when someone behind me called my name. I turned to see Howie, standing not far away, his hands stuffed in his heavy mackintosh coat.

"You're not heading out on the trail, are you, Chase?" he asked. "In this weather?"

How much should I tell him? Howie was still a suspect. I said, "It's important that I find Sally. Have you seen her?"

Howie regarded me curiously. "Why do you need to find her?"

I needed to keep my answer neutral. "Trust me. It's something only she can assist me with. I think she might be near the spot where we had our midmorning break on the first day."

"I'll take you there in my van. I know just where to go. You'll get hopelessly lost if you try to find it on foot."

I needed to make a quick decision. I didn't completely trust Howie, yet he was right; walking on my own, in such bad weather, was a recipe for disaster. If I let him take me, I could reach Sally more quickly, while possibly getting more information from Howie on the way. On the other hand, arriving in the van might tip off Sally as to my approach—perhaps not advisable. Worse yet, there was the possibility that Howie himself might be the killer. How well could I defend myself, trapped in his van? My inability to decide turned into what is known in baseball as a "yip," the sudden inability of a ball player (usually a pitcher or catcher) to throw the ball.

"Come on," Howie urged. "It's getting cold, and you'll catch your death. Let me drive you."

I began following him as a low rumble overhead told me that taking the van was perhaps the best option. Dark clouds were massing, and the last place I wanted to be in a heavy downpour was on a rural trail, especially when I was unsure where I was going. I boarded the van and sat in the front passenger seat.

"This day would have been a right cock-up if the walk were still on, wouldn't it?" Howie said as he pulled the van onto the country road, the wipers slashing in quick rhythm across the windshield. "Can't imagine a bunch of grockles walking in rain like this."

Howie must have known that rain wouldn't have stopped the walk. Even us "grockles" in the group would have been prepared with proper rain gear. Was he new to his job as well?

He glanced at me. "But you're smarter than the rest of that bunch, aren't you? I could see that right off. You're prepared for the rain as much as you're prepared to find the killer. If anyone is going to do that, I keep telling myself, it's gonna be Mr. Chasen. Certainly not that daft police inspector."

He swung the van sharply around a bend, its rear tires sliding on the wet road. I gripped my seat and expected Howie to apologize, but he laughed instead. "No, you're a keen one. No one is going to pull wool over your eyes." He paused. "You probably have even had suspicions about me, have you not?"

I watched the speedometer edge up as he sped along the winding road. "Should you be driving so fast?" I asked.

"Admit it, now. You must have seen how I throw a wobbly now and then, and lose my temper. I'm just the sort of bloke who might lash out in a deadly way, right? You know I fought with Gretz and saw me chewing out that idjit in the car park yesterday. He probably told you I also had words with that bloke who was killed in the maze. Doesn't look good for me, does it? But nor does it look good for you. If I were your killer, I'd be in a perfect spot right now, wouldn't I? Here I have the only man who could connect me with those two murder victims, locked in my van, all alone on a country road. What would stop me from giving you a quick push out the door and—"

Howie swung the van to the right, where the dark waters of the Bristol Channel churned beside us at the bottom of a high cliff. My fingers tightened on my seat, hoping they would hold me if Howie carried through with his threat. Why hadn't I fastened my seat belt?

Howie slowed the van and let forth a large laugh. "Had you going there, didn't I? You should have seen the look on your face!" He pulled into the clearing where he'd parked on Monday and brought the van to a stop.

Facing me, he said, "Sorry if I gave you a start there, Mr. Chasen. I was only having a little fun. I get my dust up once in a while, but I'm no killer. You know that too, I daresay. If you're looking for Miss Sally, I suppose you have may have your suspicions about her as well. Well, you might be right on that score. There's something not right about that girl."

"What makes you say that?"

"Too many secrets, that one. I like to get to know the guides I work with, you know? I asked Sally about her past job, her family, that kind of thing. Just to be friendly, you know, not a snoop—I'm no curtain twitcher. But she shuts up like a clam. Won't talk about herself at all. She doesn't even share her trail maps with me, which all the other guides are happy to do."

That was interesting. Sally had seemed cryptic with Billie and me as well, if not exactly shutting up like a clam.

"All I'm saying is, watch yourself around her, Mister Chase," Howie said.

"I'll be careful," I promised as I stepped out of the van. "Can you do me another favor? If you see Inspector Kilbride, please let him know where I am."

"That I will do, Mister Chase."

I thanked him and watched him drive off. Turning toward the coastal trail that led from the small clearing where I stood, I was amazed at how different it looked than it had just a few days before. Then it had been cheerful and welcoming; now it seemed dark and ominous. It was disconcerting to realize how quickly rural England, typically so comforting and reassuring, could turn threatening. I scanned the coast in the distance for the small cluster of trees Sally had pointed out—Stanley's Rest, her place of reflection—but the shadows cast by the darkening sky made it difficult to see. Why hadn't I brought binoculars?

I started walking on the coastal path until the group of alders finally came into view, looming like dark guardians in the distance. They were too far away, though, to determine if anyone was beside them.

After walking another minute or so, I spotted a path,

wedged between shrubs and ferns, that looked like it would lead me to the coastal bluff. I set forth along it, taking care not to step on branches or twigs that might signal my approach. With the rain and clouds darkening above, I was reminded of the ominous moors of legend. The wind had become as strong as it had been on the cliff path the day of Gretz's murder, but I was comforted that the sound might likely drown out my footsteps. I gave silent thanks I wasn't plagued by fog and mists this time.

The path took a bend and finally brought me to the other side of the trees that lined the bluff. At first, it didn't appear that anyone was there. Then I spotted a woman standing near the bluff's edge, turned away from me, facing the sea, bundled in a dark blue jacket, her long, brown hair whipping in the wind. It had to be Sally. I proceeded forward, steadily and carefully. When I was almost upon her, my foot stepped on a fallen branch, and it snapped.

She spun around, startled. A smile formed on her face. "Mr. Chasen. You shouldn't be out in this weather. You could catch your death." A gust of wind blew up, and she tightened her arms around her torso.

"It's 'Chase,' remember?"

"Oh yes, of course. My mistake."

"And now, why don't you tell me your name? It certainly isn't Sally Anders."

Her expression slowly morphed into one of surprise. "How . . . how do you know that?"

I stepped closer. "The tag on your luggage was the first tip-off. I noticed it the first day. We had no one in our group with the initials 'A.S.' Shouldn't that have been 'S.A.'? But it became clearer when I learned you had worked at Starling House, Gretz's senior-care facility here in Devon." I withdrew her note from my pocket and held it up. It had the establishment's name engraved right on it, and I hadn't noticed it until that morning.

She took a deep breath and looked up at the sky before returning her steely gaze to me. "I figured I could disappear by changing my name, but I'd forgotten about that notepaper. It's the little things that always trip you up, isn't it?"

It struck me full-on that I had found our killer and was confronting her in a remote spot, miles from anybody. I would have to proceed carefully. "I'd like you to tell me why."

"Why did I kill Gretz? And Chambers?"

"Yes."

She looked toward the sea, and her body shivered. "I'd have thought you would have figured all that out too."

"It's just now coming together. I could make a few informed guesses, but I'd much rather hear it from you."

Another deep breath. "Alice. That's my real name. Alice Sanders."

Sally Anders. Alice Sanders.

"Why not just go on and say it? I've made a proper botch of it, haven't I? I'd never murdered anyone before. It's much more difficult than it looks in films and on television."

"Let's start with Gretz. Why did he need to die?"

The wind blew Sally's hair across her face, and she brushed it away. "It's interesting that you put it that way. Not 'Why did you kill him?' but, 'Why did he need to die?' Because that was really it, you see. He *did* need to die. He was quite evil, you know. And evil must be addressed, even when it is too late."

Rain began to fall. Trembling, Sally plunged her hands into her coat pockets. "I'd been working at Starling House for four years as the night manager. I had grown close to several of the . . . well, they call them 'guests,' but when you care for someone on a daily basis, they become your family. You see, I never had a proper family of my own.

My parents died when I was young. I was raised by a cold uncle, who meant well, I suppose, but who had no interest in looking after a little girl."

Her body trembled again. "The guests at Starling House became my true family. Kindly Mr. Brewster with his chamomile tea—Caroline, who would call me 'Sweet Alice' and regale me with the plot of every torrid romance novel she read—and Mavis, and Jerome . . ." Her words caught in her throat. "And Thalia. Dear Thalia. She would tell me endless stories of her days in the theater . . . she always called me the daughter she never had. . . ."

Sally turned toward the sea again and fought to control her tears. Wiping her eyes, she faced me. "That's something they warn you about, you know—forming close attachments with patients. It's like . . . it's like becoming too close to animals you are raising for the slaughter."

"That's a bleak analogy, isn't it?" I said, raising my voice to be heard.

"I don't think so. That is the way Gretz and his managers viewed our 'guests'—as prisoners on death row awaiting their execution. And don't think I'm exaggerating."

As she spoke, she began a slow, steady rocking motion, stepping from side to side. As it continued, she moved herself steadily backward, toward the edge of the bluff. It was higher than the cliff where Gretz was pushed. Was she doing that intentionally? Suicide might have seemed a more tempting option to her than facing a life in prison.

I needed to keep her talking. "But the guests at Starling House showed remarkable resiliency, didn't they? Because of that wonderful new program they'd introduced?"

"You know about that?" Sally asked, cocking her head. "Yes, that was exactly it. That crazy combination of lighting, music, diet, art made all the difference. I was one of the biggest naysayers about the program at first. It sounded mad, but it didn't take long to see that it was actually working. My darlings were blossoming. Some were even becoming *younger*, engaged in life again. They looked forward to getting up in the morning—something we rarely, if ever, witnessed."

She turned toward the sea and continued her back-and-forth movement. Did she not notice how dangerously close she was to the bluff edge?

"There was only one problem," Sally said.

"That miraculous program cost money." As I spoke, I began inching toward her, preparing to reach out and grasp her should she begin to fall.

She nodded. "Yes, but it wasn't just the cost. It was greed. Gretz wanted to wring every last penny out of the place. Even with the expense of the program, Starling House was still profitable, but it wasn't enough; it's never enough for people like him. When I first heard he intended to do away with it, I was furious. Couldn't he see the good it was doing? That program could be a blessing for thousands! But my protests fell on deaf ears. The managers were on my side, but they were powerless against Gretz. All that mattered to him was money, money, money."

A shadow engulfed us as black clouds gathered above. "And then one day it was all gone," she continued. "It was if someone had turned off a switch. Everything didn't revert to the way it had been instantly, of course—the changes in décor couldn't be easily changed, for example. But everything else—the music programs, special diet, cultural and group activities—stopped. My darlings took it so hard. It was as if their new lease on life had been stripped away. They were inconsolable. I was the only one who cared, the only one who stood up for them. But my love wasn't enough, you see? When they were again brought face-to-face with their mortality, their fragility . . ."

Sobbing, Sally turned away. I struggled to hear her over the wind and rain. "I tried and tried to get my superiors to see reason. I explored every option I could—appealing to the board of directors, the regulatory agencies, family members, everyone. But I got nowhere. In fact, I was regarded as a troublemaker, a pest."

Her left foot backed slightly out over the bluff edge. I jerked my arm forward to grab her, but she stepped forward on firmer ground again. Lifting her head, she said, "It was then that the idea of murder came into my head. I knew Ronald Gretz had to die."

"Did you believe that would fix everything?" I asked.

Sally's face grew solemn, her eyes feral. "I did, actually. His replacement would certainly be more open-minded. But it was a deeper issue, don't you see? Greed is evil. And evil must be dealt with. One mustn't permit it to spread. One mustn't!"

She tightened her arms around herself, while resuming her side-to-side shuffle. "We were a small, trusting group, so it wasn't difficult to check the emails of my managers. I began perusing them and learned that Gretz was coming over here and taking this walking tour. What a stroke of luck! At first, I planned to sign up as a participant. But imagine my surprise when I found that the Wanderers needed a walk leader because theirs had just resigned. I applied for the job. I have the right background, and I knew they'd hire me in a flash."

"You also knew the right spot on the cliff path to attack Gretz," I said. "Just like you know this place."

She nodded. "I chose a spot that would give me cover and allow me to scuttle over to the Valley of the Rocks with no one seeing. I put on that green jacket just in case someone did. Stuffing it into Mr. Nielsen's suitcase was a last-minute improvisation; I hadn't actually planned that. It was rather transparent, though, wasn't it? I would have been better off throwing it away."

"It might have been found."

Rain started coming down in windy sheets. It was growing difficult to hear Sally. "I knew I had to work quickly," she said. "I explored the route of the walk and made a few changes that would bring us along the cliff path."

"Why did you send Gretz those threatening notes?"

Her mouth twisted into a sly smile. "I wanted to make him squirm. I created a fake email account. I knew he'd never figure out who was after him."

"Weren't you concerned he might cancel the trip?"

"That would mean giving in, which wasn't something he would do. I knew he had promised the trip to that new wife of his. Plus, everything was going so perfectly—my getting the job, leading a walk along a trail I've walked dozens of times. Everything was going my way, as if it were ordained. And then those other things began happening to him. It almost seemed as if someone else was trying to kill Gretz *for* me! It was mystifying, but reassuring. For a while, I thought I wouldn't need to do a thing."

Rain splashed against us. "But Gretz was like a cat. He didn't die," I said.

Sally's eyes turned colder. "It didn't matter. I knew what I had to do. The foggy weather on the day we walked the cliff path was a godsend. It made it more likely that I wouldn't be seen. Still, I put on that jacket. It was so easy to hide behind that bush beside the trail, leap out, and give him that shove. His wife was only a few feet away, but she couldn't see or hear me. The old fool didn't know what hit him."

Thunder boomed overhead. Rocking side to side, Sally again edged nearer to the bluff edge, which had become a mush of unstable sludge. "I'd never felt so powerful. I had avenged my darlings, and nobody would ever learn the truth, ever." Her self-satisfied grin then faded. "It was quite a blow to learn that I'd been spotted, though. Even in all that fog. Damn!"

Lightning flashed, and the rain increased. I was feeling

increasingly vulnerable and hoped Kilbride and his team would find us soon. I tightened the hood of my jacket, carefully monitoring Sally's movements while maintaining eye contact.

"After a while, though, it looked like I *would* get away with it," she said. "The police seemed to have no clue at all. Then I ran into Chambers in the maze." The tone of her voice lowered. "He recognized me, of course. 'What on earth are you doing here, Miss Sanders?' I laughed, treating it like an innocent encounter, but I could see him putting it together. What was I—someone he knew very well, someone who had recently caused a row at one of his facilities—doing at that hotel, not far from where his boss was murdered? He wasn't a stupid man. He figured it out. He *knew*."

The wind and rain had become so fierce, and we were so close to the bluff's edge, that we could both have been blown down to our deaths at any moment. Oblivious to the danger, Sally continued relating her tale, almost delighting in getting it out.

"I hurried away from Chambers and, before I realized it, found myself in the center of the maze. I hadn't planned it. I saw the stones around the tree. I picked one up and walked back to him. Before he could see me, I struck him— again, and again, and again. Then I dragged his body into a side passage."

She flashed a triumphant smile. How will she feel, I wondered, when she learns that Chambers was the solution she'd been seeking, that he'd been seeking a way to get the Meyerses' trial program up and running again? I suddenly pitied her: an emotionally needy and fragile young woman, forced to witness the unnecessary decline of loved ones. She'd killed for revenge, out of madness, undoubtedly, but also out of . . . love.

Sally twisted her head and looked at me as if I were a

stranger. In the near darkness, she almost resembled Allison, regarding me with icy hatred, although for an entirely different reason.

"You were the one I was afraid of," she said. "You're smart. I knew that if anybody would find me out, it would be you."

I felt more vulnerable than ever in that godforsaken place. Where the devil was Kilbride?

"The first time I suspected you was right after Chambers was killed," I said, inching toward her. Perhaps I could grab her and get us both out of harm's way. "You came toward me with your hands stuffed in your jacket. It was such a warm day, it seemed strange that you'd be cold. I wondered, could she be hiding something?" I paused. "Perhaps blood?"

Sally's eyes turned cold. "Yes, you're smart, alright. Gretz had to die because he'd killed my family. Chambers had to die because he would have told the inspector about me and they'd lock me away." In a flat voice, cold and direct, she said, "And now you have to die. You know too much."

With a roar, she lunged at me. Startled, I jumped to the side and fell to the ground, one of my legs dangling off the bluff's edge.

Sally had slipped and fallen as well. As I struggled to stand, she reached out, grabbed my foot, and yanked me down again. She tightened her grasp and began pulling me toward her. I struggled to resist, thrashing out my hands at the earth around me, but they could gain no traction in the mud, particularly with Sally using all her strength to counter my actions. She was stronger than she looked; I'd realized that when I'd seen her move the boulder from the opening of the lime kiln.

She continued tugging me toward the edge of the bluff. I struggled to grab something—anything—to hold onto and save myself. At last, my fingers passed over a wet, grassy tuft. It seemed a desperate option, yet I managed to grab hold of it. Sally gave my leg a powerful yank, but my grasp held fast. The tuft did not give. She tried again with no luck. Then she began to pull herself up my side, holding onto my waist, then my arm, and finally my shoulder until her face was beside mine. I could feel the warmth of her breath. What was she planning to do? Roll us both over the bluff together?

The rain intensified, and I felt the tuft loosening. *Damn!* I needed to get Sally off of me, and quickly. I summoned my remaining energy and twisted my body to the right, rolling the two of us far enough away from the bluff for me to reposition myself. When I was able to distance myself a little, I jerked my knee into Sally's side. She screamed and released her hold on me. I scrambled to stand, but slipped down again. She reached out to take hold of my leg again, but I was too far away. I struggled to get to my feet and this time succeeded, stepping quickly back, farther from Sally. Perhaps I could save myself after all.

But she got to her feet as well. We faced one another, both of us breathing heavily. Sally had the advantage: My back was to the bluff. I didn't have much energy left; one quick push would do it. I was prepared to dodge her when I saw her ferocity fade.

In a small girl's voice she said, "I don't want to kill you."

"You don't have to."

The next few moments seemed to pass in an eternity. She visibly wrestled with her next move as I calculated mine. If I made the slightest move, she would react. Her eyes darted back and forth, then lasered into mine with brutal intensity. Just as she was about to act, two arms emerged from the shadows behind her and pulled her back.

It was Kilbride. She screamed, writhed against his hold,

and managed to pull herself free just as a bolt of lightning, its glare illuminating her face, struck the tree beside us, cleaving it in half. As it cracked and fell, Sally let loose a wail, backed toward the edge of the bluff . . . and disappeared.

"No!" I yelled.

Kilbride and I looked down to the roiling, dark surf below where Sally's body was being tossed, lifeless, in the murky foam.

That night, pen poised over my journal, I resisted putting down everything that had gone through my mind during my struggle with Sally on the cliff. Death had never seemed so close. Many images had flashed through my muddled consciousness—Doug, Billie, Allison, and others who might miss me. I even had seen Mike. I thought of how my legacy would be forever tarnished by a case that finally proved too much for me. Fortunately, my top-of-mind thoughts at the time were about how to survive. And it was thanks to those, plus a little help from the inspector, that I was safe and warm in my hotel room.

Aside from relief and gratitude, I felt something else. I had pinpointed the murderer, and I felt vindicated. I had proven my faith in Summer Gretz, who wasn't the culprit, even though all the others believed otherwise. I'd also fulfilled, in a way, my duty to Gretz. I might not have been able to prevent his murder, but I helped bring his killer to justice, or a semblance of it. My old instincts were still in good shape. I could still *detect*. I could still perceive innocence where others saw guilt and examine clues to track down a killer. I wasn't an over-the-hill, past-his-prime old fossil after all.

There was life left in me yet. It would be a life without Doug, but I now knew that was not a death sentence. I could still cherish Doug's memory and move on to create other memories. Whether they included Mike, I couldn't tell. But that was outside of my control.

Earlier that evening, I had enjoyed a celebratory quaff of ale with Kilbride, Bright, and Billie at the Quarryman. After giving Billie a blow-by-blow account of my battle with Sally, including the well-timed lightning strike that provoked the leap to her death ("How biblical," Billie commented), I texted Mike to inform him of my narrow escape. He didn't respond. Putting away my journal, I checked my phone again, but saw no reply. My spirits fell, but I was determined not to let that bring me down. I was alive, and that was a precious gift. With a silent prayer of thanks, I slipped under the covers and turned off the bedside light.

Chapter 35

Saturday, morning,
Downsmeade Grange

Iwheeled my suitcase into the lobby and glanced at the calendar on the front desk. I could hardly believe it was Saturday. Had only a week passed since this all began? It didn't seem possible. Does murder expand time?

Most of the others were already there. Phaedra and Justin stood near the front door, she checking travel documents and he studying his cell phone. Corky and Brett sat nearby. Barker was discussing his room charges with the desk clerk.

"No, I did not request any Irish coffee to be brought to my room even once, let alone four times!" he protested. "I never drink such foul brew."

"Yes, but Mr. Barker—" the clerk countered, and the argument continued.

I hadn't any room charges to settle, so I put my bag with the others alongside the wall—Sally's noticeably absent—and joined the rest of our group in the foyer. Their mood was a mixture of relief (at the murders being solved), shock (at the identity—and death—of the murderer), sadness (at ending a walking holiday that had involved very little walking), and exhaustion.

It was a contrast to the usual scene on last mornings, typically a succession of semi-sincere farewells and promises to stay in touch with new friends. There was none of that with this bunch. I suspected they were all tired of being cooped up together and couldn't wait to return to their normal lives.

Billie came down the stairs, carrying her astonishingly small travel case. How on earth did she carry all her clothes and knitting supplies in that little thing? I would have to ask her sometime. Even with Doug's help, I never could master the knack of efficient packing.

"I finally heard from Janice," she said in an upbeat tone as she joined me.

"Good news?"

"Great news. They removed the tumor, and it looks like they got all the cancer. It was only a lumpectomy, not a mastectomy."

"That's wonderful. I just wish you hadn't had to carry that worry around with you all this time."

"Tell me about it! One of these days, we'll have a medical-care system like they do over here, and screwups like this won't happen."

I had a feeling her optimism in Britain's National Health Service might be a tad overstated, but I kept quiet.

"You're flying home today, right?" she asked.

"No, I've decided to go to London for a couple of days. Maybe see a West End show or visit some galleries. I want to finish this trip with memories of something other than dead bodies."

"I thought that dreamy coroner was going to show you around."

I tightened my lips and took another glance at my phone. Still nothing from Mike.

"So did I. Guess he had other plans." Mustering a smile, I said, "We'll do this again soon, though, won't we?"

She gave me a hug. "Absolutely. And with a lower body count, God willing."

I saw everyone turn and looked up. Summer was descending the stairs, wearing a stylish white dress with a tasteful pearl necklace and chic white pumps. Her newly dark hair was swept downward in a casual wave. She oozed sophistication.

One of the younger male staff members followed her, carrying her bags, and deposited them by the entrance with the others. As Summer sailed past us, I expected Phaedra to make another cutting remark, but she held her tongue. Summer didn't give her a glance as she walked out the front door, although she did give me a sly wink.

Barker had resolved his conflict with the desk clerk and came over to us. "We're not leaving this hellhole one minute too soon."

" 'Hellhole?' " Brett said. "Isn't that a bit strong? I like this place. Their cell coverage sucks, but they have more than three hundred cable channels."

Barker gave him a harsh up-and-down glance. "Television is for ignoramuses."

"Isn't that 'ignorami'?" Justin asked.

"Whatever," Brett said. "It's what I call a guilty pleasure. You must have a guilty pleasure, Mr. Barker. Now, let me think. What could it possibly be?"

"Brett, please," Corky interceded. "It's our final day. Let's not get into a scuffle. We all—well, most of us, anyway—have been exonerated of murder. Can't you just shake hands and walk away?"

"You're right, sis," Brett said. Extending his hand toward Lucien, he said, "What about it, pal?"

Barker reluctantly shook. A second later, Howie walked in. "We're leaving for the train station in Taunton in six minutes. Everyone into the van!"

We walked out into the bright, sunny morning, none of the previous day's storm in evidence. Howie wheeled the bags to the rear of the van and began loading them in.

Corky and Brett examined their travel documents.

"You said we were traveling first class!" Brett said. "These tickets clearly show that we're in coach."

"What difference does it make?" Corky said. "Everyone's on the same plane, after all. Face it, Brett. If you don't have the money, you can't travel any way you want."

Brett scowled. "Of course, I can. It's just a matter of playing the angles."

"Yeah," Corky scoffed. "Look where playing the angles has gotten you."

I approached them. "I hope you'll return for another English walk. You deserve one with a little more walking and a little less drama."

"That's for sure!" Corky said. "Although it was nice getting involved with a genuine British murder. This is something I can tell my grandchildren."

"Better start having children before planning grandchildren," Brett said.

Corky stuck out her tongue at her brother and turned to me. "Maybe we'll see you again, Chase?"

"I certainly hope so," I said. "Just stay out of trouble, you hear?"

Corky gave me her promise as she and her brother boarded the van.

Summer was a few feet away, taking a last look at Downsmeade. She flashed me a bittersweet smile, and I walked over.

"I will never forget this place, that I can assure you," she said.

"I hope everything works out well for you. But I have the feeling you'll be just fine."

"I owe you big-time for what you've done. You were the only one who stood up for me, and, of course, you were the one who found Ronnie's killer. If you hadn't, I never would have been at peace."

"It wasn't just me," I said. "But I appreciate your kind words." Was this it, the Bill Buckner absolution I had so long been seeking? I'd had many moments of closure in my career, yet Summer's acknowledgment felt particularly gratifying.

Summer and I traded kisses on the cheek as Howie made a last announcement for us to board the van. I was about to follow Summer when a black sedan pulled up and Inspector Kilbride stepped out. What on earth was he doing there?

I went over. "Don't tell me there's been another murder. Did some fiend mistake Constable Bright for an archery target?"

The inspector grinned. "I'm afraid not, Mr. Chasen. I only came to wish you the best of journeys. And to thank you for your inestimable help."

I was taken aback; this was a welcome and unexpected gesture. "Why, thank you. But don't sell yourself short, Inspector. I wouldn't have figured it all out if not for you. And don't forget, you saved my life on the bluff."

Kilbride eyed me with doubt. "That is something of an overstatement. Sheer luck was at work as much as anything else."

We shook hands, and the inspector got back into his car.

"I'm sorry, but I have to ask," I said.

He looked up. "Ask what?"

"What exactly is on your damned notepad? I never once saw you write anything in it."

After a pause, Kilbride pulled it from his jacket pocket and handed it to me. I flipped through the pages—all blank.

"I don't get it," I said. "There's nothing here."

"Why should there be?" he replied, taking the pad and pocketing it. "It is jolly well intimidating enough as it is."

He started his car's engine and flashed me a rare smile. "Toodle pip!" he said and drove away.

I gave a laugh and was about to join the others when I turned to give the hotel one final look. Its gray stone façade and mullioned windows, framed by tendrils of wisteria, gleamed in the morning sun. A wisp of wind ruffled my hair, and a lark somewhere let forth a snippet of song. Glorious. Not hearing from Mike still had me down, but if this was to be my last memory of my walk in Devon, it was a good one.

Inside the van, I wedged myself between Billie and Phaedra. We were bound for the nearest train station, from which we would catch the train to London Heathrow. I would go from there into the city.

Phaedra turned to me. "I never thanked you, Chase. I'm convinced that, if it weren't for you, we'd still be stuck here, being grilled by the inspector."

"I appreciate that, Mrs. Meyers," I said. "I hope you and your husband get your life-enrichment program sorted out. I might want to partake of it myself someday."

She cocked her head. "Didn't we tell you? The future of Enviro-Plus will be sorted out quicker than you think. All thanks to Mrs. Gretz."

"Summer? I don't understand."

Summer, seated in front of us, turned around. "I felt so terrible about what Ron did to the Meyerses. So I figured, well, as his widow, I have some clout with Golden Sunset. I can convince the board to reinstate the Meyerses' program, maybe even expand it. If they put up the slightest resistance, I'll remind them I now hold the controlling shares in the company."

"Summer's been the answer to our prayers," Justin said. "She's inspired Phaedra and me to make Enviro-Plus better than ever, partly because of Sally's passion. Too bad she had to resort to murder to express it."

It was good to hear that Summer and the Meyerses had joined forces and moved on. As had I. Doug would always have a big piece of my heart, but I was turning my focus back to myself.

It didn't take long before we reached the rail station. Everyone got their bags and thanked Howie for his help. My London train was due to leave in a few minutes, so I said my goodbyes to the others.

Justin said, "My wife and I enjoyed the walking, Chase, what there was of it. Don't be surprised if you see us over here again."

"If we do this again," Phaedra said to Justin, "we need to check the rooms out first. There's no way I'm going to sleep beneath an elephant all week."

"I think it had magic powers, actually," he said. "You haven't snored once since we got here."

"Snore? Me? How dare you! You're the one who sounds like he's inhaling the curtains."

"That's not true, and you know it!"

They continued to bicker, and I became lost in thought as I headed toward the platform. I saw how I had been idealizing Doug, thinking him perfect, which he certainly wasn't. We could argue and bicker just like the Meyerses, often more heatedly. Doug had been an admirable man, but he was only a man, as flawed and mortal as the rest of us.

The sharp blare of a car horn made me stop and turn. My heart leapt as I saw a green MG roar up and come to a stop where our van had been a moment before. Mike jumped out and hurried over to me, breathing heavily.

"Chase! Thank God you're still here," he said with a relieved grin. "I was afraid I wouldn't make it!" He was every bit as attractive in everyday clothes, but he'd be a welcome sight even in rags.

I felt my heart swell. "I'm so glad you did make it."

"I was never able to reach you!" he said between breaths. "That storm must have been playing havoc with wireless transmission last night."

"I tried calling you and didn't get a response. It looks like we had our wires crossed."

Mike straightened up. "I offered to be your guide, and that's what I intend to be." Then he let his shoulders relax. "Please don't tell me you're returning to the States today."

"I was planning on staying on in London for a couple of days."

Mike gave his head a scolding shake. "That overcrowded amusement park? Nothing doing. You're to be my guest here in Devon instead. I've a big warm house with a beautiful view of the moors and a room already made up for you. We can go exploring and enjoy the best shepherd's pie you've ever had in your life."

"I'd like that," I said and put my arm around him. "I'd like that very much."

Billie was still standing not far away, watching. I introduced her to Mike, and as she shook his hand, she smiled at me approvingly. Then she said, "Oh, before I forget—"

She pulled a pair of thick red-and-gold socks from her bag. "These are for you. I could tell you didn't like those green ones, so I knitted a new pair. Red socks, right? Your favorite team?"

I hesitantly accepted the gift. "Very striking. Thanks. I'll wear them on days I'm feeling adventurous."

"You do that. Now get back to your canoodling."

I laughed. " 'Canoodling'? Where do you come up with these words?"

She eyed me sardonically. "Spend forty years in a library and you'd be surprised at the words you come up with. Now, if you'll excuse me, I have a rendezvous with Ben the fisherman." She gave me a quick wink and walked toward the train platform.

Mike put my bags in the boot of his car. As we climbed inside, he asked, "Aren't the Red Sox the football team you told me about that day we first met?"

"Baseball," I corrected with a smile.

"They're not the same thing?"

I smiled as we drove off. There was a lot I had to explain to Mike. I hoped it would take a long, long time.